THE
DOORWAY

THE DOORWAY

KELLY SCANDIZZO

STONEWALL PRESS

PAVING YOUR WAY TO SUCCESS

Published in the United States of America

ISBN: 978-1-64460-125-9 (*sc*)
        978-1-64460-126-6 (hb)
        978-1-64460-124-2 (e)

Library of Congress Control Number: 2019933234

Stonewall Press books may be ordered through booksellers or by contacting:

Stonewall Press
4800 Hampden Lane, Suite 200
Bethesda, MD 20814 USA
www.stonewallpress.com
1-888-334-0980
orders@stonewallpress.com

1. Romance
2. Action and Adventure
19.02.05

CONTENTS

CHAPTER 1

"Hon, where are my snow boots? I thought they were in my closet," Nick hollered to me from upstairs, a thudding sound periodically coming through the ceiling.

"I don't know why we're packing weeks in advanced for this trip but whatever," he muttered to himself.

"They're in your black suitcase in your closet, along with the rest of your snow gear." I yelled back up to him.

Sophie sat quietly on the living room floor, playing with her teddy bear and unicorn. I could never play like her, to find it in me to have that kind of imagination without feeling absolutely ridiculous. My brother never had trouble playing like her, though. In many ways I saw him through her and my heart would tighten.

He had been tormenting my mind lately. I couldn't wait to get past the one year memorial of his death. I felt as though he was as annoyed as I, and that we were keeping him from more important things.

More thumping and a few curse words wafted down the stairs, and I gave up trying to finish my to-do list. Sophie didn't look up, so I left her to her toys and went to rescue her father.

"Nick, you don't have to tear the place apart for Christ's sake. Here, move." I shoved him aside and lifted out the suitcase.

I dropped the suitcase on our bed with a heavy sigh, and made a production of opening the damn thing. I gave him a face of *I told you so*, then, with hands on my hips, I left the room.

"Thank you!" I heard him say through the floor. I rolled my eyes and, forgetting what else was needed to be on my list; I plopped down and played with Sophie.

Once the house was quiet and Sophie finally asleep, Nick and I settled into bed. The TV cast flickers of light on the walls, but I hardly noticed them. All the check lists and plans were going through my mind. Nick lay next to me reading a car magazine, periodically stopping to watch the TV.

Sophie called for me as she had every night at the same time, for as long as I could remember. I sighed as I got up. Slipping my robe on, I shuffled down the hall and checked on her, refilling her night time sippy cup with water and tucked her back in. With a kiss and a wave, I closed the door and went back to bed.

Nick was snoring with the magazine on his chest as usual and I settled back into bed. I shut off the TV, closed my eyes, and fell asleep.

"I've got Brandi taking care of the bookstore while we're gone, and hired a couple of part timers to help her out. Everything squared away with work, babe?" I asked him.

"For the last time, Jessie, I took care of everything that I could. I need to bring my laptop to do some work while we're up there, which I told you a week ago. You need to get your head out of the clouds."

I gave him a dirty look and shoved past him in a snit. I was getting tired of his bad attitudes lately and couldn't wait to see my dad and a change of scenery.

"Like I said before, you don't have to come along, Nick. I know how you hate it up there and the people there too. He's my father so there's no need for you to come."

"And just where would that put me on his shit list? Higher or lower, you think? Besides, I know you, and I know you'd make my life hell once you got back if I don't go, so I'll pick the lesser of two evils, thanks."

"Ughh!" I stormed off to do something, anything to get away from him for a while. I found Sophie in her room coloring, got her shoes on and told her we were going for coffee. She protested until I told her there would be a marshmallow treat for her there.

I needed to pick up a few more things for the trip anyway, which, would thankfully keep me from coming home in a bad mood. Men could be such jerks.

"Are you ready, kiddo?" I asked Sophie as I strapped her into her car seat. "Papa is going to be so happy to see you, and I bet he has a big hug waiting for you when we get there. Would you like that, honey?"

Sophie nodded her head, clapped her hands, and reached for me to give her a hug. She was a great hugger, and that worked in her favor whenever she was in trouble.

I checked our bags and snacks, and made sure we had blankets and books for Sophie. She was looking at her shapes book and exclaiming over the brightly colored foil paper. It didn't take much to amuse this kid.

Nick got in, the two of us still not talking to each other, and we pulled out of the driveway and took off. It was going to be a long trip.

"I know it's been a long drive honey but we'll be there soon. Grandpa and Grandma are looking forward to seeing us, especially you!" I reached back and gave Sophie a tug on her snow-booted foot. She reached for my hand but couldn't quite reach it. I smiled one more time before facing front again.

The snow was falling heavily, and Nick slowed down. It wasn't quite dark yet. I grimaced, and hoped we'd be there soon.

"Honey, should we pull over and wait a little bit? Maybe the snow will lighten up and then we can proceed." I said.

"Jessie, if we stop now we'll get socked in. Then what happens? We don't have anything warm enough, not even with all those blankets in the back. We need to keep going."

"We can't even see the lines Nick!"

"I know where we're going, for Christ's sake, Jessie! Just sit back and talk to Sophie."

I looked back at her and smiled again. She was looking at her picture book and humming. At least someone was comfortable in this car.

I sighed and squirmed in my chair. The heater was turned all the way up but my toes were popsicles my boots.

"We should have been there by now, even with all this snow. I haven't seen a damn sign." I mumbled to myself. Nick glared at me from the corner of his eye but gave my leg a squeeze. The silence is over consuming so I tried the radio once more but there was only static.

The headlights lit up the highway sign and I took a breath. Only 50 miles to go and we'll be in Reno. As Nick drove, I recalled the curving road along the mountains and relax.

I could picture the hot bath waiting for me at our hotel and snuggling into bed with Nick.

A flash of bright lights hit my closed eyelids. I opened them to see them in our windshield, just before the jolt of our car was slammed into. Glass, luggage and other debris flew around us as we spun, then tipped over and rolled.

I woke to find myself hanging upside down from my seat, Nick next to me out cold; blood dripping from his head. I couldn't move and the only sound I heard was my own labored breathing.

I tried to turn to see Sophie but was trapped by my seatbelt. I reached back or try to but couldn't feel her. I couldn't feel anything. I breathed again then the lights go out, and I closed my eyes again.

"Miss, Miss, can you hear me? Open your eyes!" I heard someone shouting next to my ear and I turned away from the voice. I just wanted to sleep.

My body hurt everywhere and I didn't want to move; just sleep. I felt a tug and a wrench as something pulled on me. I screamed and tried to pull away but I couldn't.

"Miss please we need to get you out of here. Open your eyes, and listen to my voice. Grab my hand honey and I'll catch you. Just breathe."

I didn't know the voice but it was quieter now so I did as it asked and it did catch me. I curled into it then went rigid with pain. What happened?

I was down now and felt better. I look around and saw lights flashing around me. Then I was blinded by a bright light over my head. Faces were around me talking but I couldn't understand them.

I tried to move my hand to remove the cover on my face but my hand kept getting pushed away.

"Where's Nick? I need Nick!" I screamed to the faces.

"You have to calm down Jessica. You were in a car accident and we need to get you to a hospital. Lay still; we are giving you something for the pain."

"What? Where's Nick? I need to find Nick and Sophie! Where are they? NICK! SOPHIE! Where are you?" I fought against the hands, but then gave up. I felt light headed and the pain seemed to melt away. I felt good, like I was floating in that wonderful hot bath in my hotel room. My eyes closed as darkness surrounded me and took hold.

Snow was blowing sideways across the highway and lights were flashing blue and red. In the ravine below interstate 80, a bright glow lit the area but not in a good way. State troopers walked around, lighting flares and made a human chain to guide oncoming traffic.

A tow truck groaned as it slowly pulled up the minivan that is now a crumpled mess. One side was compressed so much that you couldn't see where the windows had been.

The driver-side door, and rear passenger door, had been cut off and showed a bloody mess. A car seat dangled sideways, also crumpled.

It was set aside, awaiting a flatbed tow truck to haul it away. A recovery wrecker came next to drag the 18 wheeler out of the ravine. Bright headlights still gleamed upwards, like spotlights through the clouds.

The shipping container, had been smashed and twisted like a corkscrew, and dangled from its attachment to the cab of the truck. The contents of the container were scattered at the bottom of the ravine.

The driver had been removed from the cab and taken to Reno's General Hospital. Another ambulance had quietly left the scene a couple of hours earlier, carrying two of the car victims. The only surviving victim from the car was air lifted to the nearest hospital.

Once the vehicles had been removed, clean up began, and the lanes were reopened. The trooper in charge left grim faced and quiet.

CHAPTER 2

I OPEN MY EYES and looked around. The walls are white with green stripes and a horrible light hanging over my head. I raise my hands, wincing as they come up I saw wires and tubes coming out of them. Bruises, nicks and cuts covered my arms.

What the Hell happened? I tried to jog my memory but things come up fuzzy and I stop because my head starts to hurt. I lay my head down again to look around. I raised the bed to a reclining position, wincing.

The sound of machines next to me, were alarming. No one had come in to check on them, so they must have been ok, but they were annoying.

"Good afternoon Ms. Lauren. Good to see you're awake. I will page the doctor to come check on you. Any pain right now, dear? I can give you a small dose of morphine to take the edge off."

The nurse who had come in spoke to me while she checked the machines. I felt like I was on "Days of Our Lives." It was surreal. I shook my head and asked for something less extreme than morphine. She nodded then exited the room.

A few minutes later, a man entered looking like a doctor, the nurse not far behind him. With a tray and two cups, she handed me Tylenol then the water. I gladly took them.

"Hello, Ms. Lauren. Do you know where you are?" The doctor asked.

"N-no," I replied. I didn't recognize my own voice. I rubbed my throat trying to loosen it up.

"You're in St. Mary's Hospital. You were brought here a week ago after a car accident. You're all right but we'll still do more tests to make sure everything is all right."

He gestures towards the bed, asking to sit. I nodded and waited. *Car accident, what car accident?* He interrupted my thoughts, continuing the conversation.

"Do you remember driving four nights ago? Do you remember where you were headed, and why at night in heavy snow?"

I stared at him, and then looked away, trying to remember. I looked up and told him we were headed to my father's house, in Reno. *We? That's right. My husband was driving us. And our daughter Sophie, she was in the back looking at… something.*

"We have called your father, and he's on his way to see you with your stepmother. For now, can you tell me what happened that night?"

"We were driving to my father's house." I paused trying to think.

"The snow was thick and we had to slow down." I paused to swallow, drinking more water. "We couldn't see the lines, but we were close to the mountain side…." The doctor sits patiently, waiting for me to continue.

"Where are my husband and daughter? Are they ok? Why aren't they here?" I started to panic and tried to get out of bed.

The doctor restrained me and pushed me back down gently until I stop fighting him. My father came in then, and I reach for him crying.

He tries to smile, but it didn't work, and he collected me into hisarms. After a few minutes we broke apart but continued to hold hands.

"Mr. Matthews, I was trying to see how much Ms. Lauren"

"She is *Mrs.* Lauren, doctor. Mrs. Nick Lauren. When can she be released from the hospital? My wife and I want to take her home!" My father demanded.

"Mr. Matthews, she needs to stay a couple of more days for observation. Her recovery is slow but steady."

"I'm sitting right here! You can talk to me about when I can leave. I want to leave now! I don't feel that much pain so let me go home."

I shoved my father and the doctor out of the way and try to get out of bed, only to end up on the floor. I hadn't notice that a full length cast had been placed on my left leg. Then the pain registered and I cried out as they lifted me back into bed.

The nurse moved in with a shot of something but before I could protest, she injected me with it and I settled down into sleep.

"Mr. Matthews, your daughter sustained internal bleeding which the surgeons were able to stop. She also had contusions to her head, and several broken bones. She can't be removed for at least another week.

"For now let's keep her comfortable. We'll keep her sedated over the next few days so her body can rest. She doesn't remember what happened to her husband and daughter; I don't think she even knows."

Mr. Matthews looked down at his daughter, who looked peaceful as she slept. How could he tell her, tell her that her husband and daughter were killed in the accident?

He'd give anything to take her pain as his own, so she wouldn't suffer. He would go with her to identify them when the time came.

He sat down in the chair next to her bed and held tightly to her hand, and prayed. The doctor touched his shoulder, and then removed himself from the room to give them privacy.

CHAPTER 3

I HOBBLED SLOWLY INTO the waiting area in the morgue to identify my husband and daughter. My father stood next to me and I felt his strength pouring out to keep me strong but it wasn't working.

We walked into a bland room which had two steel tables with two bodies, one small; the other one long. Both were draped in a green sheet.

I stopped at the first one, taking a few breaths and squeezed my father's hand. The coroner asked if I was ready and I hesitated before nodding.

What greeted me belonged in a horror movie. I gasped and heaved before looking back at Nick, or what was left of him. I nodded to the coroner, giving confirmation that it was indeed, Nick. I looked at the next table, but I couldn't bring myself to walk there. I looked at the tiny shape that lay under the sheet and prayed it wasn't my baby girl. I could see her sunny smile and hear her laughter. It couldn't be her, it couldn't.

My father pulled me forward and the coroner moved to the other side. With a nod from my father, the coroner lifted the sheet; the little form on the table was in fact, my little girl.

I reached for her but hesitated for a moment, then touched her just as I did in the past when she would hurt herself. She looked as if she were asleep. There was only one cut along her cheek that marred her form.

"How, how did she," I sobbed to the coroner.

My father wrapped his arm around my shoulder but I shook him off. I was so angry. How could my baby girl be gone? How?

"I can assure you she felt no pain, and it was very quick. Due to the impact, her neck whipped to the side and broke cleanly.

"Your husband bore the brunt of the accident since the impact was more towards the front driver's side."

He paused before saying his condolences then excused himself to give me a private moment.

I lifted Sophie half way off the table, cradling her head in the crook of my arm, and held her close to me as I cried. I rocked her gently and whispered that she would be okay; that I was there now, and everything would be all right. But it wouldn't be.

My father held me tightly and wept with me. I stroked her hair and her cheek and clasped her tiny hand in mine. I could imagine her little fingers holding mine.

After what seemed like hours, but had only been a few minutes, I gently laid her down and brought the sheet up to her chin, tucking her in for a long sleep.

I looked at her one last time and left a kiss on her forehead before walking out. My father and I collapsed together on the floor and sobbed.

"How am I going to live without her, without either of them? Why am I here, Daddy, why? It's not fair! It's not fair."

"I know baby, I know."

We raised ourselves from the waiting area floor, my aching leg tingling from falling asleep. My father handed me the cane I had to use, and we hobbled out of the hospital and into the sunshine.

Home. After months with my father, burying my husband and daughter, meeting after meeting with the police, I was finally home. But it wasn't home, Nick and Sophie weren't here. Sophie wasn't upstairs playing with her dolls or dressing up. Nick wasn't listening to a game as he worked on his novel. The house was silent; dead.

I dropped my bag, the only one that survived the wreck, on the floor and kicked off my shoes. The silence is overwhelming, so I turned on the TV for company and headed to the kitchen to put the kettle on.

My friend Kate got rid of all the food that would have spoiled, so I only had canned soup and cereal left. Soup took too much effort, so dry cereal it would be.

A knock at my kitchen door brought me out of my daydream and I saw Kate looking in, holding a large box. I rushed over and let her in, and she dropped the box onto the kitchen table, out of breath. I went to close the door but she ran back out.

"I have a couple more coming so hang on a sec okay?"

I stood there with a blank face but kept the door open. I walked back to the stove and moved the kettle to a cool burner, moving through the motions of getting mugs out, dropping a tea bag in each. Green tea, honey and lemon juice; was always so soothing.

"Hey, hon, how are you holding up? I brought you some food now that you're back. I snuck in a couple of your favorite junk foods too."

Kate shrugged out of her coat and tossed it aside onto one of the kitchen chairs. I brought over the mugs and got ready to sit when she engulfed me in a tight hug. I heard her sniff, and then we both fell to pieces.

"Hanging in there kiddo?" She repeated.

I shrugged and wiped my nose. "Doing the best I can. It's hard being here, without them here too. I don't want to go upstairs yet. It's too much." I turned my mug back and forth absently.

Kate took my hand and gave it a light squeeze before returning to stocking my fridge and pantry with fresh foods. I didn't know what I would do without her.

"Have you figured out what you're going to do with the house? You mentioned something about selling it. Did you contact a few realtors to find out what the comps are for the neighborhood?" her voice came out muffled from my pantry while she stocked it.

"I did. I've already hired a realtor. There are too many memories here, and I don't want to live in a home with ghosts. I need a new place, another town or city.

"So you would leave everyone behind and move completely?" she asked incredulously.

I sat silently, waiting for her to berate me over how selfish I was being, and that I should stay if not for her, then for my father. But it didn't come. Just silence from behind the pantry door.

"Well, when do we leave?" She yells from the pantry. I laughed ever so slightly. I'd picked out my new location already, and I couldn't wait to get there. Somehow I didn't think Kate would like it very much. She was a city girl through and through.

"What do you mean 'we'?"

"Don't be dumb, Jessie. I'm not letting you out of my life, and I am sure as hell not going to let you keep me out of yours, so if you are moving, then so am I."

"Don't be ridiculous, Kate! You are not coming with me!"

Kate came back out, sternness written across her face. I didn't back down, but met her stare. I forgot that she could stand there all day and glare. It was one of her many talents. I broke eye contact and continued to drink my tea.

"Look missy, I am going with you and that's final. You cannot be alone out there. You've never left this town except to see your father! I am a well-traveled woman and can get you around."

"Kate, please, I know you want to help get me through this, but I need to do this alone. And actually, I have traveled many times; to Scotland. I need to not talk about what happened, and God help me, you wouldn't want to, but...you would."

Kate plopped down next to me again and still wouldn't budge. I looked at her for a long moment then gave up the fight. "Fine, you can come." I glared at her and crossed my arms like a pouty kid.

"So, where to then," She grinned smugly.

"Are you kidding me?!" She exclaimed.

"I told you, you didn't have to come along," I yelled back at her.

"But why Scotland, there's like nothing there."

"There's actually a lot there. They have modernized since the fourteenth century you know," I educated her sarcastically. She rolled her eyes at me in answer.

"All right, all right, we'll go there. But why there?"

"My grandmother lives there. I haven't seen her in at least a dozen years. It would be a nice change of scenery for me. It's the best time of year to visit too." I pulled all sorts of clothing-both cold and warm mainly for the cold-from my closet, and tossed into my suitcase.

I sold my jewelry-all, except my wedding ring. This I wore around my neck just under my shirt. I checked my wallet for my cards, currency, and two photos. Checked my front pouch for my passport, then looked around one last time, then locked the door behind me.

I send an e-mail to the realtor to let her know where I had hidden the keys for her to use for the showing. Kate was waiting for me in the car, blasting her music through the open windows. I looked back once more, my heart breaking as we pulled away.

"All right, where are we staying once we're there? What do I have to pack?" Kate asked while she drove around.

"Well, it's not the Bahamas so I would recommend warmer clothing than cooler ones. It won't be snowing but we will be up in the northern part of Scotland."

We arrived on time and I couldn't wait to get my feet onto Scottish soil. This was my home away from home and

I had missed it. We rented a car and took to the roads, headed to Nana's house in South Loch Ness. The weather was unusually warm, and I found myself taking layers off as we traveled.

About a half hour later on a rough road, I turned onto the long driveway to her house. Not much had changed other than more trees it seemed.

The gardens in front were blooming and Petals flew gracefully around us as a gentle breeze bumped them off their stems. The scent was wonderful.

"OMG! Jessie you didn't say your grandmother lived in a castle! Now this I can stay in. This trip just got better!" Kate stared wide- eyed, out the front window at the magnificence of the estate.

"Well, technically it's not a castle, it's a manse, or rather a manor in American terms. I love it here."

I veered to the right, driving around the massive fountain, until we pulled up to the front entrance. There, Jasper stood, expressionless, in his butler's uniform; looking at nothing in particular.

The coachmen, as they were still called, opened Kate's door, helped her out as I exited on my side. Two liverymen came forth and removed our bags, taking them inside.

Kate stood there dumbstruck at what service she was receiving, and I just had to laugh. I took her arm, and we walked up the stairs to the main hall.

"Hello, Jasper. Good to see you after all these years."

"Aye, Miss. Welcome home," he answered back, giving me a slight bow.

Nana stood leaning against the foyer table, arms crossed and looking very displeased. Kate took a step back, and I could see amusement flicker in Nana's eyes. I couldn't help but snicker.

"And just what are ye laughin' at young lady?" Nana spoke and her voice echoed through the hall. I immediately stood straight and stopped snickering. I felt like I was a girl again in trouble.

"H-hi, Nana, how are you? It's-been a long time."

"Bet your arse it has been girl! Why has it taken ye so long to get here for a visit?" She demanded.

"I'm sorry, Nana. I have no good excuse. Dad says 'hello' "She looked at me up and down, and then stood straight. She didn't look a day over sixty, if that!

Nana was a rare beauty, especially back in the day. She was still stunning, even at her current age. Back in the day, she had beautiful ginger hair; curls abound, that fell down her back. Even the curls refused to be disobedient!

She was unusually tall but very graceful, like a dancer. Her eyes were the color of emeralds, with a touch of hazel around the irises. Not a blemish or a freckle on her porcelain skin.

Now, her hair was just as long and curly, and streaked with snow- white strands, interlacing through the red. She was a magnificent sight to see.

Kate, who was still standing slightly behind me, looked at Nana, and then looked at me, then back again. Here we go…

"It's like looking in a mirror with you two!" She said disbelievingly.

"Well I dinnae ken about that, lass. But aye, she does take after me for the most part. Just as sassy as I was too."

"Was?" I said back to her with a slight smile.

"Watch yerself missy. I can still whoop your arse just like when ye were a bairn."

Nana walked over to me, not smiling, and I couldn't help but feel as though she really was pissed with me. She stopped in front of me, almost nose to nose, and then shocked me when she pulled me into a bear hug. She was laughing, laughing!

"Och, lass, I'm just givin' ye a hard time. I'm sorry to hear about yer wee lass and husband. My heart aches for ye. A few weeks here and ye'll feel almost back to normal.

"Jasper will show ye to yer rooms. Feel free to take a rest if ye like. Ye can find me in the Rose Room, takin' tea with a wee nip." She reached up and touched my cheek, and I instinctively turned to it. I felt her warmth and love in the mechanical motion, and my heart tightened and my eyes stung.

Jasper slowly took the stairs to the third floor, expecting us to follow without being asked to. Kate held onto my arm as we ascended the stairs, looking at everything at once.

Suits of armor stood along the hallways here and there, but not the shiny kind that were in movies. Tapestries that were handmade from the middle ages and on, hung on the walls, more for decoration than for heating purposes now.

"Miss Jessica, this will be yer room durin' yer stay. Ye will find all ye need in the bathroom, but if ye do not, then ye may call upon me, or one of the maids. Ye will meet them later. They have unpacked yer bags, and ye'll find yer items in the wardrobe here.

"This is yer sitting room. Feel free to have one of the maids start the fire for ye if ye wish for one. The manor does have modernized heatin' throughout. Yer *seanmhair* still requires that fires be made on request."

I followed him around, but was already familiar with my lodgings. It had been my room whenever I had visited. Only now, there was a spirits bar set near a bookcase in the sitting room.

"Dinner will be served at 6pm sharp. Tea is currently being served in the Rose Room, if ye would like to join yer seanmhair. I will leave ye to familiarize yerself. Again, do not hesitate to call for assistance if ye require it."

Jasper handed me the key to my room, bowed, then exited into the hall. Kate looked at him, stock still. He quirked an eyebrow at her then motioned for her to follow him.

I nudged her toward him, then, closed the door behind her before she could run back in. I sighed as I leaned against the door. It was very overwhelming to be here just now.

The bed seemed smaller, but most likely, because I actually had grown since being here last. The room was a soft pink with lavender accents on the walls. The bedding was the same as when I had been a child visiting, and matched the floral print on the wallpaper. Lavender scented the rooms in crystal vases, and little lavender sachets placed in the drawers of the wardrobe. I jumped onto the bed and laid there for a few minutes. It felt so good to be home, away from all the hurt and darkness.

CHAPTER 4

A SOFT KNOCK ON the door awoke me, and I found the room was dark. The knock came again, a little louder now. As I rolled to the side of the bed, the door opened with a creek, and Kate walked in.

"Your room was so quiet that I thought you went downstairs for tea. I didn't find you there, but I did find your grandmother." She switched the night stand lamp on as she spoke.

"What time is it?" I yawned and stretched before heading to the window. I pulled the curtains back and found it was night time.

"I can tell you your grandmother is something else. At first it was quite awkward sitting there and only getting yes and no answers from her.

"And then the Spanish inquisition started. It's amazing how many questions she had. After a bit, she relented and settled into casual conversation. I guess I passed her inspection." I laughed and agreed with her.

My stomach grumbled loudly, which reminded her as to why she'd come in the first place. "Let's head down now. I am sure Nana is already waiting for us."

Nana was in fact, already seated at the head of the table; waiting for our arrival. She looked crossly at me. I slithered into the chair next to her and avoided her gaze.

"I will ignore yer tardiness tonight due to yer fatigue, but I expect ye here tomorrow on time."

"Yes ma'am."

We all made small talk, how our trip was here, what were we going to be doing while here. We hadn't thought that far ahead yet, so we agreed we would play tourists for the next couple of days.

"Nana, if you don't mind, I am still jet-lagged, and I would like to be excused." I said while in the process of yawning. Kate seconds the notion.

"Alright, ye may go. Ring for the maid to bring ye breakfast in the mornin', and I will come to visit afterwards. Feel free as well to call on the servants if ye require anythin'. Good night, lassies."

I leaned over and gave her a slight hug, and she patted one of my hands. "Oh, luv, I will have a map for ye both to carry of the area here, so ye dinnae get lost. There are certain areas off limits due to erosion. We dinnae need ye getting hurt out there. The hospital isna close."

Kate and I nodded then headed up to bed. However, sleep seemed to elude us, so I ordered up a couple of hot toddies and some biscuits.

After yawning for like the millionth time, Kate left my room, returning to her own. I soon followed suit and passed out cold, candles forgotten.

I woke to the sun shining through the window, the curtains still drawn back from last night. I couldn't help but groan. The silence was a blessing; my head pounding horribly. If only the sun would go away too.

Surprisingly, it wasn't that late in the morning, so I headed down to the kitchen, finding two maids chit chatting with their backs to the entryway.

"I heard it wasnae an accident. That she and her husband were fightin' when the car flipped and went over the cliff. That's what the tabloids are sayin', poor little girl. I hope she dinnae suffer."

I scraped a chair away from the butcher block table, announcing my presence. I sat and looked directly at them.

"Would you like to know the truth, or should I leave you to your *tabloids*?"

They looked at me, their faces going pale from being caught gossiping, then quickly became flushed and stuttered.

"We were driving to see my father, the duchess's son, when a heavy snow fell on us. We veered around a bend in the road when a semi headed right for us.

"My husband swerved, but the truck still hit us. Both our car and the semi went over the cliff. I woke up a week later to multiple broken bones, survived internal bleeding and a concussion. But that was not the worst of it. I found out that my husband and baby girl had been killed in the accident.

"But the reason for it all was that the driver of the semi had fallen asleep at the wheel. He was late with his delivery, and drove for twenty hours straight. The driver survived. I survived, but not my husband and baby girl."

They stood there with horror stricken faces. I turn around, wiped the tears from my cheeks, and headed back to my room; my appetite now gone.

I caught Kate coming down the stairs, and she rushed me, worry written all over her. "What happened? Are you all right?"

"I'm fine. I had to set the record straight with the two maids in the kitchen."

We headed out the door, Kate carrying the map Nana told us about. We looked it over, picked a destination, and then I looked Kate up and down and thought twice about hiking.

"Girl, we need to get you some shoes for actual hiking around here. These things you're wearing won't work; they'll kill you in forty minutes."

Kate looked down at her designer hiking boots then back at me. "What! The girl there told me I could."

"Maybe for walking the streets if you know what I mean, but not here. Let's go to town today and find you real hiking boots. Maybe try the local fare."

The groundskeeper brought around the Land Rover for us and we headed out.

Inverness was a great tourist town. Trinkets and baubles shimmered in almost all the windows; the shop doors open and welcoming.

"So, now that you have the correct attire and shoes for the hike, how about small one. So you can break in the boots."

Kate played at ignoring me about that topic. "Why don't we go sightseeing instead? We could go souvenir shopping later on the way back. I'm sure there is something here your parents would love."

I sighed and rolled my eyes, then relented, with the agreement that we would go hiking tomorrow. Kate sighed back at me but agreed with some mumbling.

We packed up the land rover with all our packages then went on our way. We came across the local church and immediately, Kate wanted to go in. She loved stained glass windows and old architecture.

The church was beautifully medieval. Grey stone walls and archways, wooden oak doors darkened in color from stain and age. The hinges were handmade and worn.

Kate walked around and took photos of everything while I sat peacefully in one of the wooden pews. I closed my eyes, and breathed in the scent of tallow candles and wood polish.

Kate joined me and continued to look around. "Ready? Let's go check out the cemetery," she said in a loud whisper. A few parishioners turned and glare at us before shushing us.

I nudged her until she got out of the pew and we left through the side door. It was beautiful. The sun was shining on this rare occasion and the old headstones, some broken with age, some illegible from moss, stood cock-eyed in the ground. There were a couple of crypts towards the far back of the church grounds draped in shadows.

"Are ye lassies lost or can I be of some service to ye?" Kate and I jumped and turned, finding a priest holding his bible and a serene smile on his face.

"Oh, we're just taking a look at the grounds if that's all right Father ," Kate asks.

Aye lass, I am Father Kirkland, head of this church."

"Wait, how cool is that! Your last name means *'church'* in Gaelic, doesn't it? I think?" I asked.

"You have the right of it. Clever lass ye are. How do ye ken that?" he chuckled and I joined in. Kate looked at both of us as if we had lost our minds.

"I studied Gaelic when I was in College. I'm afraid my knowledge of the language is very limited though."

"So, ye two are Americans aye? I can tell by yer accents." He said with a wink.

"I was wondering what gave us away. Yes, we're from America; however we are visiting my grandmother for a time. I, sorry, *we* needed to get away from the states for a bit."

"Ye wouldnae be Lady Eleanor's granddaughter would ye, lass? Aye, she said something about ye comin' for a visit. It's a pleasure to meet ye. Ye have to get your *seanmhair* down for a visit. I do miss our gossip sessions." I looked at him startled and he laughed.

"I admit it's a terrible thing to do, and goes against my job title, but I'm only human, and as long as nothin' is said untoward of another person, there's no harm in it. Just dinnae tell the man upstairs." He said with another wink.

I slowly smiled and gave him a wink back. I looked around and found Kate playing a game on her phone. I roll my eyes and grabbed her arm.

"Father, we were just going to walk around the grounds back here if that is all right. May I take a few photos?"

"We ask that photos not be taken. This is a spiritual place and we want the souls to continue to rest. But feel free to walk around. I will leave ye to it then lassies, and if you need anythin' I'm not that far away; good day."

Kate blew out a breath then walked on. "He's a real chatterbox isn't he? Souls need resting? I think they woke up with all that chatter."

I shoved her over a couple of steps in response then we walked slowly around. Flowers grew wild over quite a few graves, but mainly grass. It was a peaceful place.

A whisper of a breeze caressed my cheek and I closed my eyes. It felt like a lover's touch. A light sent of sandalwood tickled my nose.

My eyes popped open, expecting to find a stranger standing next to me but I was alone. Even Kate had walked off. I rubbed the back of my neck, trying to shake off the eeriness, walking hurriedly in the direction Kate had gone.

"Did you see anyone around here with us, like a man?"

"No. Why?" Kate wandered more along the path of the graveyard behind the church, only half listening.

"I could have sworn I smelled sandalwood a minute ago, but there's only flowers and grass here. Huh, strange. Are you ready to go? Nana will worry if we aren't back soon."

We headed back to the car and settled into traffic, which was a little better than when we had driven in. "What did you think about the town?"

"It was nice; quaint. It's no New York that's for sure. And the food is, uh, well that's not New York either."

"Well get used to it girl cause that's what we're eating from now on."

CHAPTER 5

So, NOW WITH THE proper hiking attire on, Kate and I opened the map and headed off up the shortest hill behind the manse. Nana reiterated the importance of following the map again and we agreed.

After about an hour of walking, we took a break at a gathering of old granite stones and had a small picnic. The breeze had a bite to it but it smelled and felt clean and crisp.

Even the sun seemed brighter here. Maybe just being in another place, where there was no pain, no clouds, and no judgment from anyone made it feel fresher. Here, I was a stranger with no history other than my grandmother and past family line.

We headed back out for a couple more hours then Kate gave up. Once we returned to the manse, she went straight upstairs, claiming she had to soak her frozen, aching feet. Aching, maybe but frozen most likely not.

I joined Nana in the Rose Room, removed my boots and stretched my toes. We sat in silence for what seemed like hours, but had only minutes until she spoke. Just conversational chit chat at first, but it soon turned to what she really wanted to know.

"Ye followed the map?" She asked over her tea cup.

"Of course Nana, followed it just as you said."

"What was out there? I havnae traveled out there since I was much younger. Ye ken, there was a tree, out on the hill just to the east. I would sit there as a lass, around maybe nine or ten years of age. I sat up there almost every day, even in the rain.

"My da would have to pull me from the tree just before dark to do my homework. I dinnae ken what it was about it, but it would call to me. I dinnae ken why, but once I was sittin' in it, I felt at peace. Is it still there?"

I pulled out the map and looked it over. I handed it to her and told her I had not walked east, but had gone south. "I will go there tomorrow for you." I'd take a few photos of it if it was still there. She handed back the map and smiled somewhat distantly.

Once she had taken her leave, I lightly placed a circle around the tree she'd drawn on it, and folded the map and tucked it away. Jasper walked in to announce dinner was being served. I nodded then joined the rest in the dining hall.

Kate looked like she hadn't slept in a week and was wearing her slippers, claiming her feet were still killing her. I rolled my eyes but sat down and waited to be served. The wine Nana had selected was divine and went well with the meal. She asked Kate as to how her hike had been, and Kate grumbled and winced when she wiggled her toes.

Kate relayed pretty much the same info I had to Nana, to which Nana did not look happy about. Nana did her best to hide the sadness she was feeling, but I could still see that she was troubled.

I assured her again that I would check out the tree and report back to her with photos in hand; if there was a tree anymore. She nodded and returned to her meal. Kate looked over at me and I could only shrug and carry on with my own meal.

Once settled for the night, a roaring fire in the hearth going and my flannel PJs on, I scooted down into my warm blankets and thought over the information Nana had given me earlier. I shivered then turned over, tightening the blankets over me.

Kate sat in the rose room, her feet up close to the fire and a blanket over her legs and said, "I think I'm gonna hang around here today Jess, if that's all right with you. My feet are still hurting some and my legs too. Maybe this afternoon we can go around the area some more."

"Suit yourself then." I shrugged then headed out. She was such a Drama Queen.

Map in hand along with my phone, keys, and wallet, I headed to the east of the Manse and up the hill there. I looked up and there were a ton of trees along the hillside, and I groaned out of irritancy.

I thought about going back and informing Nana that not only was there one tree but many, and I that wouldn't know which one she had been talking about, but I decided against it. I was already here so no sense turning back now.

The sunlight, what there was of it, dappled through the thinly-branched trees and lit the floor in spots. It soon became clear that someone had planted them there, as a kind of property line. They had been there for a very long time. Their trunks so wide my arms only hugged about half of it that is, if I had tried to hug one. The line ran about a half mile long; curving to the right slightly.

I passed through the line and came to an open field of flowing grasses and gasped. The sight was absolutely breath-taking. Hill upon hill of wheat and lavender, farmed into neat rows, went for what seemed like miles.

The grass tickled my fingers as I stood there taking it all in. I continued on up and over another hill, and there, at the bottom of a small valley, was a tree standing all alone. It was clearly out of place, being here in Scotland.

I journeyed down to it, a bit hesitant to fully approach it, but stood a few feet away from it.

What the hell kind of tree was this? There were definitely many in America, practically on every block, but not being one for horticulture, I couldn't tell an oak from a redwood; ok I do know what a redwood tree looks like but even so. I snapped a few photos from all sides with my phone, and headed back to the Manse.

I ran up the stairs and synced my phone to my tablet. The photos of the tree on my tablet seemed to glow, mesmerizing me. The colors were bold and took on what seemed like a magical aura.

I looked up different varieties of trees and came across one similar to it. It was possibly an oak. From the looks of it, it had been there for some time. I would have to ask Nana about it. It was the only tree of its kind in that area which was obviously strange. The trees that were planted as a property line were firs for sure.

In the meantime, I settled down on the settee with my lunch and my tablet, turning on one of my secret indulgences, some girly reality show. It was a nice mental break.

Nana found me found me in the tea room and sat next to me on the couch. I pulled up the photos on the tablet and handed it over to her to inspect. A little gasp escaped her and she touched the screen.

"It still stands?" She said more to herself than to me, and just stared at it.

"Are you sure this is the one Nana? It was the only one around in a clearing but I wasn't sure."

"Aye, I'm sure it's the same. But it looks so vibrant, so glorious." She ran her finger over the photo, only to replace it with another photo, one not of the tree. She looked up at me in panic.

I swiped the photo back for her, and she sighed quietly and calmed herself. What the hell was up with this tree? I looked at her quizzically, waiting for an explanation of some kind but received none.

"Nana, what is so special about it? It's just a tree?!" I exclaimed at her, throwing my hands in the air. She put aside my tablet and folded her hands in her lap, taking a few breaths before answering me.

"It's not just a tree, luv. This tree was where I met yer seanair. It's also where I lost him; so many years ago. Please, dinnae go there again. It's a place of sadness and best forgotten."

She clasped my fisted hands as she sniffed into a tissue, then stood and poured a drink. I debated whether or not to ask how exactly a tree would cause Papa to pass away, but thought better of it. Maybe I'd ask at another time.

Papa was never a topic open for discussion in this house; ever.

Nana refused to answer my questions over the years, and so I had stopped asking.

I got off the settee and hugged her from behind. I wished I could do more to comfort her. But comfort from one sad person to another wasn't worth much.

"Nana, I can understand your pain; I know it too. I can only imagine how life will be for me now that my husband and daughter are gone."

She stood quiet and tense but didn't turn around. I dropped my hand and left her to her thoughts. I needed time for my own thoughts and heartache.

I found Kate hanging around in the kitchen, trying to find something to eat that seemed somewhat American, coming up with a package of Oreos and a glass of milk.

"Grab me a glass too would ya?"

"All ready taken care of. Somehow I knew you would be coming down." Kate said over a mouthful of cookie. She loaded up a couple of tea saucers with cookies and we sat at the butcher block table.

"I saw your grandmother a little while ago. She seemed upset, and it was obviously she had been crying. Any idea what's up?"

I explained my visit with Nana and Kate sat quietly, intently listening. She ended up shrugging then continued to eat.

"She said that she had met my grandfather there, and where she'd lost him. She hasn't been back since then. I took photos of it to show her; and she wept."

"When did he die?" Kate played with her cookie, rolling it back and forth on the block.

"I think it was around 1968 or 69. My dad was about 5 years old. I'm not sure how he died. It's been a touchy subject for as long as I can remember."

We sat in silence for a few minutes then I got up and went through the motions of cleaning up. "I'll see you in the morning, girl." I called over my shoulder.

I headed up to bed, still thinking about the conversation I had had with Nana earlier. I wished she had never asked about the stupid tree period.

———⟨∞⟩———

The next morning, I got up early before everyone else; the light of dawn just touching the morning sky. I had snuck out and walked back to the tree. The sun had begun to touch the top leaves, making it look as though tiny fairies flitted about as the leaves moved in the slight breeze.

It stood there all alone, in the valley between the low hills. There was nothing else around it but a few wildflowers here and there.

An eerie feeling came over me and I rubbed my arms as if to chase a chill away. The feeling only worsened.

I returned to the manse in time to see Father Kirkland pull up in his lorry. "Father Kirkland! How nice to see you again. What do we owe to have the pleasure of your company?"

He took my hand and cupped it warmly with both of his, then led me up the stairs to the main hall. "My dear, it's so nice to see ye again too. The Duchess, excuse me, yer seanmhair, asked me to tea if ye can imagine that. God works in mysterious ways I always say."

Jasper brought us to the Rose Room for tea, but I excused myself, leaving the two of them to discuss whatever business needed attending to.

I met Father Kirkland for a bit after his visit with Nana had ended. He let me know that Nana was upset over the discussion she and I had had the day before. He assured me that it was none of my doing, just that the good memories and the bad ones were warring with each other, and that she needed some spiritual guidance.

I walked him out and waved him on as he turned down the drive, then sought out Nana. She was still in the Rose Room, standing at the window deep in thought. She looked tired.

She turned when I rapped on the door jam, granting me entry and guided me to one of the chairs. For a moment she stared into the flames of the fire, and then situated herself in the opposite chair.

"As ye can see, Father Kirkland came to see me today. He told me of yer visit to the church the other day and how pleased he was to have met ye. He wondered why we hadn't had our tea time in months.

"Anyway, I called him here because after yesterday, I needed to let all my feelin's be known, to be assured that yer *seanair* was resting peacefully still, even after all these years."

I went in search of Jasper and creepily, he popped up behind me, scaring me again. "Damn it Jasper, really! You have to stop scaring me like this."

"Terribly sorry Miss, it was not my intention I assure ye. How can I be of assistance?"

I caught my breath and asked my questions. He directed me to the third floor and to head up the stairs in the west wing. It would lead me to the attic.

I nodded my thanks and headed to my room to change clothes, trading in my day clothes for more grunge-worthy ones. I stopped by the kitchen and grabbed a bottle of water and some snacks, then headed over to the West Wing.

Jasper was arriving at the staircase just as I turned the corner to the hall. "I forgot to give ye the key. Her Grace keeps it locked at all times. I hope ye find what yer looking for, Miss," and with that, he turned and walked back down the hall.

Why keep it locked? It's not like anyone comes and goes other than Nana and the sparse staff. I shrugged then opened the door to the staircase. I was stunned to see the spiraling mason stairs instead of modern ones.

"She never changed the staircase and the above chambers. She wanted to keep a piece of the family history." I squeaked and nearly fell down the one step I had already taken at Jasper's sudden return.

"Damn it Jasper!" I snapped at him. "What did you forget this time?"

"I heard ye ask about the staircase so I came back to answer ye." He shrugged then turned and headed back down the hall again. "If I didn't know better, he did that on purpose, asshole." I muttered then turned to see if he had heard that but he hadn't.

Taking the step I nearly fell off a minute ago, I headed on up, feeling a little claustrophobic with the narrowness of the stairway. After five minutes of climbing I finally reached my destination. I nearly fell down the case while dropping off my parcels to unlock the door, but caught myself.

As old locks go, I had to wiggle the key back and forth until I heard the "click" of it unlocking, and I pushed a couple of times before the door gave way. I could only get it open enough for me to slither in; the hinges having grown rusty and tight from lack of use.

I looked up and found even more stairs and I rolled my eyes before pushing the door closed behind me. After taking only two steps, the hallway opened into a spacious room, hardly an "attic" as Jasper called it.

Dust moats floated through the sunlight that came through the two sets of small windows, two sets on two sides of the room. I open the windows to get rid of the musty smell that cloaked the room.

There were quite a few large items covered in sheets, casting eerie shadows across the floor. I snagged a couple just to ease my imaginative mind.

I walked the room, zig-zagging through the sheet covered figures, touching small trinkets left uncovered on any flat surface available. I found some kind of handmade something or other made from my father when he was a kid, and I smiled at it before moving on.

After about thirty minutes and quite a few strained muscles, I found an access door, half my height in the back wall. The hinges were handmade and the handle was a ring, slightly eroded on the surface from age. "Add a nice screech to it and it's officially ancient." I said to myself.

It looked like a door from a medieval movie or something. I wiggle the handle but of course it wouldn't budge. "Why would this be easy for me? Where would be the fun in that?" I say to the room.

With my patience running out, I twisted the handle to the left and then to the right and then back again, none too gently out of frustration. A small sliding sound happened and the door opened slightly. "Of course," I said under my breath.

I opened the door fully and a puff of dust slapped me in the face, and I could have sworn I'd heard a sigh escape, as though the room had been holding its breath since the door had been closed years ago.

Well this was cool. I felt like a little kid getting into something they shouldn't. I pulled out my cell and turned on the flash light app before crawling in.

The room was much smaller than the main one, perfect for a small child to play in. I stayed on my knees since everything in the room was on the floor anyway.

Once my eyes adjusted to the dimness that remained even with my little cell light, I spotted a few small office boxes, a large chest of some sort, and a large steamer trunk; folded military blankets resting on top.

I dragged out the blankets and spread them out to keep any of the contents from getting dusty, then slid out the three small office boxes first. Unfortunately, the chest and the trunk both had locks on them and Jasper only gave me the one which opened the attic. I'd have to ask about those when I saw him next. For now I contented myself with the boxes and settled in.

CHAPTER 6

"Jasper, I want to go into town with Jessie. Have the car brought round please. Where's the lass, now?" The Duchess inquired.

Jasper stood ready in the main hall awaiting her. "Miss Jessica is currently upstairs in the attic. She requested to know of the Master so I directed her where to look."

He didn't look at the Duchess, but continued to straighten the linen table cloth over the hall's large center table. She walked over, placed her gloves and purse on the same table and snapped at him.

"What?! How could ye Jasper! Ye know I forbade anyone to go there!"

"She has a right to ken, Eleanor. She has a right to ken where he came from; about everything! At least she wants to know unlike yer ingrate of a son." He snapped back at her. He released her arms, not realizing he had grabbed them in the heat of the moment, and then adjusted his coat.

He rubbed the bridge of his nose, trying to compose himself before saying, "Let someone in for once, Eleanor.

Share with her. If for no other reason than to show her how ye feel for her, that ye can honestly say ye ken what she's goin' through."

Eleanor didn't look at him or say a word. When he left her standing by the table, she let out a pained sob then dropped into the nearest chair.

The first box I opened was half full of aged articles as to the death of my grandfather. Some were conspiracy theories; that he hadn't passed away, but had vanished, using the fire in the valley as his way of leaving his wife and son for someone else.

I rolled my eyes over that and grunted as I continued to read. There were interviews with my grandmother as to whether he was truly dead, or hiding from the law.

One showed a photo of her, so young, beautiful, and mournful over her loss. My heart broke for the young woman in the photos, and for the woman she now was. She had so many years without him, and never to remarry. There was another article photo of both her and my father. It was weird seeing him as a little kid. Would he remember his father?

Once the boxes were done I sat and looked at all the contents splayed across the blankets. Why would people think he would have fake his death and up and vanish?

I collect the piles I made, each one designated to their boxes and fold the blankets back up. For now I shove them back into the little room but I shove the chest and the steamer against the wall to come back to later. Maybe Jasper had the keys to those locks.

The sunlight had waned quite a bit and I chance a look at my phone to see the time and grimace at it. I have missed tea time. Nana will not be pleased. I lock up the attic then head down to the Rose Room, only to find it empty and from the lack of Nana's perfume; I'm guessing she missed it too.

Jasper found me in there and let me know where I could find her. I asked about the keys to the locks on the trunks but he said I was to ask the Duchess. I decided not to bother her about them now. Feelings were still raw in her department and no need to continue picking at that sore.

We left the Rose Room and went our separate ways, Jasper repeating that he would have tea sent up momentarily to my room. My phone buzzed in my back pocket and I see that I have several missed calls and texts from Kate, and a message from Nana.

Reception I guess was not the best up in the attic I guess. I continue to my room, my phone ringing back Kate. I find her sitting on my window bench looking out at nothing.

"Hey you, where have you been?" I jokingly asked her. She rushes me into one of her rare bear hugs before yelling at me.

"Where have *YOU* been Jessie? I've been looking for you all day!"

"I've been here the whole time. I asked Jasper where I could find some information on my grandfather and he sent me up to the attic. I got kinda caught up in it all and lost track of time. And, it turns out, reception up there is nill. Have you seen Nana? She tried to ring me too."

Kate stomped back to the window bench and sat back down. "She's in her rooms. She was upset that she couldn't locate you. Jasper let her know I guess because she was yelling and crying at him.

"She was really giving it to him but then he turned on her and yelled back. I've never seen a butler behave like that in my life. I'd have fired him if he were mine. I didn't stick around to find out what was going on, but I know she was very upset after they parted ways in the main hall."

Huh, Jasper got uppity with Nana, interesting. I settled onto the side of my bed, removed my shoes and tossed my phone on the side table. Kate turned toward me and doesn't quite make eye contact with me.

"Maybe coming here was a mistake, Jessie. You're grandmother seems sadder each day we're here."

She finally looked at me and I realized there might be some truth in that statement. My being here had opened old wounds for her and it pains me to knowing I'm the cause of it.

A weary sigh escaped my lips and I settled more onto my bed. What could I say? "Kate, I can't leave. Yes she's hurting, but maybe she needs me to help her finally move on, just like I have to."

"But why go through all the past stuff in the attic? What can possibly be gained by going through it? He's gone Jessie, and he's not coming back!"

"Because he's my grandfather and I have a right to know about him! And it's good to know that I'm not the only one out there going through this alone. You can't understand because you've never lost someone!"

I felt awful for saying it, but it was true. She hadn't. Yes she's been there for me through this difficult time, but she couldn't fully understand how I was feeling, what I was going through.

Kate sighed and turned back to looking out the window. Silence filled the room for a few minutes then she said over her shoulder, "just because you've lost someone doesn't give you the right to go digging around into someone else's heartache to hide your own. Just look at her for Christ sake!"

She got up and began to pace the floor and continued to lecture me. "Once you do leave, even if it's not now, she'll be alone again. No family around, just old, once forgotten ghosts to keep her company that she buried long ago. Do you want that for her?"

"You don't think I know that Kate?! My own father never visits her. He blames her for the loss of his father." I got up myself but instead of pacing I get out of my dusty, musty smelling clothes and put on my sweats and a t-shirt.

No, I won't be going anywhere anytime soon, so if you feel so inclined to leave, since obviously that's been the case since we got here, than go. I'll be fine and so will she." And with that, I stomped to the door, flung it open then slammed it shut, scaring one of the maids holding the tea service.

"I'll have it in the Rose Room after all," and I stomped down the hall to the stairs down.

The gardens were where I found myself once I had caught my breath and massaged the stitch in my side. The cement bench I perched myself on was cool and soothing on my bruised palms, where my nails had dug crescents into them.

Still angry but more heartbroken, I sat and stared into the manmade pond, watching the dark water ripple from the late breeze and or the hidden fish in it.

The tears had come and gone, and now all I felt was a raw numbness seeping into my body. Chilled and tired, I turned to leave only to see Nana standing at the garden gate with a blanket opened for me.

I go to her as a young girl would and sobbed against her shoulder. "How did you find me? I don't even remember how I got here."

She settled the blanket more firmly around my shoulders as she spoke, "I saw ye run out of the house like there were banshees chasin' ye."

We walked back to the house, silent for a moment then she asked, "Now, tell me what yer fussin' about, lass. I saw yer friend Kate cryin' in the hall just outside her room. Did ye two have a tiff?"

"A bit of one. She feels that since our arrival, I've drudged up old wounds for you about Papa. She thinks that I'm hiding my own wounds by looking into yours. And she's right, Nana. I'm so sorry. She thinks its best that we leave and go back to the states."

We entered through the mud room and into the kitchen. She set the pot on to boil and I took a seat at the butcher block table. She went into the pantry and pulled out the package of Oreos that I've been sneaking, and I gawk at her.

"Don't look so surprised girl. Who do ye think got them in the first place? But it looks as though I need to replenish my stash." She smirked at me then proceeded to arrange them on a plate. Only she could make it look fancy.

"Lass, I love having ye here. It's been some time since anyone has come to visit, especially yer father, and it's a nice change for me. Yes, the old wounds have resurfaced, but I had put them aside long ago instead of dealing with them from the start."

She went about setting up the tea cups and steeping the tea, adding a dram of whiskey to each cup. It felt nice to be taken care of as though I were a child again. I didn't care to be an adult at the moment.

She settled down at the table with me, poured the tea and snagged a cookie. She even made that look sophisticated. I smiled and she smiled back.

"Tell me about yer Nick. I never got to meet him or yer daughter. Do ye have any photos of them that I may see?"

I take out the photo I carry with me at all times, the two of them hugging while at the park just after feeding the ducks. Sophie's radiant smile lit up even in the photo and I caressed her face in it. Fresh tears threatened to come but I held them back as I passed her the picture.

She smiled at it and fingered the photo too, just as if she was caressing Sophie's cheek. She would have loved her great- granddaughter so. Nana would have spoiled her rotten if I had let her. Sophie would have loved her too.

"Tell me about them. How did ye two meet? And, when yer ready, tell me of what happened. It will hurt quite a bit but saying it out loud will be the first step at healing yer heart."

I took a couple of breaths, trying to get enough courage to start. "I met Nick at University. You can say we ran into each other, literally, on the stairs to the entry hall of the library."

I continued on, feeling the smile spread across my face as I told her of our adventures together and how much we loved each other. There was no one out there who could take his place, no one. A fresh spear of pain pierced my heart and I catch my breath at it.

Once it was all purged from me, I wept again, how there were any tears left I'll never know but there you have it. When there were no more tears, from either of us, we consumed the rest of the cookies and skipped tea and went straight to the whiskey shots.

I found Kate in her room that evening, packing her things. "So, you're leaving then. Maybe it's for the best. I've decided to stay after talking with Nana. She needs me and I need her."

She didn't look up from folding her clothes. "It's best that I go, Jessie. You need each other more than you need me, to get through this. I can't imagine what you are going through since I've never had to experience loss, at least like this."

She continued to fold her clothes and toss them into her bags. I can see she'd been crying too. It had been an emotional day for all.

"When do you leave?" I ask as I helped fold.

"Jasper will have a car ready for me after breakfast. I'll call you after I arrive in the states so you don't worry."

I crossed over to her and hugged her tightly. What could I say to make her stay? There was nothing. She didn't belong here. She needed the city and heels, not Highlands and boots.

I let her go and headed towards the door. "Okay, once everything calms down, I'll return to the states. Maybe I can get Nana to come too, see my father. Take care of yourself Kate." And with that, I left her to it.

Fresh sorrow filled me at the thought of not having Kate here with me but it's for the best. I toughen my heart because I was damn tired of crying and head to my room.

My room was cloaked in darkness and I realized for the first time, that night had settled in and so had the chill. If on cue, one of the maids appeared and brought the fire to life while the other one appeared with a supper tray.

"Her Grace said ye might want to take supper in yer room tonight. If there is anythin' else ye may be requirin' ye only need to ring." I agreed that dining here was a good idea.

47

They exited the room and I curled up on the bed to think over the last few days' events and emotions, and exhaustion hit me like a ton of bricks.

When next I opened my eyes, it was to see the sun streaming through the windows and across the floor. The supper tray laid untouched and the fire nothing but ash. I had apparently slept through the night. Something I hadn't done in a long time. I looked at the time and shot out of bed.

I rush down to catch Kate before she left but I had been too late. I returned to my room and found a folded stationary note on my spare pillow.

> *Dear Jessie,*
>
> *I am sorry that I couldn't say 'good-bye' but I know we will see each other soon, and I can't wait to see you when you return. I hope you and your grandmother find what peace you can in each other.*
>
> *Love You Forever,*
> *Kate*

I fold it gently and place it on the night stand. Maybe it was for the best.

CHAPTER 7

I EXPLORED THE MANSE more thoroughly and in my own pace to learn more about the family. In the gallery, portraits lined each side of the walls.

At the end of the hall, I found the portrait that I was looking for; the portrait of my grandfather. He was a striking man. He stood out from all the other Dukes that came before him that was for sure. How old was he here I wondered.

"Handsome wasn't he?" Nana's voice sounded behind me. It didn't startle me though.

"This was painted soon after he took the seat to the Dukedom. The artist even captured the sparkle in his eyes. A piercing green, they were. They could look into yer soul if he got too close.

"His hair was pure silk and ye couldnae say what exact color it was because of all the different shades of reds and auburns running through it. He was over six feet tall, strapping shoulders." We stood for a moment longer, taking in his, *hunkiness* was the only word I could think of, and then we turned to continue walking.

"But had he not been handsome, his knowledge, his depth of feeling for another person before himself, would attract ye. All the children would rush him on the fields as he worked, beggin' for stories of knights and dragons and the like. It's a wonder he got any work done at all."

We found ourselves in front of the main door to the staircase to the attic. Nana unlocked that door. "Nana, I've already been up to the attic. I went through the small boxes in the hidden room. I wasn't able to open the other two because they have locks."

Nana opened her hand and in it laid two sets of keys. "One is for the chest, and the other for the trunk. Let me show ye how I saw yer *seanair*."

We headed up, one behind the other due to the narrowness of the staircase. She muscles the door open, opening it further than I had. She flipped a switch and the room flooded with light. How did I miss that when I came in the first time?

We moved some of the furniture nearest the back wall to make more room for everything, including us. As I did before, I laid out the blankets and pulled the chest and trunk into the middle. She handed me the key to the trunk and she unlocked the chest. "Let's start with the chest. Those hold the early memories."

I opened the chest and a puff of musty air, trapped all these years in the chest, hit me in the face and I sneezed sending more dust into our faces. Once the dust settled, Nana reached in and pulled out the first item.

"I havnae opened any of these things since I locked them up. I forgot what was in here." She held up a folded piece of cloth and put it to her nose; inhaled.

"This was the shirt he was wearin' when I met him. He smelled of Lavender, sandalwood and of the highlands." She passed it to me and I smell it myself. It smelled... comforting somehow.

Next, she pulled out a long folded piece of plaid and she told me it had been his kilt, the colors announcing his clan. It was rich burgundy, yellow, and black. She found his dirk in its sheath, a single Emerald pressed into the hilt.

A lock of hair that had been hers tied through a promise ring he'd given her. She laid out all the contents and ran her fingers over every single piece lovingly.

She sighed then moved onto the steamer trunk. This one she was sure about opening. Inside were poetry books and novels, three stacks of letters bound with ribbon. There were photos of the two of them and pressed flowers.

I found little wooden toys, handmade with love and smoothed over time from being played with. "Those belonged to yer father. Yer *seanair* and Jasper made them for him. He played with them day and night. He wouldn't go anywhere without them."

"Does Daddy know about all of this stuff Nana?" I turned a wooden horse over and over in my hand, tracing a finger along the intricate details of the carvings.

"I dinnae think so. He was so verae young then, lass. I saved these for him in case he ever wanted to ken about his father, but he never asked."

She looked down at the letters bound by ribbon. "I'm sure he could care less about love letters, but here, feel free to read them."

Nana stood up and rummaged through an old wardrobe. She nearly fell over in the process of pulling out what looked to be a sword!

I rushed over and helped her pull it out, almost falling over myself in the process. "This was his claymore. This is what he used to do battle with. He was so strikin' when he held it, especially when he wore his kilt." Her cheeks flushed then mine did from seeing hers. She actually giggled like a school girl!

"Wait, what? What battles? There haven't been any battles involving swords since, I don't know, since the middle ages?"

She ignored my comment and went on to say, "Jasper put it in there as if it weighed nothin'. How men fought with these is beyond me. But it sure is beautiful to look at."

I agreed silently; with a nod then went back to questioning her. "Did Jasper know Papa?"

"Oh aye lass, he did. He was yer Papa's man at arms; bodyguard if you will. They were thicker than thieves they were. What a pair they made. They grew up together. In many ways, they saw each other as brothers, and fought like brothers too. Ye've never seen such stubborn headed idiots in yer life when they disagreed."

I sat gawking at her; speechless. Man at Arms? She caressed the sword gently, careful not to slice a finger off and claimed the metal felt warm to the touch.

"Lass, there is somethin' I need to tell ye. Somethin' even yer father doesnae ken." She looks at me as though waiting for me to do or say something.

"Okay…," I said.

"Yer *seanair* isnae dead, I mean he is now, but he dinnae die when he left us. He just, disappeared. I saw it with my own eyes or I would have agreed with the ones who though he'd run off."

I look at her silently, hoping my facial expression was, well, expressionless, while my brain thought she had gone bat shit crazy. "What do you mean 'disappeared'?"

"The map I gave ye, with the areas marked dangerous and safe, the dangerous areas are portals. They're doorways to different places in time. I dinnae add the tree because the last time I had seen it, was when yer *seanair* had set it on fire to it.

"For the longest time I had had a hard time believin' him, but I fell in love with him and dinnae care about anythin' else. When Jasper was goin' on about the same stuff Jonathan had, I couldnae help but think there was some truth to it.

"There had been stories, urban legends and the like from the verae old folks, mostly from the male pub members, who would swear they saw someone just vanish."

"After digging into history records at the library and city hall, we located the Campbell family of Devonshire and found his name among them. We were able to convince the government that he was the current Duke of Devonshire; that he had gone missing as a boy and we had documents fabricated for proof. She pulled out the forged birth certificate record for my grandfather and the records on his family as added proof.

"We also found that the church had the portraits of his family and a few of their belongings locked up in the cellar. The one we saw upstairs was a 'dead ringer' to his looks and so there were no more questions asked. It was so much easier to do that back then.

"Papa was the Duke of Devonshire, fifth of his lineage. When we met, I was a young lass myself, and a commoner.

I was wonderin' over the hills, evadin' my work on the farm, when I found him walkin' the hills.

"I watched him for a while wonderin' what he was doin' out and about without a horse, or some kind of tool for farmin', but just himself. He'd spotted me and I turned to leave to avoid him, but he caught up with me in short time. Vera' long legs ye see. He'd asked me where he was and then for my name. I couldn't answer right away since he was speaking in Gaelic, a language long since spoken in these parts. He had to repeat the question a couple more times before I figured out what he was askin'.

"I asked him where he thought he was and he told me that he was in Devonshire. I had to inform him that he was not. He insisted he was and I felt my anger rise over his dismissive manner.

"I turned away and headed home, ignorin' him as much as possible, but he decided to follow me home. My parents were none too pleased that had I brought home a stranger; a man in particular.

"He introduced himself as Lord Jonathan Campbell, fifth Duke of Devonshire. My parents laughed at him at his outlandish declaration."

"Why did they laugh? That was incredibly rude, even if he was a stranger and a bit vague in the head." I shook my head and crossed my arms over this thoughtlessness. I couldn't believe my family would have behaved in such a manner.

"Back then, it was not a fashion faux pas to insult a lunatic. But they humored him and asked him to stay for dinner. In the meantime, my father had called for the constables to figure this all out."

"Anyway, I had let him know that he was a few miles away from Devonshire, but there was nothin' there and hadnae been in a couple of centuries. Just ruins of an old manse. He insisted that we travel there to see for himself. I can still see the look on his face when we had arrived, and, just as I had told him, there was nothin' left but a few stones markin' the layout of the former manse."

"But he insisted that his home was there? That you had taken him to the wrong place?" Stupid man.

"I stood my ground about where we were. For the first time, he actually looked at me and noticed I was different. He asked why I was so scantily clad, and that a woman should be completely covered. At least I had my hair up." Nana had the good grace to roll her eyes at that.

"'What happened to the Manse, do ye kin?' He had asked me. I told him that it had been overtaken and burned down in 1803, but that had also been a replacement for the first one that had been built in 1321. The first manse had been destroyed in a siege.

"He actually asked what year it was and all I could do was look at him stupidly before answerin' '1963'. He fell to his knees at what had once been the entryway to the manse, and clasped his head in his hands."

He built onto this Manse which was abandoned on the Devonshire lands but kept this," she looked around and spread her arms out, "he wanted to keep somethin' to remember of how and what it looked like from the time it had been built."

"So, Jasper, he traveled too, to your time? A Man at Arms? He's a glorified butler, Nana. He doesn't even look like he's seen a sword in his hand before. This is too much, Nana. This is a lot to take in."

She shook her head and agreed with me, that she felt the same way when she met my grandfather, but it did eventually sink in. I guess I would have to wait for it to fully sink into mine.

"Anyway, yer father went for a stroll and came across the tree. Jonathan had just reached him in time before yer father had thought to climb the thing. That's when he decided somethin' had to be done about it before anyone else got 'lost'.

"I followed him up and into the valley where he proceeded to douse the tree in petrol. He tossed a couple of matches but when he got too close, he tripped over a root I guess, and went to catch his fall, absently putting his hand against the tree and, vanished. He didn't die in the fire.

"I stood there in shock then raced down to the burning mass searching for him, but there was no sign of him. I cried for him, callin' his name as tears streamed down my face, but he never came back. I sat there long after the flames had been washed out by the villagers."

"Night had fallen before my father came to fetch me and I refused to go, but then yer father was there, holding my hand and fast asleep with his head in my lap. I don't remember when he had come to sit with me. There were tear streaks down his smoke covered cheeks. He was all I had left of Jonathan."

I sat there not sure what to say about the story I had just heard. It was something out of a novel; of make believe. Nana, kept her eyes downcast, absently twirling the lock of hair that had been in the chest.

"But the tree is there now, hale and hearty." I said in confirmation.

"That's why I marked the map after you showed me the photos of it. No one can go there. It's too powerful it seems. Ye must not go there Jessie, please, I forbid it."

She was frantic now with the thought. I promised her I wouldn't to appease her but I had to check this out for myself. This was insane?! I look at a couple of the photos again, one of he and Nana so happy together, another one of him holding my father and beaming a smile.

"So, let me get this straight. Papa is from the past, and Jasper too. What year?" I asked hesitantly.

She took a breath and said, "1503."

I felt the blood drain from my face and opened my mouth to speak, but I just looked like fish breathing.

"If ye dinnae believe me ye can search the family archives down at the town hall, and there are some in the church as well. His birth was the year of our Lord 1476, born to His and Her Grace, the Duke and Duchess of Devonshire the IV."

"But why did he, they come to your time? There must have been a reason."

"The only thing I could come up with was to continue the family line. I think Jasper was an accident though. Followed his Master's footsteps and poof, here he was."

"If all of this is real and true, why is my father living in the States instead of reigning as the current Duke?"

"He doesnae want the responsibility. He wants a simple life and so he went out in search of one and found it. So it's left to me or until I can find someone to take it over from me."

We sat in silence, looking over all the contents that now lay before us. I began to pack them back up but she stilled my hand. She handed me the three stacks of love letters and told me to bring them down and read them. She would pack the rest back up in a few minutes.

I agreed and headed to the door, stopping to turn and look back. She was still sitting on the floor, breathing in the scent of the yellowish colored shirt that was my grandfather's. She sobbed into it. I wished there was something I could do to make it better for her.

CHAPTER 8

IT HAS BEEN AN emotional few days and I needed to get out and clear my head. Without care I headed out in some direction but thankfully it was away from the cursed tree. This side turned out to be more rugged terrain and the wind seemed stronger here.

Along the way I passed ruins of once beautiful homes and castles, what once had been a chapel. I pulled out the map and searched it until I found the names of the places I was exploring.

As I wondered the ruins, I couldn't help but feel as though I had been given special permission to explore closely. After all, these ruins were of my own ancestors' blood, sweat and tears.

I wondered what it had been like to have lived in their time. Hard I was sure and I cringed at the thought of living without toilet paper. Yes, very hard indeed.

The chill from the wind seeped into my bones so I headed back to the house. I could almost feel a soothing warm bath calling my name to chase it away.

Jasper was hanging outside, instructing the landscaper what needed to be done. Once he was done giving instructions I waved him over. There were some answers I needed to a few questions.

"Aye, Miss Jessica, how may I be of service?" He looked down his nose at me.

I cross my arms and stood my ground, "Cut the crap Jasper, Nana told me everything about you and Papa."

He actually blanched as though offended; he even sputtered. Once he saw that I was unmoved about his "delicate sensibilities" being offended, he shut down all together. Even the emotionless butler was gone. What stood in its place was a glaring highlander instead.

"What do ye want with me, lass," he snarled. I giggled and he glared at me even more.

Once I got my laughter under control, I told him I had some questions for him about him and Papa's travels. His face drained of color then he turned and walked away, telling me he didn't know what I was talking about.

I stomped behind him determined to get those answers, and after nagging and nagging and more nagging, he finally relented. "Yer vera much like him ye ken. Alright I'll tell ye, but not now. Her Grace, I and now ye, are the only ones who ken of it.

Since the attic has been busy with visitors lately, we can meet there say at midnight. Dinnae tell yer Gran about this meetin'."

I nodded at him then we split up, going our separate ways. I could hear his grumbles as he strode away and I shook my head then rolled my eyes; men.

I headed back in, bath forgotten, and head for the library instead. I roamed the room slowly, not sure exactly

60

what I was looking for. I came across a rather thick tome, the gold wording almost rubbed off from use and age. The leather was a milk chocolate brown and the paper, creamy parchment.

On the front what I could make of it, was the family crest of a soaring falcon with a thistle clasped in its talons with a claymore crossing over it. The binding creaked as I opened it and to my surprise, the information was written in Gaelic. I mentally smacked my head for my stupidity. Of course it would be in Gaelic.

Well that's that for now I guessed. I would have to bring my laptop down to help with the translation. This was going to be a long night. Before closing the tomb, I caught sight of a page showing the family-tree.

The tree was pretty impressive, recording all births, marriages, deaths. There were a few showing dates of birth but not of the deaths, including the missing Duke that Papa took up as replacement.

I also spotted the entry of my grandfather's birth and death, and did a double take at the death date. There were two, but the first had been crossed out and the second written in. He lived to be in his late seventies; never remarried nor did he have any other children.

Did Nana know about this? I wondered. I closed the tome and race up to my room for my laptop. Once back, I took a few photos, downloaded them, and then found a translation application that scanned the documents then translated them.

After a couple of hours of reading, I took a break, and saw that it was close to the meeting time with Jasper. However, just as I stood to go, Jasper entered the room.

"Oh, Jasper, I was on my way to me," I trailed off as I studied him.

He wasn't dressed in his usual attire, but in a workman's shirt, sleeves rolled up over sinewy forearms, and light brown worn breeches and stable boots. I looked him up and down then did a double take when I saw that he had shoulder length black hair, streaked with white.

When I hadn't said anything, he looked over at me and glared. "What? Cat got yer tongue?" He raised a brow then snapped his fingers at me.

"You look so....so different that's all. I didn't even know you had long hair. What else aren't you telling me?"

He looked up as to think then returns his attention back to me. "I can speak six different languages includin' the old ones. I've been trained for battle in broadsword and archery, and I like to cook."

I mumbled an "hmm", impressed with the list. "Sword fighting you say, really?"

I laughed at him but sobered up when he threatened to leave and forget about everything. He pulled out a flask and took a couple of swigs then offered it to me before closing it. A little liquid courage never hurt anyone.

"I thought I'd find ye here. I figured it was best that we met here; saves me havin' to climb all those cursed stairs. My back isnae like it used to be."

I pulled out my own liquid courage in the form of a warm can of Coke that I had forgotten in my coat pocket, and took a couple of sips. The Coke had magically appeared in the pantry one day, but no one thought to put them in the fridge.

"Have you or Nana looked to see if he made it back? I think he made it home."

He looked at me confused. "What do ye mean, lass?"

"Have you looked in history books, in the family archives to see if he did make it back? I found something you might want to see."

"No, we havnae looked. It never crossed my mind to search. Lass, yer a genius! Can ye do that for me? I wouldnae tell yer Gran about this though, not until ye find him, if we find him. I can help with the archival ledgers, but ye would be better at the whole computer thin'."

He actually beamed a smile for the first time I had arrived and it wasn't a bad thing to see.

Stretching and not bothering to hide a yawn, we both headed up the "cursed stairs", and went our separate ways. Without a word we nodded our farewells for the night and retired.

Tomorrow would be a long day of searching and trying to keep Nana out of it was going to be tricky; especially since she'd begun checking in on me often of late.

During the day I searched online, and during breaks, I walked to the library and dug through history books and articles. And in between that, I took my daily hike around, taking photos, etc.

On the fourth day, Jasper handed me one of the family tomes and smiled. "I found him!" He dragged his finger down a column of names and tapped.

"That's him there. He made it home!" He danced a little jig over his findings.

"How do you know it's him and not another family member named after him?" I asked, not getting my hopes up.

He leaned over and tapped another name near it. "That would be his younger brother there, Thomas, his half brother; several years younger than Jon."

Thomas had three live sons and two live daughters. His wife had three stillbirths after the youngest girl. One of the daughters had died in childbirth and one of the sons had died of consumption at the age of sixteen.

As we read through the pages, reading of births and deaths of all types. It was surprising how many children had died; more than adults. No wonder they would have so many kids back then besides lack of birth control.

I felt tightness in my chest and I swallowed a few times to try and relax it but it didn't help. Jasper, sensing my unease, rested a comforting hand on my shoulder in understanding.

"Jasper, do you ever regret not having children of your own?" I asked over my shoulder.

"At some point I did but I was blessed to take over the rearing of yer Da so in many ways, I did." He cleared his throat then returned our attention to the book.

"He fought in the battle of Flodden, an English victory that one.

Good King James IV died that day. He was a young King but so naïve in the ways of war. He had potential though."

We took a break, he going about doing his daily rituals of managing the household staff, and I went down to the kitchen to scrounge for the makings of a sandwich. I thought over the information we'd found, and did the math for my grandfather's age then. He had been forty.

He had been twenty-five when he came here if the year they were from was 1503 as Jasper claimed. Why after all the years of being in that era did they come through to 1963?

Nana found me stuffing my face as a true American only could, with mayo at both corners of my mouth and my cheeks swollen from too large a bite.

She looked as though she might laugh but recovered quickly and instead, found a napkin for me to clean my face. "Where have ye been hidin' yerself these last few days lass; and Jasper for that matter?"

It took me a few tries of swallowing before I could answer, "Not doing much, just a lot of hiking, and reading about the family. Nothing woo hoo. I could ask the same of you Nana," I said, turning the tides onto her.

"Aye, I've been doin' some of this and some of that myself. I visited the tree yesterday. It seems bigger than I remember, gave me quite a chill."

I rubbed her shoulder then continue with my lunch. She settled next to me and sipped her tea. "You drink a lot of tea. You should eat something instead." I commented.

She chuckled, "Lass, I'm seventy years old. What would I want with food?" She looked over at my plate and returned, "Besides, it looks like yer eatin' enough for the both of us. How ye keep yer figure is beyond me."

I blushed even with my cheeks full and keep silent. "So, anythin' good come out of all that readin' on the family?" She asked.

"Not much. I found out that you're the only commoner to marry into the family. How was that received?" I said.

Nana had the good graces to snort over that question. I smiled at her. "Och, lass, it was not verae welcome to be exact. There were plenty of blue-bloods here, and what was left of the family tried to convince Papa not to marry me."

She shook her head at the memory of the gathering, of the Campbells and the available nobility for him to choose from. Even after telling them not to bother.

"It was quite a day at the Campbell gathering. Granted it was 1963, back then Scotland wasnae like the states. Old beliefs were still strong then. Anyway, the nobility were dressed in their finery, the men in their kilts and the ladies in their family tartans over their gowns; jewels dripping from their ears.

"We caused quite a tizzy. He looked so handsome. He wore the kilt he arrived in, linen shirt that my mother had made for him in starched white, huntin' knife at his hip, sporran strapped at his waist and a dark blue surcoat. His hair lay over his shoulders in black waves, such a no-no then.

"A few feminine gasps were heard among the crowd and I inwardly beamed. They couldnae have him. My parents were there and he joined them immediately, forging our connection even tighter.

"Louder gasps echoed throughout the crowd as I made my presence known. My mother had given me her wedding dress, handed down from generation to generation."

Her eyes had glistened over with the memory of her special day. I could see the young girl she was, sitting in front of me. She looked into her tea cup, turning it back and forth.

"The gown was dark blue velvet; somehow it matched his surcoat perfectly. The threading was gold and tiny creamy pearls sewn on to mirror a midnight sky of stars. No frilly things or petticoats. The back trailed three feet behind me, and the scooped neckline and bodice enhanced my bosom. It seemed the dress was made just for me.

"My hair flowed behind my shoulders in vibrant red waves, braids woven through the top to keep it out of my face. I felt like royalty. Dinnae matter what they thought; only what he thought and by the look in Jon's eyes, I was all his and, he mine."

She took a few sips of tea and I unknowingly had stopped chewing and coughed when I tried to. She patted my back and gave me her tea to help the food's progress down my throat.

When she didn't continue, I blurted out, "Well? That's it?!" She laughed at that and settled back down to continue.

"While everyone was busy looking at me, the town priest had joined my parents and Jon. Once I joined Jon, the priest married us on the spot, or so everyone thought.

"Jon knew how the gathering would go so we made the plans for our marriage to occur on the day. Jasper and my parents and a few cousins on my side, knew about the weddin'. Once the ceremony was over, there were unhappy Campbells and quite a few unhappy prospective maidens glarin' at us.

"We dinnae care, we loved each other so much. Couldnae wait to start our family. My parents had dinner set up for all of us, including the Campbells but they chose not to partake. Dancing to folk songs and current music too, God help Jon when it came to dancing to rock n' roll!"

We both laughed at that and she went on to tell me that watching a sixteenth century highlander, brawn and tall, trying to dance to Elvis in a kilt, was truly a sight to behold.

I had a laugh over that myself, letting my imagination take flight on the idea. Once we calmed down, I cleaned up and sat back down. I warred with myself about telling her about finding him after his disappearance.

She would be so happy at least to know that he never remarried, nor fathered any other children other than my father, that there was record of. How lonely he must have been. Without his friend, wife, or son back in his time. She wouldn't have wanted that. I decided not to tell her for now. I hugged her, thanked her for sharing her memory of that day with me, and then excused myself.

CHAPTER 9

Lately, I'd been on edge, like something was on my mind but I couldn't quite put my finger on it. Today it was stronger and it felt as though the house was closing in around me. I needed to get out.

The walks always seemed to help calm the edginess, but for some reason it only got more on my nerves, to the point of bringing on a headache. I began to head back in to get something for my head, but once I got to the door of the mud room, the pain dissipated and I took a shuttering breath of cool air.

So I wouldn't tax myself with a hike after all, but contented myself with walking the grounds; I headed into the gardens. My mind wondered over the last few days' events, the information Jasper and I were able to find and collect.

After awhile I notice my head was completely better; fantastic in fact and breathed in the crisp, cool air and scents of the flowers. Wait, what? "Oh what fresh hell is this?!" I yelled and put my fists on my hips when I saw where I had ended up. The grasses brushed along my jean thighs and the lavender filled my nostrils strongly, almost to choking.

And down the low hill into the valley, stood the cursed tree, leaves rustling in the brisk wind that had started; the leaves shimmered without the sun shining on them.

I walked down furious with myself for coming here again. This time I wanted a closer look. I wanted to yell at it.

A slight tickling sensation began to annoy me under my breastbone and I absently rub at it. As I continue my way down, muttering, the tickle got worse; spreading like an itch that goes unscratched. By the time I'd gotten to the edge of the border of grass that circled the tree, I was out of breath. But, it wasn't from exertion, but from this feeling of a sexual build up; to a climax that wouldn't come.

Two burly hands yanked me back and were followed by the sinewy arms attached to them. I struggled, reaching out; trying to find release but the arms wouldn't let me go.

"Lass, lass; can ye hear me? Jessica, can ye hear me girl?" A deep angry Scottish voice repeated over and over as I was being dragged away. I wept and struggled once more but in vain.

"Jessica, snap out of it! Do ye hear me?" A sharp slap across my face had me snapping out of it all right, finding both Jasper and I standing on the hilltop; Jasper glaring down at me while still grasping my upper arms almost painfully.

He grabbed me into a bear hug, stripping me of breath and I squeaked. He dropped me just as quickly but caught me before I fell on my face. "Wha-what happened?" I ask shakily.

"Oh shit my head!!!!" I fell to my knees and grabbed my head with both hands. The headache was back and it felt as though it had doubled in size.

"Why on earth did you slap me you asshole?!!!" I gasped out, wishing it had been delivered with more force.

I sat and placed my head between my knees, trying hard not to puke my guts up. Jasper stood next to me as if he were a standing stone and his face was set like one too. I asked him again what happened and finally he sat next to me and huffed.

He stared down the hill at the tree before answering, "We almost lost ye, lass. What were ye thinkin' about, comin' down here?"

"I wasn't. I came out to get some air and then my head started hurting. I went back for medication and as I continued my walk back to the house, it dissipated when I reached the back door. So, I continued to walk just the grounds, and then, well…,"

I hesitated in telling him the rest but he gave me a knowing look and his next comment confirmed it.

"Ye felt it then. The Tree. What is it for ye? It's calling? For me, it's this nagging high pitch screech that gets stronger the closer I get to it. I've grown tolerant of it. Most people can't feel it.

"It's more of a dull nagging now for me after all these years. I avoid it as much as possible; only comin' on the anniversary of his Grace's disappearance. Even then, I cannae stay long for fear my ears will burst."

My head feels a tiny bit better but I kept it between my knees while listening to him. I looked up briefly when he had stopped talking and asked, "Does Nana know about this? Does it 'call' to her?"

"No. At least she's never mentioned the like to me. She doesnae come here."

I looked around, feeling only light headed now. "She came a few days ago. She told me to," I added after seeing the disbelieving look on his face.

"She didn't mention anything about a 'feeling' to me and I would have assumed she would have to prevent me from going out here again."

"Yer verae observant, lass. Aye, I dinnae think so either. She visited many times with Jon but she dinnae show any signs of sensing anything unusual. Some can and some cannae. Are ye good now? Can ye make it back to the house or shall I carry ye?"

I actually blushed at the thought but not in embarrassment but in temper at his thinking me so weak.

"No, I can make it on my own thank you," I said smartly and got up to show him. My head spun but I bit my lip and straightened none the less, then headed on down to the house quickly before I fell on my face.

I could still feel the tickling sensation in my chest and I rubbed at it hard, trying to relieve it but to no avail. Once I got into the house, my head felt ten times better and the tickle had finally gone away.

Nana came rushing into the kitchen snaring me in a tight embrace before she looked me over for any visible signs of injury. "I'm fine, Nana. A slight headache again but I'm fine." I said now more for myself than for her.

Jasper was leaning against the sink, arms crossed and scowling at me. I made a face back at him but he didn't react. Damn him.

"Ye need to stay away from there for the last time. Look at you girl, ye look as though ye visited hell itself. Thank the Lord, Jasper caught ye before it took ye." She hugged me again.

"What happened to me there?" A chill ran over me and I start to tremble.

"Some people can sense portals. Some hear them, like me, but it's different for everyone. Some can actually see them; but those are rare. Yer Gran doesnae feel or hear anythin'.

He handed me something in the shape of two pills, and a dram of what turns out to be Scotch. "You do know you're not supposed to mix alcohol with medication right," I quirked an eyebrow at him.

"Och, shite, lass just drink it!" He bellowed at me. I winced from the pain in my head and downed the pills. I thought whiskey was awful but I was wrong, Scotch was worse.

I coughed and cleared my throat, mumbling under my breath as to how anyone could drink the stuff and like it; were crazy. "But why now for me? When I've been there previously, I haven't experienced anything."

Jasper looked at Nana before speaking. "Lass, why do ye think ye've been makin' multiple trips there? Somethin' has been callin' to ye from the start, whether ye felt it or no. It will be Samhain in a couple of weeks. Plenty of 'magic' around that time; could be that's the cause…" he trailed off.

"What is Samhain?" I asked.

"It's a seasonal festival that marks the end of the harvest season and the beginnin' of the winter season. It's said that during the seasonal solstices, the portals are stronger. No one knows why."

I was having a hard time processing all this-nonsense; nonsense being the only word I could come up with. This stuff was only in stories and songs and the imaginings of kids.

"I'm going up to bed. This is a little too much for me." I got up slowly and pushed through the swinging door after bidding them a good night.

"So, it's callin' to her now, but why? We need to keep her away from there." Eleanore rolled the snifter between her hands.

Jasper placed a hand on her shoulder and absently massaged it. She gave a deep sigh and bowed her head into her folded hands.

"I will keep her safe my Lady, at all costs."

"I ken, Jasper. I ken...

After Jasper was done doing his directing of the staff, I pulled him aside to tell him of my thoughts last night and he pondered them for himself.

"That would be interestin' indeed. Once he left and the tree was gone, I gave up all hope, that I was stuck here. It never occurred to me to try and go back. I took the sound I kept hearin' as a warnin' to not to pursue it.

"The sound is quite horrendous to listen to, so why would I want to go towards it only for it to get louder. Had yer Gran been able to travel I wouldnae have hesitated on tryin', bringin' her with me."

He rubbed his chin and I noticed the shadow of growth covering it and his cheeks. He obviously didn't get much rest last night either if he forgot to shave. He's usually impeccably dressed and groomed.

"Jasper, what if I'm supposed to go back, to find him and bring him back? Or maybe I have something to do for the family in the past, not involving him at all?"

"I swore to yer gran that I would keep ye safe lass, so no, I willnae let you try. What if ye don't go to that time?" He demanded.

"Look, if my calculations are correct, it's been a little over five hundred years since your time, seventy years since he went back."

"No! Ye promise me ye'll no try it, lass," he bellowed at me, finger shoved in my face. Stubbornness warred between us and our tempers clashed. *Promise, promise?!!* Ha, not bloody likely.

"Dinnae try to lie to me either girl, ye have the same look yer grandpa had when he was up to no good."

"Fine, I'll try not to go." I spit out over my shoulder. "Wait, why don't you come with me? A woman wondering around could be mishandled. You're more familiar with the area too." I suggested.

"Absolutely not! I cannae be leavin' yer Gran by herself. We're all she has! No, that's not happenin'."

"She's not an invalid for Christ sake; she can take care of herself." I rolled my eyes at him. His face turned beet red then moved into a deep shade of purple. I swear I could see smoke coming out of his ears.

"She couldnae bear to have the rest of her family up and leave her. It would break her." At that he stomped out and slammed the door. That man was truly impossible sometimes. I growled as one of the maids came in and she immediately turned and exited the room.

I found my laptop, snagged my car keys from the main hall closet and took off into town. I needed to be away from this place and all its *magic* and beliefs for awhile.

The weather matched my mood and I punch the gas and sped up. By the time I reached town, my temper had cooled down enough to be around others in polite society, but hoped no one would bother me.

Parking turned out to be a bitch and I could feel my temper rising again and once I found parking, I sat for a few minutes. The rain came down in sheets and the sound of it crashing on my car seemed to help calm me down completely.

I looked out the side window, noticing that my parking space was right in front of the church. And none other than Father Kirkland stood standing in the alcove of the doors, speaking to one of his parishioners. The candle light behind him in the chapel looked so warm and welcoming; like a beacon for a lost ship in a storm. As if sensing my presence, Father Kirkland motioned me to come in. I pull out my umbrella and after locking the car, jogged up the stairs to the entry way.

"Why, Miss Jessica, what a pleasant surprise. But of course it's always a pleasure to see ye here. How is yer gran? I'll be seein' her in a couple of days for tea." He ushered me in and down the main isle between the pews, taking a seat in the second row in the front.

"Now child, ye seem to need a weight lifted off yer shoulders. How can I be helpin' with that?"

Rain water dripped from my bangs and I notice soon after that, that the rest of me was dripping onto the masonry floors.

"Oh, Father I'm sorry! Just look at me, I'm making a mess on the floor."

"Nonsense lass, the stones will soak it all up, not to worry. Now, tell me what ails ye." He gently took one of my icy hands into both of his warm ones, and rubs lightly.

I sat quietly, looking at the large cross that hung over the altar, and bit my lip. How do I go about telling him all of what's been going on? He'd call the cops and have me in an asylum in five seconds.

"Something has come to my attention, something quite extraordinary and I'm being torn in different directions over it. I feel as though I must leave my gran and I'm not sure for how long; if I'll be able to come back to her. Anyway, Jasper doesn't want me to go, and I asked him to come with me; to help me, but he refuses.

Where I'm going I am unfamiliar with the territory and he's very knowledgeable of it. I might even find what I'm looking for a lot sooner if I had his help."

He looked at me; trying to gauge where I was going with my story. "What be it ye lookin' for?"

"I'd like answers to start with. I'm in search of answers as to what happened to my grandfather. You know of my grandfather's err, passing, I'm sure. Well, I'm in search of him." He looked at me confused.

"What are ye sayin', lass? His body was burnt to ashes in the fire. We have an empty plot for him in the cemetery. That's all yer goin' to find on him." He shook his head in sympathy.

I ground my teeth, trying to grasp patience after a long day, and not lose my temper in the house of the Lord. I shifted on the pew and quivered from the chill rising from the stone floor.

"I'll be right back. I'll bring ye a dry blanket to chase the chill. Stay here, lass."

I watch him go through a side door in the altar wall and silence fell upon the chapel after the echo of the door closing. I saw for the first time that the room was lit by candles everywhere; shadows playing in corners the light couldn't reach.

Father Kirkland returned with a large wool blanket and wrapped me up in it. "The church is old and loses power during these storms, so we light candles, more for warmth than for seein' for just in case during the storms. Most people stay home in weather like this so why waste electricity." He said sheepishly.

"Thank you Father. This is very kind of you, I'm feeling better already." I rubbed the towel over my hair fiercely then twisted it into a turban.

He waved me off then joined me again, but sat in the pew in front of me instead of next to me. "Now lass, as ye were sayin'. Why does Jasper need to go with you? Doesnae he needs to be around for yer gran?"

Obviously I'm not making much sense so I gauged my next words carefully. He was a religious man after all; someone with strong beliefs and familiar with all types of mythology and the like. What if I were to be straight with him?

I walked up to the altar, and tightened the blanket around me. "Father, my grandfather didn't die in a fire. Yes he's dead now, but he lived a long life."

Silence greeted me and I turned to see if he was even there. He was and was sitting patiently, waiting for me to elaborate more. I cleared my throat and stood facing him.

"The tree he burnt down, well it wasn't just a tree…," he still sat quietly.

"It's a doorway, a portal to another time. I know it sounds crazy but it's true. Jasper came with him. He couldn't return once the tree was destroyed. He can now, with me."

"So yer sayin', the Duke and Jasper; traveled here through a tree. And that yer grandpa went back to his time instead of stayin' here." He steepled his fingers and tapped his lips.

"He didn't go back intentionally." I said a bit heatedly. I gasped at my outburst towards him and quickly apologized for it. "So, if this tree is callin' to you, then you must go. If what you say is true then there is somethin' for you there. If God gave me the chance to do somethin' spectacular such as this, I wouldnae question it."

Stunned, I just stood there mouth gaping wide and speechless. "What? Did ye no' think I would believe ye, lass? God works in mysterious ways and who am I to tell ye nay or yay? I give ye my blessin' for a safe journey. Is there anythin' I can do to help with yer journey?"

I shook my head no, too emotional to speak. He took me back to the main chapel doors. I handed him back the blanket and towel only to have the blanket pushed gently back with directions to keep myself dry and warm.

The rain had stopped while I had been talking with the Father and now my eyes were blinded for a moment from the rays of the sun peeked through the rain clouds.

I questioned my sanity at the angelic scenery in front of me, wondering if I had actually left the church, or had passed out on the altar floor. But no, it was real and I had to admit, it was pretty breathtaking.

For now, I chose to believe in signs and took the scene before me as a sign that all was right with the world for the moment. I thought over what the Father Kirkland had said. It looked like I'd be going on a journey, and I was going to be damn sure Jasper went with me.

Father Kirkland gave me information on the time period that I hopefully would land in, and said he would try and find period clothing for me. A soft knock on the door announced my dinner but I ate without tasting the food. There were too many things on my mind now to simply enjoy it.

Another knock later came and before I could reach it, Jasper shoved his way through it to stand over me; glaring and snarling. "What do *you* want Jasper?!" I snapped at him before he could tear my head off first.

"So, yer hidin' like a stubborn wee bairn I see."

"How did you find me? I didn't tell Nana where I was staying." I snapped again.

"Ha, that's what's nice about bein' part of the help. We ken each other and relay information."

I still didn't budge, but continued to glare up at him. "Alright! Father Kirkland called me and told me, ye happy?" He snarled.

"Why are you here? Go back home Jasper. I just wanted a good night's sleep without a damn headache and ghosties flitting about. And 'magical' trees calling to me every waking and sleeping moment."

I sat back on the bed and continued to eat my dinner, ignoring him as he continued to stand there in the door way. Finally he left, closing the door quietly behind him.

Father Kirkland joined me for breakfast, carrying a parcel with him. I guessed right that the parcel was of the time period clothing. It looked as though he was successful.

"I borrowed these from the threatre. I thought it best that I get clothes suitable for a young farm hand rather than for a woman. I hope ye dinnae mind. It would be much safer for ye, traveling in disguise."

"Lass, since magic is being dealt with here, maybe find out what date yer *seanair* left and see if ye can get as close to it yerself. It just might help."

"Thank you, Father, for everything. I can't believe I'm doing this. It's insane!"

He squeezed my hand and took his leave. I packed the parcel into my car before heading back to the manse. There was someone I needed to talk to; a much overdue conversation was needed.

CHAPTER 10

JASPER STOOD AT THE door, uniform impeccably in place however, on closer inspection, there was a gap on the right side between his collar and neck. So, he'd been tugging it for some time, awaiting my arrival.

I turned my nose up at him and waltzed through the front door and into the entry hall. Since one of the maids passed by me, I directed her to have my things brought to my room. Before she continued on, I inquired as to where I would find my grandmother.

Nana was in her private solar, writing at her secretary. She was so deep in thought, that she hadn't heard me come in. The sun was streaming in at just the right angle to touch her hair, setting off the different hues of reds still visible through the snowy white curls.

I watch a minute more, and then I reluctantly cleared my throat, breaking the spell, and she turned to see me in the doorway.

She looked me up and down, still sitting at her secretary, pen poised over paper. I came and sat beside her. Could I bring her love, her life, her soul, back to her? I took her hand and squeezed gently.

"Nana, I've a few things to tell you; about the family history. I've been studying it. Nana, I think the tree wants me to find Papa and bring him home."

She looked at me a bit startled. "Mo Ghradh, he is gone and willnae return. He would have tried if it had been possible."

She cupped my cheeks with her hands and tears shimmered on her lashes. "Besides, there is no tellin' if he even made it back to his time; or if he ended up somewhere else. Please Jessie, dinnae think any more of it."

"I found him," I stated matter of fact.

She sat slowly and looked at me, a little unsure as to what I had just said. "What, did ye say?"

"I found him, Nana; he made it home." I gave her a hopeful smile.

"I found him in the family archive tomes in the library. He returned five years later than when he left."

"Are ye sure? But it cannae be," she exclaimed in panic. "I poured over those damn books for years, tryin' to find anythin' on him, but there was nothin' that I could find?!"

"You couldn't find anything? Did you look in the right ones?" I asked puzzled.

"Aye! When I wasnae raisin' and beatin' yer da and takin' care of our home and lands, I would be up into the wee hours of the mornin', books surroundin' me in the library. Paper cuts on my fingers and hours and hours of little sleep tryin' to find him."

She began to cry hysterically and I tried unsuccessfully to calm her down. It got so unmanageable that I had to take her by the hand and dragged her to the library. I found the tome I needed, still on the desk where I had left it and sat her down.

"Jasper and I both found him. Here, here he is, right next to his younger brother." I pointed to the page but she only cried harder.

"What's the meanin' of all this cryin' and blatherin' about?!" Jasper bellowed from the doorway. Once he laid eyes on Nana, I knew I was in for a severe tongue lashing.

"I told her about finding Papa. I'm showing her the proof."

He and I went over to her, opened more books, finding other pages to show her.

"Where, I dinnae see him, I dinnae see him anywhere!"

Jasper and I looked at each other and the truth settled over us. Not only could she not feel anything from the portal, but she also didn't have the capability of seeing the information in the books either. The gravity of what we had done overwhelmed me and I sank into a chair.

Jasper collected Nana into his arms and settled her on his lap while she sobbed. Tears streamed down my own face and I laid my head down on the desk in defeat. I've broken her heart for the second time. Why didn't I think of that before?

"Mo Cridhe, Jessie is right it is there. I have seen it myself; with my own eyes. Please believe me. I wouldnae lie to ye." He rocked her in his lap and her sobs seemed to grow more painful.

She pushed away from him then stormed out of the library, Jasper still seated, and glared at me. He warned me to keep all of this from her but I didn't listen and look where it got all of us; especially her.

"Well I hope yer pleased with yerself. I warned ye but you dinnae bother to listen." He got up and stomped out, slamming the door behind him.

I sat on the floor huddled and crying myself into a puddle for an hour or so, and my own heart-broken and beaten. I got up, straightened up the desk and the books; putting them back on their shelves since they were no longer needed.

I shuffled on to my room, stopping by Nana's door after seeing light under her door. I went to knock but I stopped, hearing muffled sobs behind the door. I had to make this right, for the both of us. I moved on and collapsed onto my bed, fresh sobs wracking my body anew.

Since neither Jasper nor Nana was going to help me, I'd have to do all of this on my own. I collected my jewelry, including my engagement ring and headed into town again.

Once I'd done my business of removing the stones from their holdings, I headed over to the church to say good-bye to Father Kirkland. I spotted him and he summoned me over to join him.

"I spoke with Nana about everything and it did not go well. Jasper is furious so I'm afraid I'm on my own with my journey."

"Well maybe it's as it should be. When do ye leave?" We walked through the small garden, my hands in my pockets, his; clasped behind his back. It was so peaceful here. I hated to leave it.

"Oh, I almost forgot, ye might need this to get ye started once ye've arrived. It's not much but it should last ye a couple of weeks." He handed me a leather pouch and it clinked as I opened it. As I up ended it, coins trickled into the palm of my hand and I gasped. They were period money!

"How did you get these?" I asked as I fingered the few that I held. I poured them back into the pouch, adding the smaller pouch that held the stones and lumps of gold from the jewelry.

"Och, never ye mind where I got them. I have my ways." He walked me back to the front of the church and bid me farewell.

"Thank you for all your help and kindness and support. I'm glad someone believes that I can do this." I shook both his hands then headed back to my car.

I finished packing and changed out of my modern clothes. I packed those as well, in case I end up in a more modern time rather than in the past.

Jasper came into my room unannounced and I chastised him for it. When I informed him that I could have been naked his reply was a dismissive snort followed by a "not bloody likely," comment.

"So, are ye ready then? We need to get a move on if we are to make it by sunset." He collected my satchel but I snatched it back.

"I don't need your help thank you. You were right, she needs you." I tried to go around him, but he stepped into the doorway, blocking my exit. I growled at him and tried to shove him. No such luck.

"Dinnae be daft woman! How do ye plan on findin' him, *if* ye find him? Ye dinnae ken the country like I do. It doesnae look the same as it is now."

"I'll be fine. I have money enough and with my attire I should blend in as a farmhand."

"Do ye not think highwaymen willnae take a fancy to a…" he looked me up and down, "a little boy?"

I growled at him and tried again to shove him away but he was as solid as a statue. "Oh my God you're incredibly strong for your age. What are you now, a hundred?" I hoped that had offended him but he only smirked.

"No, I'm" he stopped to think about it and I laughed. "It doesnae matter how old I am. I'd still do better out there than ye. Besides, what if ye do find him and bring him back? I couldnae bear to see them together. Their love would break me. Let me die in my own time in my own home. Please." He asked quietly.

That hadn't crossed my mind and I felt horrible for it. He'd had so many years with Nana, loved her from afar; and to have that life shattered for him, I knew how that felt.

After a long moment of standing there, a cough sounded behind him and he nearly jumped out of his skin. How much had she heard of what he'd just said.

"My Lady, how long have ye been standin' there?" He actually stammered and blushed. I can't help but hide a smile.

She walked in and strode over to me. "This is for ye. It brought me luck on my weddin' day; may it bring ye luck wherever yer travels bring ye."

She handed me a folded piece of fabric. I gently unfolded it. Tears collected in my eyes as I ran a hand over the blue velvet gown that had been her wedding dress. I embraced her tightly then folded the dress with care before putting it in my satchel.

She turned to Jasper and placed her hand on his cheek. "Jasper, ye have been a constant companion for me and I too have loved ye. Not as you would hope, but love all the same.

"I know it calls to ye as well, and ye should have returned years ago. I regret that I kept ye here, but it's time for ye to go home. I'll be fine my dear friend. Take care of her and if ye see Jonathan, please tell him I never forgot him, nor did my love for him fade."

Nana handed him a package wrapped in tanned leather, directing him to give it to Jon if he were to see him. He nodded then embraced her. He hadn't done that since the day Jon had gone back.

"Lass, it's time. My Lady, will ye walk with us?" Jasper asked.

Nana shook her head no, saying she could not bear to see two more of her loved ones taken from her. She'd much rather remember us here. She walked us to the kitchen, handed us another parcel which contained food. Jasper took it and flung over his shoulder.

We embraced Nana a final time then left as she watched us from the kitchen doorway. Before I left, I had handed over an envelope asking her to send it to my father.

Jasper and I headed off into the sunset as the saying goes; not speaking. I wouldn't say it was a comfortable silence but it wasn't uncomfortable either; just the two of us with our thoughts.

As we got closer, my heart roared in my ears and the tickle spread through my chest and soon through my body.

I hoped for release once I'd touched the tree. Jasper shoved what appeared to be cotton or cloth into his ears and I wished it would have been that simple for me.

We stepped to the edge of the grass circling the trunk of the tree and clasped hands without thought. We looked at each other, both out of breath from the pull of the portal and we reached out and touched the tree.

The release I wanted; no needed, hit me with such a force that my head snapped back and I could no longer feel

Jasper's hand in mine. When breath filled my lungs again, my vision dimmed in and out, and then faded out to black. Now there was only silence and darkness.

The sound of a growl had awoken me and I didn't move. I couldn't tell if my eyes were open or still closed; the only thing I could see was darkness. The growl sounded again, only to be followed by what sounded like curse words. I heard shuffling near me and I tried to sit up.

"Jessie, are ye there lass?" a horse voice asked me.

I swallowed a few times, tried speaking but had to clear my throat a couple more times before I was able to get a word out. I croaked out miserably that I was, in fact there, but where was another matter; I had no idea.

I felt a strong hand cup the back of my neck, and the feeling of cool water rushed over my lips and I thought I was in heaven.

"Where are we," I managed to croak out.

He looked around and shrugged. "It's too dark to tell. We need some rest anyway after all that business." He laid me back down, thankfully feeling a makeshift pillow behind my head. He wrapped me in something warm and I soon fell asleep.

I woke up to the smell of meat; bacon to be exact and my stomach grumbled loudly. I opened my eyes and sunlight flashed into them. I slapped a hand over them quickly and cursed from the sting throbbing in them.

"How are ye feelin' this mornin', lass?" Jasper was sitting across from me making breakfast. He looked like hell, and I could only imagine how I must have looked.

I sat up and stretched, every joint in my limbs popping left and right. I rubbed my tearing eyes, then, squinting at him I answered, "Just dandy."

I got up and walked around to get the blood flowing again in all of my extremities, and then plopped back down; closer to him and the fire. I closed my eyes at the smell of the bacon.

He handed me a cup of what smelled like coffee, and I told him that I could possibly be in love with him for this banquet. He chuckled and handed me a plate with the bacon and a biscuit.

So, any idea where we are or, rather, *when*?" I took a bite of both bacon and biscuit before continuing with, "Do you recognize anything?"

I took a minute to look around our little camp, and noticed that there wasn't a fresh dead pig lying about with its flesh missing. "Where did we get bacon from?"

"Yer gran packed us some staples so, hence the bacon and biscuits and coffee. We have more and other foods too, but we need to pace ourselves. We don't know when we might reach the next town or home."

He took a large swallow of his own coffee before answering my earlier questions. "As to the year, I have no idea, and as to where, well I am verae sure we are in Scotland. I would ken the smell anywhere."

Once we were fed and caffeinated, we closed up camp and just began to walk.

We walked for what seemed like hours but turned out to be only about two, thanks to my watch; one of the few things from my time I took with me.

It was either Fall or early Winter; small amounts of snow clung to the higher cliffs and terrain. A light dusting had started and I huddled more under my coat for warmth. I cursed quietly that I hadn't counted on what the weather would be like, and wished I had brought at least gloves.

We trudged on, stopping every four hours to rest. The light was waning and we needed to find a place where we would be out of the elements. Jasper found an overhang of rock and so we laid claim to it for the night.

One thing I was good at was starting a fire and with the fire- starter that had also made its way here with us. I got one started quickly as he set up a canvas tarp for our shelter. It wasn't the Plaza but it would have to do.

He made tea and added some whiskey to each cup and more bacon. We ate silently, both going over what had already transpired and what we may face tomorrow or in the near future. I had come across a few large rocks and put them into the fire once it had started. Now that we were ready to settle in, I took two out for him and two out for me, setting them next to us under our blankets.

Jasper sighed audibly and I smiled to myself. "Where did ye learn that trick, lass? I'm goin' to sleep like a wee bairn tonight!"

I chuckled at his compliment and told him I had learned it while camping as a child. He voiced his approval once more then snores soon followed. I feel asleep soon after him, hoping we would find something tomorrow to help us.

Our second morning was just like the first but less stiff, thanks to the heated rocks. We continued on and once we were over yet another hill, and I tell you, I have had about enough of these "hills", Jasper had spotted something familiar.

I looked around myself, trying to see whatever he was seeing, but nothing stood out to me. Just more rocks, snow, and a few trees. It was mid afternoon when Jasper called for a short break. He looked around as he'd been doing since we'd left camp. Then he abruptly halted.

"What? What are you looking at?" I asked, still scanning the area.

"We're close to where Jon and I traveled. I can hear the static from that portal!" He began walking in that general direction, and updated me every ten minutes that the static was either getting louder or softer depending our direction.

When he announced that we had arrived at the portal, I took several steps back quickly. I didn't hear or sense anything from it myself, but I could see Jasper was getting more and more uncomfortable being next to it himself. He yelled at me to follow him.

I cringed at his bellowing of instructions, but I followed him anyway, walking past him to shut him up. My own head was starting to pound from him. Once his bellows became a normal tone we stopped to catch our breaths.

"You didn't have to yell at me, Jasper; I could hear you just fine back there! Now I have a headache."

He was hunched over, hands on knees and tried to catch his breath. After about five minutes and a few chugs of water, he stood up and scanned the area.

"I'm sorry. I forgot ye dinnae hear them. We head North from here. This will take us to the Manse." We picked up our gear then proceeded northward.

After a mile or so I asked how long it would take us to get there. I was none too happy with the answer.

"About a week." He looked at me and got defensive after seeing my facial expression.

"What? We dinnae have horses to get us there faster." He started walking, not looking back to see if I would follow or not. I secured my stuff over my shoulder then started behind him, grumbling.

To pass the time, I asked him questions about what to expect once we got to the Manse. "Well let's see, women were more obedient for starters," He looked at me with a scowl.

"Food isnae like back where yer from; quite borin' in fact. There are no stores but town markets. There ye bargain before payin', mind. You pay the merchant the original price he quotes ye, news will get around and they will take ye for every cent ye have.

"It's usually the staff of the manor that go to the market, though so unless there is something you really need, which I can tell you, you won't, stay away from the market."

"Once Jon had taken on the title and responsibilities after losin' his father, he took his job verae seriously. He would come down to the market at least twice a week to visit with the people."

"Anyway, men do the hunting, takin' home boar, cow, deer, rabbit, things of that nature, and the ladies of the house do their women stuff, needle-somethin' or other. Dependin' on yer position in life, from peasant to lady of the house, the rolls are many. Child rearing, wet nurse, maid, lady in waiting, chamber maid, Mistress of the keep, etc."

He fell silent for a moment, lost in thought. We stopped for a break and ate, resting only for a few minutes this time. He was eager to get home I guess.

"Ye ken we used chamber pots for doin' our business right? And unfortunately, there's no toilet paper for wipin'. Och, but dinnae fash lass, we use cloths for our bums. We're not savages." He laughed at seeing my look of horror at the thought of no toilet paper.

CHAPTER 11

I READ UP ON the time period of living, and so had a general idea of what a day in being a lady was like, and found it was going to be very difficult for me, being from modern times and that time being of liberation and speaking one's mind, male or female alike.

Most importantly, I was to stay at his side the whole time. I was posing as a young farm hand but even young boys experienced brutality at its finest. I had some training in the fine arts of sword play, fencing in high school; so I had no problem agreeing to stay with him.

It was beginning to darken into nightfall and about a mile or so ahead, the twinkle of lights brought us to sharp attention. Finally! Civilization! I could practically run the rest of the way if it meant food and a room with a bed to sleep on; my legs thought otherwise.

The village was small, what we could see of it in the dusky background. There were about ten small houses, community stables, and on closer inspection, a well that sat in the middle of the courtyard.

Jasper headed for the stables and looked around. "Hello, anyone about?" He called out. I stood behind him looking over his shoulder.

"Aye, I'm here. Who might ye be, sir?" A rotund man exited a stall and gave the horse in it a rub of the nose.

"I am Jasper Campbell and this here is mo ogha, Jessie."

"I ken everyone in this area, and never heard of ye. Where are ye from, and where are yer mounts?" the man asked suspiciously.

"We were taken upon by a group of highway men. They took our horses and our supplies that were on them. This is all we have now. We are verae tired and we are seekin' shelter for the night." Jasper jingled a few coins that were in his pocket and waited.

The man stood there, looking Jasper up and down then drew his gaze over to me. I shuffled my feet and tried to hide more behind Jasper. I didn't care for the look that was currently in the man's eyes.

"We are a small community so we dinnae have an inn. If ye dinnae mind the smell, there's a stall down there that's empty. It isnae much but it is warm and dry."

"We'll take it. Thanks be to ye, sir." Jasper handed over the coins then proceeded down the aisle. I followed him, keeping an eye on the man.

"My name is Niell; my house is to the right of the stables. Come and see me in the mornin' if ye will. Guid nicht."

Once the man had left us, I entered the stall and laid out my cloak. There was a nice mound of hay just waiting for me and it would feel so good not to sleep on the hard ground for one night.

Jasper had already settled down and his snores soon filled the stables. I rolled my eyes then did all I could to ignore them. I'd placed dirk just under my blanket for protection. I really didn't have much knowledge in the use of it, but I felt better having it there all the same. Once comfortable, I finally let sleep take hold of me.

I woke to the sound of a tinkling sound. I stiffened immediately then told myself to relax; that it was most likely some kind of gear for the horses.

I stretched then took a look around our stall, noticing that Jasper had already risen and gone. Where was he? I stood in panic, looking around in hopes of seeing him. I knew he wouldn't leave me but I couldn't help feel the panic fill me.

The tinkling sound came again and looked down at where it was coming from. A little girl stood watching me and her doll was what was tinkling when she moved it.

"Hello." I said then crouched down to her level. She didn't answer but tilted her head in curiosity. I forgot they didn't speak much English here in the countryside.

"Awrite," a male voice said, and Jasper appeared next to her. He bent down to her. The little girl handed him the doll for him to inspect and he took it a smile.

"an-dáthúil." *Very pretty*, he'd said in Gaelic.

"Go raibh maith agat." *Thank you very much*. She replied shyly then beamed a smile at him.

She turned back to me and held it up for me to see next. I took it and gave it a little shake, making the doll jingle and dance. She giggled then reached for it.

"dol air ais gu d 'mhàthair, a ghalad, lass." *Go back to your mother*

95

She scurried off, shaking her doll as I had.

"What did you say to her?" I asked him.

"I told her to return to her mother. Pack up yer stuff and let's get a move on. I was able to purchase some food from our host. We still have a couple of days before we reach Rowen Castle."

As we'd packed up our things, we'd come up with the story that I was Jasper's *ogha* in case anyone asked while staying here, in this time. The story was to continue on, once we'd arrived at Rowen Castle.

Niell and his daughter waved us on as we took our leave of their village. The little girl held out her doll and shook it violently. I waved back then turned away. I little did I know, the next time I'd see her, there would be no sunny smile to greet me.

It had been dusk on our third day of traveling, when we'd arrived just outside of a much larger village. Music and laughter poured out through the pub's door as it opened continuously. Since it seemed lively there, we headed on in and inquired about getting a room for the night.

Once that had been taken care of that, we stashed our belongings in our room and took our valuables with us before we headed down to the pub.

Jasper looked so pleased with his supper. I couldn't tell what we were eating; it was just one gelatinous lump and weird shades of brown. I poked at it with my fork, and then sent up a prayer that I didn't die from Dysentery before I took a bite. It wasn't bad and I was too hungry to care anymore. The tankard of ale helped get it all down along with some bread.

I scanned the room and saw that the dress code was optional for many of the women loitering on a few of the men's laps. I cringed at seeing their bared breasts being groped by the dirty men. Jasper seemed oblivious to it all, being so focused on his second helping of supper. One of the women sashayed over to him, gracing him with a mostly toothless smile, the smell of stale sex and body order clinging to her, and I had to try hard not to bring up my dinner. He swatted her away which only brought her over to me. I did the same.

"So, I suppose ye'd be wantin' to ken more about yer seanair; other than what yer Nan told ye I mean."

"Tell me everything. What was it like to live back in this time? What was my grandfather like? Tell me all."

"Well let's see now, yer *seanair* was born in the year 1476 in the middle of winter. I have forgotten the date after all these years but we dinna do birthday celebrations anyway. I'm sure it's written down somewhere.

Anyway, we celebrated milestones and gatherin's. Now that's a celebration ye'd have to see." He grew quiet, and a look of nostalgia played over his face.

"Our time wasnae a peaceful time; celebrations were far and few between. We always found ways to have a good time, being in pubs and the like if you ken what I mean." He winked at me. I make a grossed out expression and he actually chuckled.

"Anyway, Jon and I were not much older between each other, a couple of years only; I bein' the younger. We studied and trained together, learned battle strategy, and so on. His father would tell stories of his fight in the Sack battle. That was a proud day for the Scots. The English tried in vain to take Douglas' army but we won," He looked off again and his eyes began to glaze over, and I cleared my throat to bring him back.

He focused back on me and cleared his throat again before continuing. "We would spend most of the day comin' up with strategies, only to have either his father or his father's Captain critique them, finding weak areas and have us start over again.

"At the age of eighteen, he became the next Duke of Devonshire, his father being taken upon my deserters of Northumberland's army and murdered. One of his father's men returned not in verae good shape himself, and succumbed to his wounds soon after his return, but before he did, he was able to report to Jon what the murder looked like.

"Jon gathered a few of his men, including myself and we set out to find them. It took us a couple of weeks but we found them camped on the border and took them by surprised while they were in their beds.

"We brought them back, held them until we ken to do with them. He ordered to behead them, except for the murderer. Jon spent days torturin' him. I won't go into details as to how but ye could hear the screams for hours straight. Jon got tired of him soon enough and had him made a lesson to all who thought to betray his house, and had him set up, disemboweled then beheaded."

He sniffed as though trying to remove a sour smell from his nose then continued to eat. My stomach turned at the image my mind painted and I shuttered. I pushed aside my dinner, no longer hungry.

"Yer *seanair* is, was, not a brutal man; quite the opposite. It was a dark time until the execution. Things got back to normal a few weeks after and Jon, myself and our usual group of men, visited the tenants, collectin' rents and offerin' assistance to any of them in need.

"He knew everae one of his tenants, even the new bairns that came along. He took care of his people, just like his father had. His father raised him well." Jasper took a few swigs from his tankard of ale. "He adored yer Gran. He fell in love with her the minute he saw her. He would say she took his breath away that day. Standin' in the lavender, hair blowin' free from her braid, and her bewitchin' green eyes."

I cleared my throat, not sure what to think about what he'd just told me. "Uh, Jasper, it sounds like you fell in love with her too. Sorry," I said immediately at the sharp look he gave me.

I actually felt myself shrink as much as I could, into the bench. I thought my dad was good at scolding. Man.

"As I was sayin', in the short time they had together, they're hearts were for each other. They never left each other's side. They were married soon after they met and a year later, yer Da way born.

Jon got right back into bein' a Duke, visitin' the tenants; only difference was the modern technology. Things we would normally have helped with were taken care of by professionals. He filled his time with yer Da, teachin' him sword fightin' and how to ride, and things like that.

"Once the locals heard about his equestrian skills, they asked him to teach their lads and even some lassies. Mind, he dinnae need the money, he enjoyed the work and the children.

"Yer grandparents had planned to have more children, but sadly, yer Gran couldnae carry to term any other bairns. They contented themselves with yer Da and the local children."

"I'm sorry Jasper. He meant so much to you both."

"Aye, lass, he did, that he did."

I excused myself and headed upstairs to our room, so exhausted from all our walking and nights out in the cold. I don't know what time Jasper joined me in the room, but I vaguely remember hearing the door open and the bolt sliding into place. A familiar grumble sounded and then a belch.

When I woke in the morning, I found him snoring loudly, enough to wake the dead, wrapped up in his tartan on the floor. I pulled on my clothes quietly, flung the blanket from the bed over him then headed down to break my fast.

CHAPTER 12

"The Manse is about four days from here. I purchased a couple of horses, not verae good ones but they'll do.", Jasper checking the cinching of the saddles. We secured our belongings to their backs then hopped on. He looked so graceful when getting on, where as I; well let's just say I hoped no one saw it.

"How did you pay for these?" I asked, as I reached for my money pouch like Gollum from The Lord of The Rings.

"Och, dinnae fash yourself; I dinnae use yer money. I did come here with my own from when I was last here. There wasnae any use for them in yer time."

An audible sigh of relief escaped me and I pulled my hand out from my coat pocket. He rolled his eyes.

"Is it a bad time to tell you that I've never ridden a horse before?" I said to him sheepishly.

"The horse is tame and will follow mine. Just hold these." He handed me the reins with instructions to give a little "click" sound with my mouth and assured me she would move. "Tug the reins not too tightly to get her to stop."

"How do I turn?"

"Dinnae worry about that now. As I said, she will follow mine. Dinnae get nervous either. She will sense it and get agitated and that's when you lose the control and she takes over."

He clicked his horse into motion, going slowly to make sure he didn't run anyone over in the street. I followed suit and once out of town, he gave another round of clicks and a quick snap of the reins and we were soon in a slow steady gallop.

I almost lost my balance a couple of times when we first started galloping and I had a few choice curse words for the horse. The whole time while on the horse, I prayed for a car. It didn't matter what kind of car, just a car. How I took mine for granted in my time. My ass hurt down to the bone and all I could do from bitching was to curse some more at the horse.

When he called for a stop to water the horses, I slid off and crumpled to the ground. There was a fleeting thought of kissing it, but I just lay where I fell; sprawled out in a snow angel pose.

"I can see I'll have to set up camp by myself, again." He said over his shoulder while unloading our food stuffs.

I gave him a thumb up but stayed where I was until I could feel the blood rush down to my lower extremities. As I sat up, my back cracked in several places and my knees kinked as I tried to stand. "Man I must be getting old," I said as I dusted off my breeches.

"Old?! HA, if yer old then I must be a ghostie followin' ye around; old my arse, girl."

I stuck my tongue out at his back and he advised me to put it back in my face which had me doing it real quick and gaping instead. How the hell did he know I was doing that?

"We'll not be stayin' long here lass, just long enough to eat and see to the horses. This isnae exactly a place ye want to be out in. An hour at most then we saddle up again."

I started to balk but shut my mouth at the stern look he gave me. I began to feel like I truly was his grandchild, what with all the admonishing he'd been giving to me lately.

All too soon it was time to saddle up and once again he helped me up onto mine. He calmed my horse as it didn't seem to like my being on its back, and I could relate to its feelings.

When my butt hit the saddle seat I gasped and I felt tears fill my eyes but I sucked it up, took a few breaths before loping off behind Jasper's mount. There was no crying allowed in this harsh time.

The countryside was so…lacking in color; and trees. I was thankful for the latter. I'd had had enough of trees for awhile.

We rode until we could no longer see the landscape due to the night creeping over us, and so we settled in for the night.

Jasper gathered what belongings we really needed and stashed them under some small boulders to hide in case we were set upon.

He unhooked his cloak and tossed it to me for added warmth which I was grateful for. I had a fire started but we dared not have a large one.

Hopefully while being here, I would learn to toughen up mentally, emotionally and physically. Jasper handed me bannocks with some cheese and an apple for dinner. I watched him break his bannock in half and make a sandwich with the cheese in it. Coffee came next and that settled my nerves.

It had been a long day and I couldn't believe that I was looking forward to sleeping on the grass covered ground, but it seemed that the softness of it made my body feel cozy. I settled in close to the fire and snuggled into my blanket.

We arrived at the Manse mid morning on the sixth day of our travels and I was glad for it. My butt had lost all feeling by the fourth day, and was glad I wouldn't have to get on one again for some time.

"Let me do the talkin'. Even for a lad yer voice is vera' femine and we dinnae want any trouble." I nodded my acknowledgement and followed close behind him.

He seemed to know exactly who to ask for by his authoritative tone. One of the guards on duty stepped up; claiming to be the person in charge, but Jasper blew him off with a wave of his hand and continued into the main hall.

The man sputtered as we walked by, but he didn't follow; just stood there with his mouth agape. I thought that had been strange, considering we were complete strangers and no telling what kind of mischief we might be up to. Another guard stopped us in our tracks, and asked what our business was here.

"We are here to see the Duke; I have business with him. This is *mo ogha*. Tell him Sir Jasper Alexander Campbell has come to call upon him."

"And what business would ye be havin' with the Duke?" The guard asked.

"That's none of yer concern. Go and fetch the Duke forthright!" Jasper demanded.

I was very impressed with how Jasper took to his former authority; like riding a bike. It was too bad I couldn't understand a word he'd said. While we waited for the Duke, we walked to the main hearth to warm ourselves.

I was thankful for the warmth. My fingers started to thaw, and I contemplated bending over to roast my rump, but all too soon we were being escorted to the Duke's private study. Jasper would have to translate the dialogue later since everything they said was in Gaelic, and I didn't speak Gaelic.

After being kept waiting awhile, someone entered without looking at us. He sat behind a large desk, the color of espresso and polished to a gleaming shine with intricate designs carved along the trim. It was stunning. Nana had the exact same one! It was nice to know something lasted into the future.

We continued to stand there, ignored, until Jasper cleared his throat in impatience. The stuck up man looked up with a bored expression.

"So, sir," the Duke began. "What business do we have together then?"

"I have business with the Duke of Devonshire the IV, Jonathan McKenna Campbell. And who might ye be, my lord?" Jasper informed him.

"Whoever ye are sir, how dare ye come into my home and insult me like this! What is yer name?!" The Duke roared. I took a step back but Jasper caught my wrist.

"My name is Sir Jasper Alexander Campbell, son of Rorick Campbell; Man at Arms for Master Jonathan."

"My brother has not been in these parts for ten plus years, nor do I ken where he might be. He wasnae man enough to keep his chair, so it fell to me to take his place."

"Well, my *Lord*, takin' and keepin' it needs improvement posthaste. Had I been yer Man at Arms, I would have personally hung myself for the lack of security here." Jasper leaned over the desk and glared at the man.

The Duke slowly stood and matched Jasper's glare. They stood there for a few minutes, but then Jasper stood back to my side. I'd stayed obediently silent up to this point.

"Sir Thomas, I mean my Lord, my *seanair*," I began, using the Gaelic word for grandfather, " means no disrespect to ye. We need to find Lord Jonathan to hand him a parcel from his wife. We have been travelin' for some time and my *seanair* is verae tired and hungry."

His Grace looked at me as if seeing me for the first time, and cleared his throat before speaking. "Aye, well, at least ye seem to have some manners, boy. We havenae seen him in ten years plus. Last I heard he was killed in some wee battle on the borders."

I gave a slight bow at the waist, hoping that's the customary thing for a boy or man to do, then nudge Jasper's side, making him do the same.

He looked back, warning me; but I ignore him. I thought my Scottish brogue was quite decent. I was grateful that the Duke knew English since that was how I had spoken to him.

The Duke rounded the desk, and then leaned back against it, folding his arms and crossing his legs at the ankles. He looked over us both, lingering more on myself. I felt a chill run up my spine and I shivered.

"I remember a Jasper, ye say, back when I was a wee boy. I dinnae ken if I can remember a face from back then."

The conversation carried on in Gaelic between the two men and once again I was invisible to them. I moved over to the fire, leaving them to it since I couldn't understand. Every once in a while the Duke would glance at me and I'd turn my attention to anything but him.

After about thirty minutes, the men stood, and I collected my gloves then stood behind Jasper. I pulled the bill of my cap more forward to cast a shadow across my face. We had tied my hair in a queue after cutting half of it off, but the hat added more to my appearance.

"The snow is to get heavier as of tonight. Out of respect for Jon, I will turn a blind eye to today's behavior, and offer ye the hospitality of my house and staff. I will have Liam bring ye to the kitchens, and Mrs. O'Connell will have a room made up for ye and yer *ogha*." He said while leering at me. The chill came back.

Liam came in; somehow knowing he was needed and I gave a sigh of relief. The Duke's attention had been averted away from me and onto him. "Please escort Sir Campbell and his *ogha* to the kitchens. Have Mrs. O'Connell see to it that a room is prepared for them."

"Aye, my lord. If ye will please follow me gentlemen." Liam stepped aside and swept an arm in the direction we were to go. Jasper looked back at the Duke, nodded then proceeded out to the hall, I practically glued to him.

We were placed in a far corner of the large room and told to stay there until Mrs. O'Connell came to collect us. One of the serving women brought us both trenchers of food and drinks and as expected, Jasper dug right in.

A few of the maids periodically looked at me and I wasn't sure if they were admiring me, or at the face I was making over the food in front of me.

"Just eat lass. Ye'll get used to it soon enough." Jasper whispered between bites.

I looked around for a fork but none were in sight. Jasper laughed then wiggled his fingers. I grimaced but did my best to give it the old college try.

If I didn't look or smell the mystery on my plate, it wasn't so bad, along with a tankard of ale to go with it. The more ale I drank, the better the food tasted. "We have to come up with a story as to where we've been all this time. 'Travelin'' isnae something talked about here. We'd find ourselves tied to stakes and burned alive, or disemboweled."

"Ye two being the arrivals seekin' shelter, alright then come along," A very elderly but very robust woman stood over us, hands on hips and sweat dripping down her face and bosom.

"Why Maggie O'Connell, just as feisty as ever before I see. Why not come sit on my lap and teach me a lesson." Jasper teased her and her face turned red from indignation.

"How dare ye, sir! Who the hell are ye to be speakin' to me like such." She demanded.

"Och, lassie ye dinnae remember my handsome face? Now I'm insulted. Come and give me a kiss and maybe I'll forgive ye." Jasper cajoled.

The woman walked closer to him and he stood up and over her. Her eyes lit up and she pulled him into a bear hug, slapped his back a few times.

"Why Jasper Alexander Campbell, where have ye been keepin' yer handsome self? It's been how long, sixty years?"

"Aye, it's been a long time lass, but yer just as beautiful. Will ye steel away with me in the night and marry me?" He winked and she giggled like a young girl.

I cleared my throat before I gagged over this flirtatious commentary. Both separated immediately and looked everywhere but at me. She smoothed out her apron and patted her damp hair as he collected our things.

"Well, come along then. There's a room waitin' for ye both." She led the way, taking us to the third floor and down a long corridor; stopping at what I assumed was our door.

She pulled out the key and with a turn of the ring handle, the heavy oak door squeaked open. She apologized for the stiffness of it and the terrible noise, but assured us that the room was quite fresh.

Yet another masonry stairway appeared before us and I rolled my eyes and heaved out a sigh. "Better get used to it lass, there are stairs everywhere." Jasper whispered over his shoulder.

Thankfully the stairway wasn't that long, and we were soon entering our bedchamber. I found it quite spacious but had a homey feel to it.

A roaring fire was going in the hearth, and beautiful tapestries covered the stone walls.

There was a side table next to the bed with a candle burning; and a pitcher in a bowl. I ran my fingers over the porcelain and studied the beautiful hand painted pattern in hues of blue.

A large, dark wooden wardrobe that was intricately carved stood across from the bed, which was a monster in itself. Heave robes were pulled back with braided cordage. The posts were twisted and gleaming.

I had dreamed of this as a little girl, what castles in Camelot would look like. I thought I was dreaming again but Jasper broke the spell when speaking to Mrs. O'Connell. I returned back to them, thanking her for her assistance.

"If there be anythin' ye need, the bell-pull is by the bed. Ring twice for the maids, and three times for me-self. I had the lasses put fresh clothin' in the wardrobe for both of ye; *mo ogha* is about the same size as yerself lad. Supper is an hour after sundown. Get some rest." Mrs. O'Connell left us to it and I sat down on the bench at the foot of the bed.

There was something bothering me about the room, and I could feel my head and heart start to pound hard. My breath came out labored and Jasper came over to see what I was about.

"Oye, what's the matter with ye, lass? Take it easy, head between yer knees." He shoved it down for me before I could do it myself and kept it there with a firm grasp on the back of my neck. Once I had calmed down, I pushed against him until he let me up.

"Jasper, do you see what I see?" I said to him.

He looked around then back at me with a look of confusion. "What?" He asked back.

"Look around you!"

He looked around, still confused, and then looked back at me. He touched my forehead and I push his hand away and got up. I ran my hand over the wardrobe's doors then went to the window openings and looked out. The landscape looked familiar.

I rolled my eyes at him in frustration and snap out "It's the attic! At Nana's! We're in the attic. Look, the windows are in the same place, the wardrobe was over here. The pitcher and bowl were inside the wardrobe next to the sword.

"And, and look, this table had all those nick-nacks Nana used to collect. Oh my God I can't believe it!" I exclaimed.

He walked the room, inspected the wardrobe. It finally dawned on him that it was in fact the attic. We both looked to the wall, where the small hidden room would have been located in Nana's attic. However, the bed was blocking the area and it was way too heavy for us to move.

Most likely since the room, not to mention the rest of the Manse was all made of stone, there wouldn't have been a hidden room. I was sure there were secret passages dug through the castle though.

Night came soon enough and Liam came to collect us for supper. We headed down as a trio but I couldn't help but feel like we were prisoners, he being our guard, rather than being guests of the castle.

Apparently the Duke wanted to keep a close eye on us. Jasper seemed to feel it too.

CHAPTER 13

WE WERE SEATED AT the head table, being guests of the Duke. The Duke had yet to grace us with his presence. Trenchers were placed in front of all of us, piled with meats, and what scarce vegetable matter that could grow here. Piles of breads covered the open spaces between the rest of the food and pitchers.

Thankfully there were forks available, but no one seemed to know what they were for since they all used their dirks for both cutting and forking the food into their mouths. I accidentally left my dirk up in the room; another reason to be pleased with a fork.

His Grace finally joined the room along with his wife and a baby in her arms, newly hatched it seemed from the size of it. She handed it off to what I would presume was a wet nurse before she sat down. There were no other children following behind so I gathered this was the first of many to come.

Thomas raised his glass in acknowledgment of us, his sight lingering on me; a leering smile splitting his face. I looked away quickly and focused seriously on my food.

I ate without tasting, constantly rubbing my neck from feeling the Duke's eyes on my back. I scooted closer to Jasper but he shoved me back.

Once supper was over, at least for me, I asked Jasper to walk me up cause I was exhausted from all that we'd gone through, but he'd gotten way too into his cups and lost his judgment. He handed me his dirk and shoo'd me away.

I glared at him, and the men around him who saw it laughed loudly. I turned to leave; not waiting to see if he followed or not. I would not be humiliated by the likes of a drunkard.

I exited the room, trying hard not to run out in tears. Somehow I managed it.

"Och lad, dinnae get yer knickers in a bunch." I heard someone yell, followed by more uproarious laughter.

Another one yelled, "Runnin' off to nurse at yer mother's teat? Run along then."

More bellows of laughter and I took off running once I knew no one was around. I didn't know why I started to cry but I did and couldn't have cared less.

I arrived at our room, tears streaming down my face and I shove the heavy door open then slam it closed as hard as I could. I rushed up the short flight of starts to the room and slammed that door too.

I removed my boots and stalkings, and then my jacket followed, placing them on the bench. As I began to unlace my pants, I heard the door open and I quickly turned my back to it for modesty.

"Jasper, so help me I'm going to lash your hide clean from you ," I halted what I was about to say when I saw the Duke standing in the doorway; arms crossed over his chest and leaning against the doorjamb. I took a step back and bumped into the table next to the bed.

He stepped into the room and closed the door, sliding the lock home behind him. The sound of it had the blood draining to my feet and set my heart to thudding. My intuition of this man had been correct.

"Ye ken lad, ye shouldnae take their teasin' with much merit."

I couldn't move away. I felt around for the dirk Jasper had given to me, but I had forgotten that I had put it in the wardrobe with my jacket.

"I am here because someone failed to teach ye more manners than what ye showed me earlier. I should lash ye first, for not bidding my lady, nor I a good eve when parting from the dining hall.

"And second for how ye were speakin' to yer seanair just now, or at least what ye would have said were he here."

He began to walk toward me, no; more like stalking, only to come to a stop a foot away from me. He was not a tall man by any means, but he was still taller than I. My heart felt like it was going to burst out of my chest and my hands behind me were shaking. I tried to hide my fear, but he smiled as if he could smell it on me and took great pleasure in it.

"So, what punishment should I use for yer insolent behavior lad, hmm?" He ran a couple of fingers up my arm, and then my neck. I tried to slink away which turned out to be a terrible mistake.

"Och, are ye denyin' yer Duke's attention, lad? Yet another mistake I'm afraid." He tsk'd tsk'd tsk'd.

"Alright then, turn around." All humor had left his voice. His eyes flashed in irritation and excitement when I hadn't moved.

He took a step closer and I slowly turned. I wasn't fast enough for his liking so he spun me around himself and in doing so; I lost my balance and fell to my knees. I tried to get back up by grasping the bed sheets, but I soon found myself with my wrists bound quickly with one of the bed robe cordage and tied to one of the bedposts.

My shirt was wrenched open, exposing my back to him, and fresh fear shot through my body. I tried to stand up, fighting my restraints. I soon stop my struggles when something sharp bit into my back and I hissed out a breath.

There was another sharp bite, but in a different area this time. I started to cry and scream but the bites kept coming. I turned my head to see what it was that was cutting into me, and caught a flash of metal at the end of a strap.

The blows kept coming and soon I lost all fight and my voice, just cried and cried. Either blood or sweat ran trickles down my back in several openings where the belt had struck home. My vision blurred and I stopped moving all together, somehow leaving my body to escape the pain.

I felt the floor vibrate under me and I thought hell was opening up to either swallow him or both of us. Either way, if it stopped the blows and the pain then I prayed it would take me.

"What the hell is goin' on in here, get yer hands off him ye blackguard!" Jasper stormed over to the man and grasped his wrist firmly before the Duke could strike me again.

He shoved the Duke back, causing him to trip over a stool and falling to the ground. Jasper strode over to my limp form hanging from the bedpost and draped on the floor.

Blood smeared Jessie's back, fresh rivulets flowing with every muscle twitch, opening the gashes anew.

He didn't know where to start, she was such a bloody a mess. When he went to touch her, to sooth her she shied away immediately and his heart broke for her. Instead, he used his dirk to cut her loose and she curled into herself on the floor, fresh loud sobs wracking her body as the cuts opened again.

The Duke had recovered from his fall and brushed off his pants and shirt. At some time during the beating he had removed his jacket and had thrown it somewhere. He brushed at his hair that had come loose and now clung to his face.

"How dare ye talk to me that way, sir! Yer ogha was in sore need of learning some manners; such as how to respect his elders and people of higher station! Now, be gone and don't interfere any further or ye'll be next." He bellowed at Jasper.

Jasper stood slowly and stalked over to him. The Duke actually took a couple of steps back and turned ashen in the face.

"Why I should thrash yer Grace for beating a boy like this. How was this boy so disrespectful that he would deserve this?"

The Duke stuttered his words, and then cleared his throat before he tried again. "He left without stoppin' to bid my wife nor I a good eve before leavin', and when I came up to discuss the matter, he thought it was ye comin' in and was speakin' disrespectfully to ye, not realizin' it was me. Ye should be thankin' me that someone finally took him to hand."

"There was no reason for ye to come up here to discipline the boy in the first place! Ye should have come to me about the matter and I would see fit to decide his lesson.

"Be gone before I thrash ye to within an inch of yer life." Jasper said quietly.

The Duke didn't need to be told twice. Jasper stopped him at the door with, "And before ye threaten me again, keep in mind, I may not have been here for some time, but the people are more loyal to me than to ye. Ye'd be amazed how many still remember me and mine."

Jasper returned to Jessie as the Duke removed himself posthaste from the room. When he didn't hear the door close he turned to find it still open so he slammed it closed and shot the bolt home.

"Mac Strìopaich." *Son of a Bitch*, he swore out loud. He paced the room as he watched the small quivering, bleeding, form huddled next to the bed whimpering. Her back was turned towards him and he grimaced, almost vomiting from the sight.

Once he got his stomach back in control, he slowly walked to her and crouched down as he got closer.

"Jessie?" He said her name quietly, trying not to spook her, but she flinched away again.

Damn. He should have gone up with her, but no, he had to sit with a few of his old mates and drink. Whimpers came from the huddled form on the floor and he went out to the hall in search to see if he could find someone, anyone to help him.

Why? Why did this have to happen? He wanted to collect her in his arms, like a wounded child or animal; to give comfort but he refrained. He could murder the bastard for this!

He went back in, remembering the bell pull and gave it three tugs, informing the staff that Maggie was needed. It felt like forever before Maggie showed and when she did come he nearly bit her head off about taking her sweet time getting to them. She rounded on him, not taking any of his nonsense, but was interrupted by the sight on the floor.

She rushed to Jessie's side, and in doing so, gave the bell pull five tugs to sound the urgency of assistance. While she waited for the maids to arrive, she told Jasper to get some more wood for the fire and to bring up some whiskey for Jessie.

He grumbled his reluctance in leaving Jessie, but Maggie turned sharply and ordered him to do it. On his way out, the two maids from earlier came in with a third not far behind carrying a basket or something like it.

Maggie sank to her knees facing Jessie's back and coo'd to her in Gaelic. The maids all gasped at the sight, but set right to work, placing a large kettle on the fire, one ripped clean linens into strips and the other was sent to get the healer.

Jasper came back in fairly quickly with an arm full of wood and a bottle under his arm which was starting to slip down. One of the maids caught it before it hit the floor and he nodded his thanks.

He saw that Jessie was still not on the bed; but still on the floor with her back towards them. He strode over, halted for a moment but there was no way of helping it, he had to get her on the bed and quickly. He picked her up under both arms, Maggie grabbing her feet, and placed her on the bed as quickly and as gently as they could.

She screamed then passed out. They all blew out a sigh of relief, and then got to work. But, work came to a halted after Maggie, with another maid's help; removed the bloody shirt and caught sight of what was underneath.

She looked up sharply at Jasper and he immediately glared at her and shook his head to keep her mouth shut. She turned to the maid and did the same and got back to work.

The healer came in with his box of medicinal and got to work making a salve for the wounds. One of the maids brewed willow bark tea, and since Jessie was out cold, there was no need for Laudanum to drink. He did add it to the large pot of tea as they used the linen strips to cover the wounds.

When Maggie noticed Jasper standing in a corner, she hustled him out into the hall and slammed the door in his face. He stood there like a zombie; just staring at it. This was his fault, all his fault. He leaned his head against the door, wishing they had never come at all.

CHAPTER 14

"Shh, shhh, there now lass, it will be all right. I'll take care of ye." Maggie O'Connell coo'd to Jessie. The poor thing, she thought to herself. She kin how cruel the Lordship could be but that was with grown men, and the whores he'd been with; but this, this to a girl. Hopefully he dinnae notice that she was in fact a girl.

Seeing how there were no guards with the Duke when he slipped into the door, so the girl's secret was safe with her and the maids; for the moment. The lass was coming to, Maggie hearing her moans every now and then when being touched.

She returned to Jessie's side and removed the cold bandages and replaced with fresh warm ones. Once done, she went into the hall to speak with Jasper. He had a lot of explaining to do. She found him sitting in the chair across from the door, head in hands, and elbows on his knees.

He looked up when he heard Maggie clear her throat then shot to his feet at her worried look.

"What, what's wrong? How bad is it? Tell me Maggie!"

"Sit your arse down and stop yellin' at me. She's sleepin'. We got the worst taken care off. I had to stitch quite a few of the lacerations. We gave her a bit of laudanum with whiskey so she's sleeping now. Ye'll not be botherin' with her now."

Jasper slumped down in the chair and scrubbed at his face.

"What happened?" She asked.

Jasper told her and both shuttered and looked at the closed door worriedly. He paced the hall and Maggie watched him. He'd always had had a soft heart for children and women. He'd do anything to protect them, even kill if need be. Right now, he was a pacing bear, anxious to seek out his prey.

"Why hide her? She's yer grandchild."

"I cannae tell ye now lass, but I will seek you out when I can. I need to stay and protect her in case the Duke comes to finish what he'd started. I hope he tries so I have an excuse to kill him." Jasper walked to the door but Maggie stopped him.

"She's not decent yet. I will fetch ye when she is." Maggie patted his arm before returning to the room.

Jasper caught a glimpse of Jessie sprawled on the bed, bloody bandages covering the lash marks. His face paled and he tried to force his way in, but Maggie managed to shove him back out and slammed the door in his face. The hall grew quiet once the door slammed home and he was left to his own thoughts.

It took most of the night to staunch the bleeding. The constant changing of the bandages until the inflammation went down. And the oozing of blood to stop so the salve would stick. Maggie was sure that Jessie was going to pull through, at least physically.

Jessie had woken up for a few minutes so they were able to get some Laudanum laced whiskey into her. She fell back to sleep quickly after.

Now she was sleeping deeply. Maggie had the maids take turns throughout the day, changing bandages and replacing the salve.

When Maggie could get away she came to check on her too, finding her asleep and still on her stomach. Thankfully the bandages only had salve seeping through now instead of blood. Jasper sat the whole time by her bedside holding her hand.

By the third night, Jasper took a break to bathe in the stables then sought out food and drink in the kitchens. Maggie found him there, brooding in a corner while eating. This was going to be the perfect time for him to explain what was going on.

"Spill it Jasper," Why are ye hidin' her? When he didn't budge she yanked him by the arm until he got up then had him follow her to the stables for that chat.

She shoo'd the stablehands out, checked the stalls for any hang abouts who might want to eavesdrop. "I'm waitin', ye Dolt." She snapped at him.

"Oye, there's no need for name callin'." He snapped back at her but it had no affect on her. She fisted her hands on her hips and her glare smoldered even more.

He huffed out a breath and found a bucket to sit on. He advised her to do the same and so she did. "Do ye ken anythin' about Jon and why he left his home and title to this Dobber? I need to find him and I'm runnin' out of time."

Maggie shook her head that she did and he waited for her to explain what she knew. "What does this have to do with the 'lad'?" She looked up at the ceiling, and gestured in the direction where Jessie was currently recovering.

"It has everythin' to do with the 'lad'." He snapped but apologized immediately from the look she gave him.

"Alright then, I dinnae ken where he is now. It's been some years since I last seen him or heard of him. He set out a few years after he came back to us after ye both disappeared. He wouldnae talk about what happened, just that you two had lost each other."

She looked down at her folded hands, "he was a lost soul after he returned here."

They sat in silence for a minute, both trying to figure out how much to tell the other. He didn't know what her beliefs were in regards to the supernatural. She couldnae trust him either about the whole situation currently.

"He would come home without a scratch on him, in search of somethin', but always deflated in spirit and in mind. I ken ye two were like brothers, but the way he mourned; that was for someone that ye give yer heart to." She looked up at him suspiciously. "Ye ken something don't ye."

Jasper nodded. "Aye, I do but I dinnae ken how to tell it to ye without soundin' like a madman. Ye'd run screamin' through the castle that I was one."

"Try me. I've heard and seen many a thing, some of them loony; and some not. Why are ye with the 'lad' up there? Where have ye been all this time, Jasper?"

He got up to pace the length of the stable, returned in front of her. "Not *where*, Maggie my girl; but *when*. We're here to bring him back to his wife and son. The 'boy' up there, is his '*ogha*'."

Maggie didn't ken what to say. Jasper told her as much as he thought was necessary and waited to see her reaction. She sat quietly for a few minutes, looking at him, trying to gauge whether he was pulling her leg, mad in the head, or was, in fact, telling the truth.

"So why now? Why wait so many years to come back?" She asked.

"I was scared mostly. His wife had no one. No one to help her take care of Jon's son nor to help her with the estates. I couldna leave them to fend for themselves.

"The only reason I'm here now is because of Jessie. 'He' was determined to get him back to his wife Eleanor. After losin' his own family recently, he got it into his head that he had to do this. He was goin' to come either with or without me, so here I am. Great job I've done so far protectin''him'."

Jasper scrubbed his face with a hand, anger and frustration boiling under the surface. He felt helpless. They hadna eve been here for a day and already Jessie was nearly beaten to an inch of her life. She could still die from her wounds if not from infection.

"Jessie canna stay here, live in this life style for long. I need to find Jon and get both of them home. What men were here when Jon was last here? Did any of them ken where he might have gone next?"

Before Maggie could speak, one of the stable lads interrupted them, letting her know that one of the maids needed her. She nodded to the boy then turned back to Jasper. "I will ask around and send them to find ye."

Before exiting, she turned again but this time with a warning, "Ye dinnae ken what Thomas is capable of. I do. What's upstairs is nothing compared to the horrors I've seen of him. Keep Jessie close." And with that she was gone.

CHAPTER 15

I WAS FINALLY ABLE to lie on my back after four days and nights on my stomach and side. Using the bathroom was quite a painful process for all involved too. My back felt like something had ripped pieces of my skin off slowly. I gasped every time I accidentally stretched, and occasionally would pop a stitch and feel a trickle of blood run down my back.

When I had been conscious for the first time since the incident, Jasper was right at my side, singing something in Gaelic, a lullaby or the like. It was very sweet and it brought tears to my eyes, feeling comforted and safe.

Now he was just plain annoying me with all his "mothering" of me. I knew he meant well but there was only so much I could take being fussed over, especially by a scowling old highlander.

"Get out!" I yell at him when he tries to feed me. That was the last straw. "I can feed myself damn it!" I snatched the bowl and spoon away from him, pulling a stitch free from one of my many lacerations but I grit my teeth and eat.

"Fine ye ungrateful little," Jasper began to bellow but I interrupted him.

"Ungrateful? Ungrateful? I most likely wouldn't be like this if you had just brought me back to our room when I asked you to!"

"Ye should have had yer knife with ye for safety!"

Before I could retaliate back Mrs. O'Connell came in yelling at the both of us. "Will ye two stop this nonsense! The whole castle can hear ye. Jasper, leave, and you; eat." She pointed a finger at me, shutting my mouth before I could yell again at Jasper.

"I need to check her back. Jessie, put that down and roll over, and dinna glare at me Missy."

When neither of us did as we were told, she actually yelled louder than us. Jasper actually ran like his butt was on fire and I flipped over like a fish out of water.

She tsk'd me when she saw the fresh thin line of blood but thankfully she didn't need to stitch it again. Fresh salve covered linens replaced the ones from the night before, a quick wipe down cleansing my skin first. It felt good now to have them on.

Tea was brought up for me and I was so thankful that it wasn't the crap they had me drink the first couple of days. It helped with the pain but it tasted awful. There was Chamomile with a touch of Lavender. The scent was wonderful.

"When can I get the hell out of this room Mrs. O'Connell? I need to get some fresh air and see something, anything, other than Jasper's ugly mug."

"I HEARD THAT, GIRL!!!!" Came Jasper's voice through the door and we both started to laugh.

"When ye stop splittin' yer stitches for one! I think in a day, although, I would advise that ye dinnae leave yer room too far. The Duke will do all he can to get to ye again."

She pulled a clean night shirt over me then covered me up in blankets. I grumbled over not getting up but thanked her and the maids. I yawned, and taking that as a queue, they left me to rest.

Once I knew the room would be left only to me, I shimmied out of the bed and over to my satchel. I rummaged through it until I found what I wanted then tip-toed back to bed.

I pulled out the photos of Nick and Sophie, lingering on the one of Nick holding her a few hours after she was born. It was of the two of them standing in front of my room window, the sun shining in, putting them in silhouette. He was showing her to the world.

I moved to the next and so on. I placed them back into the envelope they came in and slipped it under the mattress. Mrs. O'Connell came back in just as I finished pulling the covers over myself and wiping my eyes. She rushed over ready to check my back for more pulled stitches.

"No, no I'm all right, Mrs. O'Connell. I was just reminiscing about my husband and baby girl. I miss them so much." I broke down crying. Who knew I had tears to shed after what had happened a few days before.

She sat down next to me and gripped my hand in hers. Once the tears had subsided, she unearthed a hanky for me. "Mo Leannan, where are they? Were ye separated?" She asked softly.

"They're dead. They were killed in a uh…carriage accident not too long ago. I'd give anything to have them here with me."

She patted my hand then got up and straightened the bed linens. "I will check on ye in awhile luv but for now, get some rest. Jasper has a guard outside so no one will bother ye."

She left me to my thoughts and after shedding more tears, I fell into an exhausted sleep.

Maggie found Jasper in the great hall with a group of men enjoying a mug of ale. They were in deep discussion over something. She had found a couple of soldiers that had gone into battle with Master Jon before he had left the castle for good. She'd come back later to let him know. There were other matters to attend to.

Jasper was waiting in the library when Maggie brought the first soldier in. He directed the man to have a seat, offered him a drink, and when the man declined; shrugged before he poured one for himself.

Jasper waited at first patiently but when the man didn't come forward with information, Jasper gestured him to get a move on with it.

"The last I saw of him he was insertin' himself in the Leith Siege. After that he vanished. It was said that he found an abandoned house down south near the cliffs."

Jasper took this information in and stored it away. There was another man to see before he decided as to where he and Jessie would travel to. The other man had just as much information as the first which wasn't much help.

The sooner they could leave here the better. He hadn't seen the Duke since the incident and he was concerned about that. For now, he would use the time to draw out their travel directions from the information he gathered from the two men.

He checked in on Jessie before heading to the main study. He spent a couple of hours there looking over property and territory maps, trying to plan out the best coarse to take. He wrote out a long list of items they would need for their trip, and handed it over to Maggie. After that, he headed to the main hall for supper. He found Liam seated in the back of the hall by himself, brooding over his mug. He left him to it.

"So where's that scamp of a *ogha* of yer's, Campbell? We've not seen him for days now." One of the men asked. The table roared with laughter.

"Och, probably under some lassie's skirts I bet," said another one then snorted out a laugh. This was followed by even more raunchy comments. He had to remind himself that he and Jessie were hiding the fact that she was a woman, so he weakly joined in on the lewdness.

The Duke made an appearance for dinner along with his wife, sans infant. He glowered at the Duke as in warning and the Duke looked away quickly.

Coward. Why would Jon abandon his home, his people and leave them to this wretch of a man? He was determined to find out, but first, he had to find Jon. It seemed he was the only one who could answer the question.

He bowed to his Grace and his Lady before he exited the hall after spending a few hours with the men. Liam had left a while ago and he wanted to get up to the room before the Duke left the hall himself. He sought out Maggie to see how the list was coming along, and she bit his head off that she had her own responsibilities to tend to, and she would have the list done when it was done.

When he entered Jessie's room, he found her awake and sitting up in bed looking at something; photos it seemed.

He walked the room a few times then told her they had to go over the agenda for our next move.

"We need to leave this place. The sooner we find Jon, the sooner we can get back home."

I found it odd that he considered our time his home instead of being here, where he was born and raised. I watched him pace the room which in turn made me antsy. "How's yer back now? Do ye think ye can ride tomorrow? Maggie has my list and said it shouldnae be much trouble to round up."

"I think so, but it might take a couple of days before moving fast. I'm sure Mrs. O'Connell will pack more salve and bandages. You'll have to help me with those if we are to leave tomorrow."

He grimaced at that thought but he stood firm and agreed to it. "I added the salve and extra bandages to the list earlier with you in thought, so no worries there."

I nodded my thanks. I got up and closed the bed robes on one side of the bed to have privacy in relieving myself. I was still getting used to that but it wasn't that bad. It still sucked that there wasn't any toilet paper.

Once I resurfaced from taking care of business, I walked to the window and looked out to the courtyard. It was dark but there were still men practicing sword techniques and such, the flames roaring upward from the smithy's fire pit when he plunged something into it.

Life carried on and it made me feel better somehow. I returned to the bed and climbed in; using the step stool Mrs. O'Connell had found for me.

Jasper assured me that no one but a handful of people knew of what happened here. He told me the men were joking around about my losing my virginity, and having not left the bed since. I rolled my eyes but kept quiet.

"The Duke made an appearance tonight at supper. He's not been around since…,"

"Where's he been then?" Not that I cared.

"His Captain had one too many drinks tonight and spilled the gossip that his bairn came down ill and he and the Duchess were by its bedside. They came down tonight without it." His face was grave at the last bit.

"Probably well enough to be left with its wet nurse." I said casually. When I didn't get even a grunt, I looked up at him to see what got his attention. "What's wrong, Jasper?"

"The bairn has most likely died." He looked away, busying himself but I could tell it bothered him.

"Why would they just act like nothing happened? Hold a service or something to mourn the child?"

"Jessie, times here are verae different than your time. Many bairns die within days, sometimes weeks; after they're born. It's not for the faint of heart to have children, only to lose them to, well, anythin'. There's nothin' else to do but breed again and hope for the best."

I scrunched up my face in disgust but he only shrugged. My heart ached for the baby. How a parent couldn't be overly bothered was beyond me.

"We should get some sleep. There's no telling when we'll be able to be in a room with a bed and a fire. Good night, Jessie." And with that, he lay on the floor, rolled up in his tartan and began to snore. I shook my head at him then blew out the candle on the side table.

We didn't end up leaving today. We needed the rest of the items on Jasper's list, which had taken some time to get.

Jasper came in on me changing into the clothes that had been put in the wardrobe our first night.

"And where do ye think yer goin'?" He demanded.

"Look, if we are leaving tomorrow, it would be a good idea to see how long I can stand on my feet. And I'm tired of being cooped up in this room. I need fresh air and away from a sick bed. My back barely bothers me now." I lied.

I tied my short hair back in a queue then stood patiently in front of him, waiting for him to move from in front of the door. When he didn't move aside but crossed his arms I countered with, "Okay, the window it is. I'd hate to ruin Mrs. O'Connell's bed sheets. She does spend a lot of time cleaning them and such."

I began to pull the sheets off, tying one end to the bedpost then tying the next sheet to the first. "Of course, I'd have to tell her it was you to blame, keeping me locked up here, but I know she'll completely understand." I look at the bed robes next and "try" to unhook one. That's all it took for him to give in and I sent him a smug smile.

"Fine, let's go then but keep yer trap shut."

I shined an innocent smile at him as I walked to the door. I found Liam jumping to attention, bowing when he saw Jasper. He turned to me and said, "Good to see yer up and about lad. Shall we eat?" He began to walk down the hall not waiting for us. I shrugged at Jasper and so we follow.

We jogged down the stairs and entered the hall to joyous cat calls from the men. The lewd teasing began at me and I just roll my eyes. Men were men, no matter what century it was.

Liam sat down next to me so I was sandwiched between him and Jasper. I was sorely tempted to loosen my collar with my finger but there wasn't one.

"So, why are ye lookin' for Master Jon? He's not been here for some time. I ken of him but never spent time with him." Liam said between bites.

The Duke saw me immediately and I stared him down. I was not going to be the victim. His gaze was taken away when someone called his attention to something else.

My thoughts were running wild about our trek for the next day. Liam told me to slow down and I hadn't noticed how much and how quickly I had been eating. I guessed I was really hungry. All I had had was soup, tea and bread while on bed-rest.

After three tankards of ale, Jasper took my cup away and glared at me. "If ye drink yerself under the table 'lad' ye willnae be able to ride sittin' upright. Here," he hands me a chunk of bread. "Eat this; it will soak up the ale in yer stomach." I did what I was told but I still glared at him.

Liam continued to eat, and I was rather disgusted by his table manners. But, considering there were mostly men in the hall; they didn't care about their eating habits. Even the maids and women of lesser means weren't turned off by the grotesque visual before us.

"My, uhm, *seanair* was his best friend. They grew up together here and have been searching for him for a long time."

When Liam looked at me in confusion I told him that I was responding to his earlier question. "Surely after all these years ye'd have crossed paths."

"You'd think but we've been in the New World since I was born. He won't talk to me about how he got there and trust me; I've tried getting it out of him." I sent a sidelong glance at Jasper, but he was lost in conversation with the others.

"Hmm, so when are ye leavin' then? Ye seem to be hale and hearty."

"I'll live. So, what's your story Liam?" I asked between bites. I looked at my plate and was surprised to find it almost empty and that I could possibly eat more. Reading my mind, Liam slapped another slab of venison and potatoes onto my plate before adding to his.

"Not verae interestin' I'm afraid. Raised on a farm down south then was brought here by *mo athiar* to train for the Duke's troop should there ever be another uprisin'. So I've been here going on about fifteen years now."

"So, in all your time here, you've never come by Lord Jon himself? We've been told he's been here in the last ten years."

"I never said I dinnae met him." He continued to eat without looking up. I stared at him trying to gauge whether he was telling the truth or not.

"Really, Mrs. O'Connell asked around and only two men came forward about knowing him. Why not speak with Jasper of what you know?"

"Because I dinnae ken anythin' about him. I met him in passin' durin' his last visit, but I dinnae speak with him."

I still felt he wasn't being completely honest with me, but I left the subject be for now and continued to eat my dinner. Jasper nudged me and I sat up straight, not realizing I had begun to doze off.

Jasper feigned exhaustion and so we said our good nights to our table mates, and then stepped in front of the Lords of the house, bowing to his and her Grace then escaped to our room.

"He wouldnae tell me where. Said he'd have to take us there bein' he knew a lot of people in the South. Plus, he could check in on his own family too."

I let Jasper know that Liam had met my grandfather and that he might know where he might be. "So he wants to come along then I presume. Probably a wise idea since I'm not half the soldier I used to be."

"I'll need to talk with the Duke tonight about borrowin' his man. He will not be so givin' after what's gone on. I'll call Liam up to discuss payment for his use." He gave three tugs on the bell-pull summoning Maggie to come up.

"What do you mean 'payment' exactly? Why should we pay him when he wants to join us?" I asked disgusted.

Maggie knocked on the door then, letting herself in without waiting for admittance and Jasper yelped. I burst out laughing. "*Daingead* woman, I could have been naked in here! Ye just dinna barge in!"

"Oye, as if ye have anythin' I havenae see before. Besides, ye rang for me so why would ye be naked, especially in a lady's presence." She countered.

I covered my mouth to hide my giggles but he still heard me and shot me a warning glance which only made me laugh harder. "So, what ye be needin' of me now. I got my own work to do without comin' to ye every minute."

"I need to speak with his *royal highness* about takin' a man with us. Liam seems to think he may ken where Jon is, but he willnae tell us unless we take him." Jasper informed her.

"Also, send Liam up. I need to speak with him." When he didn't hear her leave he turned to find her still standing there with arms crossed.

"Did ye not hear me or did I stutter?" He said impatiently.

"No, but ye could ask politely. Believe it or not, but I dinnae work for ye; but for the Arse down there."

His face turned red from being reprimanded by her and ground his teeth before asking politely. When she was satisfied with that she was on her way. It was going to be a long night.

CHAPTER 16

"YER GRACE, I AM in need of one of yer men for the trip south. We leave on the morrow preferably at sunrise." Jasper said.

"Why would I give ye one of my men at all? What are ye prepared to give my house for yer stay? Ye've eaten my food, slept under my roof, and seen to yer every need. The lack of discipline in regards to yer *ogha* is lacking to say the least. No, I think not." Thomas sat smugly behind his oak desk, and steepled his fingers.

Jasper was ready for that response. Earlier in the day Liam came to see him about this matter and before Jasper even asked, Liam plunked a pouch of coins down on the bed and told him that this should cover any "hardships" the Duke might have when losing a man.

"In that case yer Grace, we shall take the two thousand pounds with us and find more men not in yer employ. Sorry to have bothered ye. I bid ye farewell." Jasper turned and walked towards the door.

Before he took two steps he heard the large chair scrape across the stone floor and he snuck a quick smile before turning around. "Well, Sir Jasper, I think that we can work out an arrangement here. My House could use a large donation such as the money ye just informed me of and would be most welcome. It would cover the cost of yer stay here as well."

The Duke came around the desk hurriedly and stalked over to Jasper. "So, do we have a deal then?" He held out a goblet of wine to Jasper then picked up his own and toasted.

Jasper waited for the Duke to drink then posed as if he were drinking himself. He wouldna put it past him to slip somethin' into the cup. "I'll hand over the money tomorrow once we are saddled and ready to go. We will be leavin' at sunrise. Oh, and Liam will be comin' on with us.

Business completed, Jasper headed to the door. He was stopped in his tracks though. "Liam willnae be goin' with ye. I'll send Robert instead. I need Liam here."

"See, here's yer problem yer Grace. There was no stipulation on yer decidin' who would be goin' with us. So if ye want the 'donation', I would suggest ye let me make the selection. From what I've heard in the halls, the House could really use the money." And with that, Jasper took his leave.

I awoke to someone nudging me in the shoulder then snatched the blankets clean off me when I refused to get up. "So help me lass, if ye dinnae get up right now I'll douse ye in toilet water and have ye shiver on yer horse. Now get yer arse up!"

I cursed at him under my breath and he beamed a smile at me. I glare at him then got up.

"Glad to see yer learnin' yer Gaelic right fast. Who taught ye to swear so I may thank them."

"What are you talking about?" I asked through a yawn.

Thankfully I went to bed in my clothes for the trip so all I had to do was relieve myself, put my boots on and tie my hair back.

"Och, lass, ye dinnae ken ye swore at me in Gaelic?" He barked out a laugh. " Yer either too tired or so used to hearin' it from the men that ye dinnae realize it." He laughed heartily.

We collected our things and entered the courtyard, finding our horses at the ready. Liam rode up next to mine; another horse being led behind his. The supplies Mrs. O'Connell had gathered for us were neatly bundled on the spare horse.

The Duke came to the courtyard to retrieve the "donation" Jasper had promised him. Jasper took his time inspecting the side satchels, getting a kick out of hearing the Duke's impatient sighs.

"It seems all is well. Yer Grace, yer donation to the House as promised. Dinnae spend it all in one place now."

Jasper's comment was met with hidden laughter from the people milling about. They were silenced immediately when the Duke shot a look around the courtyard.

We saddled up, impressing myself as well as Jasper, on how easily I managed it, especially since I've been abed for a week. It felt good to be moving on.

Jasper tossed the bag at the Duke and unsurprisingly, he missed the catch and had to fish it out of the mud. He didn't bother to count it either; stupid man.

Jasper and I sent knowing looks to each other, and then click our horses onward. I took a deep breath once we passed the gate, not realizing that I had been holding it. Liam pointed in the direction we needed to go and so we turned our horses and followed his lead, hopeful and impatient to find my grandfather.

We traveled for days, stopping only to water and rest the horses, and at night. Winter was upon us now and I thought we'd freeze to death right on our horses. The nights were far worse. Jasper did the best he could do, putting our makeshift tent up and a fire going.

The chill still seeped through the flap that was our entry and exit of the tent. Large fires were still out of the questions; bringing unwanted attention to us being the biggest concern. What was nice was that both Liam and Jasper slept on each side of me, adding additional heat besides the hot rocks we slept with.

Jasper used the salve for his blistered, frost bitten feet. The bloody pustules that had started as small irritants were now the size of marbles, oozing when touched. The smell was just as horrible.

I looked out the small gap between the canvas flaps, watching the snow swirl angrily around us. My body stiffened as the accident back in my time, that had killed my husband Nick and baby girl Sophie, came rushing full force into my thoughts.

I could still hear our screams. I could remember Nick telling me to hold on even though that would have done little to help. I shivered at the memory, becoming aware of the silent tears that had fallen, and of Liam staring at me.

I got up and went outside, not caring that I only wore my jacket to keep warm while walking. I needed to feel numb for awhile; to push the thoughts of what had happened; away from me. The tears that I had not bothered to wipe away, turned into frozen tracks down my cheeks and ice crystals on my eyelashes.

"What's wrong with him?" Liam asked Jasper.

Jasper had to think for a minute before answering, "The lad lost his uh, father and sister in an accident not long ago. The weather was like this when it happened."

Liam stayed quiet but looked out through the tent flaps. He couldn't see Jessie but sensed movement close by and relaxed when the horses whinnied quietly.

After checking on the horses, I collected more branches and twigs, what I could find of them that still stuck out from the snow. When I returned, my emotions were back in check, and I started feeling better when the scent of coffee assaulted my nose.

Liam passed on a cup and made a face of distaste as Jasper and I sipped, and groaned in pleasure.

"How can ye drink that that shit? It's awful!"

I just grinned at him before taking another scalding sip. We sat in silence, exhaustion slowly overtaking us. I wrapped myself in my furs then drank more coffee.

"This *shit* works well in trickin' the stomach into thinkin' it's not hungry. Somethin' that will come in handy once our provisions are sparse."

I nodded in agreement to Jasper's statement, but Liam still grimaced. "Aye, well so does ale, whiskey, and scotch."

I shrugged and told him that that left more for Jasper and me. Jasper laughed, and joked that he'd have to fight me for the last drop.

I looked at my wrist to see what time it was, but forgot that I had packed my watch away for safe keeping.

Jasper saw me rub my wrist and informed me that it was getting on toward midnight. "How do you know that?" I asked.

"I can tell by the night sky, the position of the stars and such. Somethin' I picked up while at sea."

"I didn't know you did that, Jasper. What did you do out there?" I asked over bites of food.

"Well I was an apprentice; a greenhorn as they are called now. I worked on many for years to help support Eleanor and yer da."

"But what about da? I thought you were around to raise him."

"Aye, I was, but once it was time for his education, his mother dinnae need me as much and so I would sail out, and send the money I earned to them."

Huh, Dad never said anything about that. At the thought of him, I grew mournful. I shook it off though, knowing I would see him again; hopefully. For now, it was time to toughen up and pull myself up by my boot straps.

"When yer da was old enough, he came on board for a few years too. Said he wanted to save for university. Turned out, he just wanted to move as far away as possible from here." Jasper looked mournful himself.

I could hear the hurt in his voice at the memory. What could I say? That I understood my father's dislike of the family history, I couldn't. My father believed in hard work and to work for what you wanted, not to be given a silver spoon instead. He instilled that in me too.

We left that topic alone for now and turned in for the night. Liam had passed out awhile ago, his snores filling the small space we all shared. Somehow, they were no longer annoying, but a sense of comfort, knowing someone was with me.

CHAPTER 17

"We will reach Rhys Castle in a couple of hours. My cousin is Laird there and he'll put us up for a few days." Liam informed us.

I sent up a Hail Mary at hearing that and kicked my horse into gear, eager to get to the keep. Jasper and Liam looked at each other, and then shrugged; kicking their own mounts to keep up with me.

We arrived just before sundown, at least I thought so. It was hard to tell through the winter gloom. The snow had yet to let up but thankfully, it wasn't thick like it had been the last few days. Liam took the lead, announcing our arrival and that he was cousin to the Laird.

It took a few minutes before we were granted entry but once we were in, I gave an audible sigh at the sight of buildings and people.

"Ah, Cousin Liam it's good to see ye man!"

I nearly fell off my horse, startled by the booming voice coming from across the courtyard. Liam hurriedly jumped from his mount and walked over to the large figure that had spoken.

Both men grasped forearms then gave each other pounding pats on the back, jovial laughter filling the courtyard. The Laird was young by the look of him. He was older than Liam by about ten years though.

Liard Rhys, not named after the castle, had to have been at least six foot four and about two hundred pounds of pure muscle. Shoulder length jet black hair, and jade green eyes. He had a ready smile for anyone, even grumpy Jasper.

I took a bow in front of him, paying respect, and the courtyard erupted into laughter. I shrunk into myself trying to become invisible. Jasper took pity on me and brought me up to shake hands with Rhys.

"Lad, ye dinnae need to bow to me. I'm nae a king or anythin' else so fancy." Rhys corrected me.

I flushed as I shook his large hand firmly, hoping it would pass as manly. I looked up at him and thought I would develop a kink in my neck if I didn't look back down.

"Sir Jasper I take it. McGuinnis here has informed me that ye are in search of Lord Jon. Fine gentleman, but I cannae say I've seen him in a long time; years in fact." Rhys rubbed the stubble covering his chin.

Jasper and I quickly lost hope. There would be no information coming from our host. "He was here about eight years ago, and stayed on for about four years. He took up breakin' the horses in for me.

"After that, he one day sought council with me, thankin' me for lettin' him reside and work for me, but it was time that he moved on. He dinnae say where he was goin' though. I dinnae think to ask either." Jasper and I blew out matching frustrated breaths.

"Sir Campbell, ye and yer *ogha* may stay with us until the snow lets up. Come; come into the hall for food and drink and warmth." Rhys warmly invited us in.

We followed behind Liam, and were instantly engulfed in warmth, provided by the huge hearth blazing with fire. It was wonderful. Rhys spoke with one of the maids who rushed off to do his bidding.

"Follow me, there's food in the study and we can talk more of yer ventures. Tell me Liam, how fares his *Grace*?" Rhys inquired acidly.

We found seats where we could in the study, stripping off our layers then settled down with food and ale. I never thought I'd be glad to see a plateful of meats and cheeses and fruit. I ate as if I hadn't in weeks.

Rhys saw me chowing down like an animal and let out a bark of laughter. "Och, lad, there's plenty to go 'round, slow down or ye'll choke!"

I blushed and slowed down my chewing. I turned to the fire that roared behind me and fell into a daze as I ate. The last month and a half ran through my mind. I tried to push them aside and concentrate on the now. I grew sleepy while sitting in front of the fire, my body warm and full with food and drink.

"So, Jasper, tell me all about this mission to find Lord Jon. What business do you have with the man; that you travel now in the winter?"

"Well, I dinnae ken how much ye ken about his first disappearance, but I've been searchin' for him for many a years."

"I ended up in North America, following a lead there, only recently returning with my *ogha*." Jasper nodded in the direction of Jessie. Rhys leaned over and directed Jasper to do the same, then saw that Jessie had fallen asleep, snoring peacefully in the oversized chair.

"Aye, the lad has been through a lot since our arrival here in Scotland. Things are very different over in North America. I hope he'll adjust quickly."

Liam dropped into the armchair adjacent to Jessie's, feeling fatigued himself. The combination of ale, food, and the warmth of the fire had him nodding off into sleep as well.

"Liam," Rhys called over to him. "Ye may retire to yer chamber, lad. Get some rest. We have much to discuss later."

Liam got up and nodded before taking his leave from the room. The room grew quiet, the peat logs, crackled now and again. "Tell me friend," Rhys asked more quietly. " What plagues ye so? Findin' Lord Jon surely couldnae be weighin' so heavily on ye."

Jasper rubbed his eyes, exhaustion setting in. "Aye, it's more troublin' than our search. But, for now I need to be with my troubles alone awhile yet."

Rhys nodded and fell quiet for a moment. "That's fair enough. Yer rooms are ready for ye both, ye can collect yer *ogha* and get some rest. There's time enough to speak."

Rhys stood as Jasper pulled himself up out of his chair wearily. They stood over Jessie, deciding how best to proceed. Jasper opted in waking her so he wouldn't have to carry her. He didn't want to embarrass her further. When she didn't stir, he sighed grudgingly then picked her up and slung her over his shoulder. She hissed and moaned but settled back to snoring.

He got her settled on her bed and removed her boots, stalking and jacket, hanging them close to the fire to let them dry out. She automatically rolled over and cuddled one of the pillows, lying on her stomach to avoid her back touching anything.

He stirred the fire, adding a couple more peat logs before retiring to his own chamber. Even though he was extremely tired, he knew sleep would evade him for a few hours more. It would be a long night.

CHAPTER 18

LIAM ENTERED THE STUDY a few hours later, finding Rhys still sitting at his desk working. "Have a seat cousin. Fill me in on everythin' goin' on over at Rowen Castle."

Liam plopped down in the chair he had occupied earlier, and Rhys joined him with two cups of wine in hand. They both stretched out their booted feet in front of the fire and drank. "Well, he has managed to go through his coffers in quick time. His allowance as usual, is completely gone and the Crown has denied his request for an advance. Because of this, there is talk that he is raisin' the rents on the tenants. But again, it is only talk; for now."

Rhys steepled his fingers together, thinking on the information he was just given. "What are yer thoughts on it? Should I be plannin' for anythin' untoward?"

Liam shrugged, telling him at this particular time, the rumor was just that; a rumor, but advised Rhys to keep his ears open and plan ahead just in case.

Once business on that subject had been concluded, Rhys asked about his thoughts on his two traveling companions. What information he could provide if any.

"My da told me of Lord Jon and his friend, Jasper, disappearin' one day and then Jon's reappearance, just as queer, a few years later. His friend had not joined him in his return."

"Lord Jon trusted him with his life and the lives of his family and people. He hasnae given me any reason not trust him." Liam thought about Jessie and what to say about that.

"As for his *ogha*, he unfortunately got a taste of Thomas' cruelty." Liam shook his head at the thought.

At his hesitation, Rhys waved him on. "I dinnae ken the full truth of the cause of the punishment, but Thomas took it upon himself to teach the lad some manners. He lashed him to within an inch of his life.

"If it had not been for Jasper arrivin' at the right time, Thomas most likely would have killed her." Liam grew quiet, and sat and watched Rhys, waiting for his cousin's reaction.

Rhys was horrified over the news and got up to pace. He was mumbling curses then abruptly halted. "What do ye mean her?"

"Jessie is in fact, a *lass*." Liam got up and poured both of them another cup of wine.

"And just how do ye ken he's a 'she'?" Rhys raised an eyebrow in skepticism.

"The first night out of Rowen Castle, I was returnin' from gettin' water and seein' to other matters that needed seein' to. When I was on my way back, I caught site of the two of them."

Rhys turned sharply and a dark look crossed his face, making Liam quick to continue. "He was cleanin' her wounds, changin' the bandages and so on. Nothin' untoward the girl. Anyway, she signaled him to find somethin' and in the process, the arm that had been holdin' up her shirt for modesty, caused the material to fall, exposing a breast.

"I did a double take of the scene before me, not expectin' to see a woman out here, let alone a half naked woman."

This news was a bit shocking. "Why are they hidin' her as a lad?"

Liam didn't know but he would find out once they gained each other's trust. But that would take time. They still had a lot of ground to cover. "The best I can come up with is that because they're travelin' they're less likely to come to any harm, such as rape."

Rhys nodded in agreement but his thoughts were elsewhere. He dismissed Liam once he had given all the information he could give then sat quietly by the fire. He'd take Jasper out with him for a ride, check on his tenants, and see what he could get out of him.

I slept for two days. The nightmares of my ordeal at Rowen were all too real still, but at least it had pushed the ones about Nick and Sophie to the back burner.

I must have gotten up at some point to use the chamber pot, the sheets only damp from sweat. However, I did reek of sweat, horse and God only knew what else so I rung for a bath. One of the maids came in with food and ale. She rushed back out as soon as I'd put in the order for my bath.

I wolfed down the food and drank several cups of ale before she and another servant had come back. She brought with her a bucket of ice cold water and fresh linens and clothes, laying them on the bed before they both rushed out again.

I needed to constantly remind myself that I was posing as a boy, not as a woman so things were going to be different in many ways. Obviously, bathing would be one of them.

When she didn't return after about ten minutes, I put the bucket over the fire thanks to a cooking hook in the hearth, and waited for the water to heat. In the meantime, I drank more ale as I looked out the window slit, thankful I wasn't on the ground floor for prying eyes to look in.

I slid the bolt home on the chamber door before disrobing, then pulled up a stool and took my very first sponge bath. It was so relaxing. I massaged my leg muscles then arms, then cleaned my hair before soaking my feet.

Once dried and clothed, I took another look out the window slit to find that dusk had fallen upon us and, seeing the direction many of the people were headed, it was time for supper.

I saw Jasper in the courtyard moving among the throng, so I headed there too.

Liam was training with one of the prepubescent boys, others watching on and either cheering or jeering depending on who they were hoping to win. In one of the moves, Liam caught the boy on the butt, swatting him firmly, and the courtyard erupted in laughter.

There was a kind of darkness over and through Rowen Castle An evil that filled every lit corner. But here, here there was nothing to fear. I'm sure there were reprimands for poor choices in behavior, but other than that, people seemed at peace here.

Jasper spotted me coming to join him, and strode over, pulling me to a quieter corner. "Feelin' better? Did ye eat yet? Supper will be upon us in about half an hour."

I nodded my thanks, assured him I was feeling much better before getting closer to the training area. He followed behind me, taking up my right side, arms crossed over his chest.

"Have you found out any other information, Jasper?"

"No. Rhys and I went ridin' the other day, ye ken, to get acquainted I'm sure. He said the people who would have ken Jon or ken of him, have either died or have moved on since Thomas took over."

It was as if he'd just up and vanished. None of the few towns we'd visited before coming here had ever heard of Jon. This troubled Jasper greatly. I could see the thought of my grandfather meeting his end cross his face.

If that were the case, then maybe we'd at least come across a burial site or something, that's if anyone would have taken the time to dig one and erect a marker of some kind.

I tried to reassure him but he only grumbled and walked off to the stables, most likely in search of a game of some kind. I settled down on a hay stack and continued to watch Liam wear the poor boy out.

A couple of little girls, no more than say twelve, giggled at Liam; whispered to each other. Their own Lionheart I supposed.

I saw a shadow of Sophie, running in circles in the dirt, her favorite doll in her hands swinging it as she twirled. Just as quickly as it had come, the shadow faded, and the little girls came back into sight. This time though, a smile touched my lips instead of tears.

CHAPTER 19

"Oye, Jessie, get yer scrawny arse over here and learn a sword." Liam called over to me. I shook my head in refusal but he insisted. "What are ye, afraid I'll beat ye?" His face fell at once, regretting what he had just said.

I quirked an eyebrow at him then hopped down from the hay bale. I sauntered over to where the boy he'd been toying with now stood, panting and sweating. He all but shoved the offensive sword he'd been using at me, before running off to lick his wounds.

I swung the sword from side to side, checking the weight and balance of it in my hand; to see how my arm muscles worked with it. It weighed more than a rapier but still manageable.

"Are ye goin' to fight with it or draw pictures in the dirt with it, lad." One of the soldiers called out loudly, making the courtyard erupt into laughter.

Liam stood standing with the tip of his sword in the dirt while he waited, making a show of inspecting his nails. Quieter bouts of laughter sounded here and there.

"On guard!" I lashed my sword at him catching him off guard, knocking his sword out from under his hand. He nearly landed on it but caught his balance in time.

"Well, well, well Liam, looks like ye might be needin' some lessons yerself!" This was met with more laughter.

"Seems as though I just might," he said with a half grin. He tried to run me through, feinting to the left then right, like lightening, but I saw it coming and had already dipped and covered, his blade missing the top of my head by a couple of inches.

"Don't tell me you want me dead already, Liam. I thought you wanted to play for bit." I teased.

"Aye, but I want ye tired out and beggin' for mercy before we really play."

"If ye want to play with him, then find a bedchamber!" The crowd roared with laughter at that one and Liam actually blushed.

We ignored them all and focused on each other. Feinting and parrying, lunging, followed by another parry, then pulling back. I hadn't felt this alive in a long time.

Sweat ran in rivulets down my face, neck, ribs and back, causing some discomfort on a few of my raw scars. My shirt was plastered to me. Thankfully my breasts were bound tightly against me so they didn't make their presence known. I didn't care though; I just had to keep hacking away at him until I couldn't anymore.

"Cease!" Rhys' deep voice reverberated off the inner walls of the courtyard, silencing everyone at once. The quiet was deafening but Liam and I paid no notice. The only thing I could hear was the blood rushing in my ears.

Jasper charged me, knocking me to the grown, air bursting from my lungs as I hit the ground. I tried to push him off of me but he was like a stone.

"Get off, get off! I_I can't breathe." I gasped out painfully. Jasper pulled me to my feet and I bent over immediately, trying to gulp in air and not puke at the same time.

"What the hell is goin' on out here? Why are ye all standin' here gawkin' at these idiots for? Get where ye need to be; all of ye!!!!" I was waiting for him to snarl like the Beast from the movie "*Beauty & the Beast*", when no one moved. But, just as quickly, everyone scattered in every direction.

Rhys stormed over to me and picked me up by my shirtfront, bringing me within eye level with him. I stared back at him, fear filling me from the look on his face. It was like the terror I had felt at Rowen.

Liam limped over, wiping sweat off of his brow and chest with his discarded shirt. Even through my blurring vision, I could see how magnificent he was. I must have hit my head or something.

"Leave off, Rhys. It was all in good fun, right Jessie?" Liam winked at me as he continued to wipe away. I was a bit occupied being terrorized by a beast so I didn't feel like answering at the moment.

I gulped and could feel my face turn red from oogling him. I hoped no one else saw my action or there would be a lot of questions for the two of us.

I nodded then tapped Rhys' hand that still held me in mid air. A look of surprise crossed his face and he quickly set me back on my feet, a little too forcefully and I fell to my knees, off balance.

"Aye, well I cannae be havin' my men and workers standin' around willy-nilly. Ye have a job to do ye not, Liam?" Rhys crossed his arms, trying to look formidable but Liam paid him no notice.

Liam collected my coat and after a quick pat here and there, my somewhat wrinkled shirt was no longer hanging from my right shoulder. He handed over my coat and walked off, sending me another wink before doing so.

Rhys looked down his nose at me then at Jasper, before telling us we were to follow him. He didn't look back to see whether or not we followed.

"I cannae have my staff and men kept from their tasks unless there's reason for it. So, please, pray tell me why they were this evenin'." Rhys reiterated.

We sat before Rhys, looking like troublesome children, which would have been funny, I'm sure, under different circumstances. However, I didn't think it was the appropriate time to tell Jasper my thoughts.

"Liam challenged me to a friendly fight is all, sir." I said rather bravely.

"That's not how it looked to me, boy. Had I not intervened, Lord only ken what kind of bloodshed might have been done."

I sat there silently, not sure what I should say next. Sorry? No, I didn't think that would make things better.

"I cannae be havin' this kind of thing goin' on again in my keep. The lad will spit someone next time if not he's no' careful. For now, lad, ye'll be workin' in the stables with Sean, he's the stable master. He'll keep ye out of trouble."

When I didn't move he looked at me as if I was an idiot. When I still remained seated, he mouthed the word 'go', and so I did, as if the hounds of hell were after me.

"Jasper, I need to ken what's goin' on here. Liam trusts ye and he's usually a good judge of character. However, after today's performance, there's more than meets the eye here, at least where yer *ogha* is concerned. Come out with it. I dinnae have the time myself to babysit ye or the boy."

Jasper worried a loose thread on his tartan, trying to figure out the best way to start. He didn't even know Jessie could fight like that. Damn the wench!

"My laird, I do apologize for his behavior. Had I'd ken what he was about I would have shoved him into the stables myself. Thank ye for confinin' him to muckin' up shite." Jasper smirked at the thought and Rhys did the same after a minute then cleared his throat.

"Yer his *seanair*, how did ye not ken how extensive his train' was? He nearly beat Liam, a soldier of years under him!" Rhys rubbed his eyes and leaned back in his chair, waiting.

"The boy has suffered much in a short time. His experience with Lord Thomas was a grievous one, and that's puttin' it delicately." Jasper began to pace, on edge now with the memory of that night clear as day in his head.

"Wait, what happened? What does this have to do with that monster?" Rhys demanded, his hands slamming down on the desk top in rage.

Jasper took a sip of his whiskey before continuing on, stalling from not wanting to relive that night all over again. He'd not spoken of it to anyone, not even at depth with Jessie since she didn't remember much.

"I walked into our room to find Jessie tied to the bed and Thomas...," he paused, trying to swallow the bile that came up, and then downed the rest of his whiskey before continuing, "lashing the boy's bare back with his belt."

"And how does that make the lad go half mad with a sword? We've all had our hides tanned a time or two." Rhys waved off what Jasper had told him.

"Then ye dinnae ken Thomas' cruelty at all. The man hadnae just given him a few marks, he beat him to where both were covered in blood. Skin hung limp in jagged strips over the waistband of the lad's pants. Bloody rivulets ran from the open wounds, collectin' on the floor."

Jasper wiped the back of his hand across his face, not realizing tears of anger and fear had fallen while telling Rhys what happened. He could still hear her screams, then weak pleas to make it stop. He feared they'd never leave him. It would serve him right for it.

"What the hell did the boy do?" Rhys gasped out, trying not to vomit himself. They both took two more shots of whiskey to get rid of the taste.

"Nothin' that warranted bodily harm such as that. Thomas claimed that Jessie had been rude to him and his wife by not biddin' them good night, but got up and left the room. Then there was the issue of Jessie talking disrespectfully to me, thinkin' it was I who had entered the room instead of Thomas."

Rhys brooded over all that he'd been told. Jasper brooded for different reasons all together. Rhys added another mental check mark to the growing list of Thomas' misdeeds. If he could, he'd kill him, but unfortunately, it could not be done by his hand, or he would lose everything and most likely hanged.

"I'm sorry for what yer *ogha* has been through, its more than any child should go through, however, the lad needs to get his temper under control."

Jasper let out a breath he hadn't realized he'd been holding, then nodded in agreement. He replaced his cup to the side table just to the side of the tray then asked, "What service might I offer to ye, for my own lodgin'?"

Rhys sat quietly for a moment, brooding over ideas then tossing them aside until he found one he thought would suit Jasper. "I've heard that a Risin' is potentially in the works on Rowen lands. Thomas is considerin' raisin' the rents on the tenants and shopkeepers. He's managed to run through his allowance the Crown pays him every quarter."

Jasper studied him for a minute, wondering where Rhys was going with this information. He was getting a sneaky suspicion he wouldn't like it.

"I can see ye have no love for the man considerin' everythin'. I want ye to take a few of my men out to test the waters, as it were. Find out if the rumor is more than just a rumor. Send back word when ye get anythin' of import."

"All right then, when do we leave? How close to Rowen Keep do ye want us to get?" Jasper raised an eyebrow.

"As close as possible. I cannae have Liam go, as I suspect many of the people there would recognize him as one of Thomas' men. Whether he is or no', they willnae trust him."

Rhys poured himself another dram of whiskey, offered the bottle to Jasper who declined. "Have the men ready by mid mornin' and we'll head out." Rhys nodded at this then Jasper bid him a good night. He went in search for Jessie to join him for supper.

CHAPTER 20

As promised, a team of twelve of Rhys' men sat mounted and awaiting instruction. Two carts were filled, one with food stuffs and the other with bedding and items to make tents for them. Jasper gave explicit instructions to me that I was not to engage in any type interaction with Liam, and to mind my superiors.

"If Liam should find ye, just walk away."

I feigned being insulted. "I just lost my husband and child. How could you accuse me of such a thing, Jasper!" I snapped at him.

"I've seen how ye been lookin' at him and no good will come of it. Yer suppose to be a 'lad', and buggerin' is verae much frowned upon, especially in this time.

"Jessie ye'r still human. I'm not sayin' yer forgettin' yer family. Losin' someone is verae hard, and losin' a child on top of that… It's not uncommon to seek out affection to forget for a little while, whether they ken it or no'."

He hugged her then shoved her in the direction of the stables. He crossed himself and said a silent prayer asking for patience when it came to her.

He mounted up and called the team forward, filing one behind the other through the portcullis. With one more look behind him in the direction of the stables, he saw that she stayed put and so he kicked his mount into a gallop and was soon out of sight.

"Sean, are you in here?" I called out. When I didn't receive an answer after my second call, I checked in on the stalls to see what needed to be done. Obviously, the other stable hands decided to take the last few days off, seeing how disgusting things were.

Sheep were in ankle deep shit with snotty noses and bleating. The horses all hung their heads over their stall doors expecting to be fed. I had my work cut out for me today.

I stopped for a minute to pet one of the smaller sheep; the only black one in the pen. It seemed like it was the "black sheep of the pen" as it were, completely ignored by the others. "I know how you feel little guy."

As if in answer, he bleated out to me then nipped at the cuff of my coat. I produced an apple I had been saving for later, cut it into slices and handed him a couple before moving on.

"Dinnae get too attached to them lad, ye'll be eatin' them soon enough." A male voice came over the stall door and I slipped in the remaining sheep shit.

"Damn it! What do you want?" I snapped at Liam.

He stood leaning on the stall door, hands folded together and a half smile on his face. He was trying very hard not to laugh at the scene before him.

"Nothin'. Just came to check on ye, see if ye'r hungry. Sean is in the hall, along with the others havin' breakfast. Although now well, maybe ye should stay here instead."

I got up, almost slipping again had it not been for Liam grabbing me by my upper arm. I shook him off and continued on.

"I'm fine thank you. I ate earlier with Jasper. You go ahead and tell Sean I'm already here."

He moved aside, holding the stall door open for me then followed me down the main aisle. I ground my teeth and did my best to ignore him.

"Is there something you needed Liam, because if not, I have work to do." I said impatiently.

He backed away, hands held up in the air as in surrender, and headed to the main stable doors. "No, no I'm off then. I'll pass yer message to Sean." And with that, he was gone.

I finished my awful job and moved on to the feedings, coming back to my little friend. I sat in the corner, taking a break with him.

"I see ye made a friend there, lad." Sean leaned on the door just as Liam had earlier, and tossed me an apple. My stomach growled loudly as I bit into it, cleaning it to its core.

"Dinnae be spoilin' her lad or she willnae eat her own food. Cannae have skinny sheep for dinner now can we." He winked. I grimaced at that.

Sean backed away from the stall door, laughing at my reaction. "Come on then lad, I'll teach ye how to groom a horse." He walked off, so I gave my friend a final pat before following behind him.

CHAPTER 21

THE TEAM ARRIVED TO the first small village on Devonshire lands. Jasper and the men found lodging for the night at the only inn, and after taking care of their horses and parking the carts, they sat in joyful noise with a warm fire, food, drink, and half naked women.

Jasper didn't feel all too joyful at the moment. He was tired and irritable about having to travel yet again, in the snow. His feet had yet to fully heal and he could feel the blisters coming back from his damp boots rubbing them.

He was also not one for small talk. He' rather get right to the point and then be on his way, but, after today's example, he was going nowhere fast. None of the people were interested in giving information to him about the Rising. Even though he wore Rhys' colors, they still didn't want to talk to him.

One of Rhys' men, Merrick if he recalled the name, sat down at the table with him and poured them both another tankard of ale.

"Ye'd catch more flies with honey than ye would with vinegar."

Jasper only grunted. He continued to brood over his cup. "Ye'r a man of few words I take it, unless yer interrogatin' someone that is." Merrick commented.

"Aye? And do ye have a problem with that?" Jasper snapped back.

Merrick sat back and drank deeply from his cup, studying Jasper. Jasper returned it with a glare until Merrick broke it. He knew Jasper didn't want company, which made Merrick stay put.

"Look Campbell, look around ye. The men are getting' the information for ye. It may not look it but they are." Jasper didn't, but continued to nurse his cup and glare at the table top.

"All right then, ye and the others will report to me what information ye do get out of these people. I'll send word to Rhys once the reports are completed." With that, Jasper got up and walked out.

Once settled for the night, he rolled over to poke the fire, wishing he could throw his thoughts into it. God help him, if Jessie was causing grief at the castle. He'd ring her skinny little neck if he heard anything other than her behaving.

His thoughts turned to the search of Jon. He didn't like the fact that he was out, gallivanting around for Rhys, and if it hadn't been for Jessie and what had happened to her at Rowen Castle, he and Jessie would already have been south now.

The man had to pay for what he had done to her. If Rhys could find something on him that was chargeable, that would be a slap on the wrist compared to what he wanted to do to Thomas.

He was not one to believe in karma, but if it did exist, he hoped it would visit Thomas, and soon. The fire crackled and snapped and he added another stick before removing the hot stones for warmth. Hopefully, there would be news in the morning from the men.

—◦◦◦—

"Aye, it looks as though that's his plan. Many can barely make the current payments. At least half the families are talkin' about leavin' to find placement with other members."

Jasper was not happy about hearing this news, and grew less and less with each accounting. Once documented, he sent the notes back to Rhys:

> *I hope this finds you well. After several discussions with the people here, the rumors seem to be true. Thomas will be raising the rents.*
>
> *Many of them have begun to search for new areas for lodging, shacking up with other tenants or family members, which at this time of year, is not an ideal action. Many of them can barely afford their homes now as it is.*
>
> *We are moving on to Killin to inquire more, to see if there's any other news than what we already have. If not, then we will return post haste. No point continuing on.*
>
> *I cannot say when he plans on doing this, I don't know him well so I don't know the way he operates. However, seeing how agitated the people here are, it will not be long.*
>
> *There are some who speak of heading in your direction, so keep a look out. Tomorrow we will head out, and will report again in a few days.*
>
> *Jasper Campbell*

Rhys put the letter aside; thoughts running in his mind. So, he'd have an uprising in the making on his hands soon. He'd have Liam do the rounds, get the men ready, have an inventory done on supplies and weaponry.

Liam entered then, interrupting Rhys' thoughts. "Och, lad, is there a witch about in my Keep?" At Liam's confused look, he brushed his comment aside and gestured to a chair.

"Word has come. Thomas does intend to raise the rents. Durin' mid-winter it would seem. People cannae leave and find another place before keelin' over dead in the snow. They're trapped and he kens it. "

Liam didn't like the sound of this news either and grimaced. "What is it ye'd have me do?"

"I need ye to round up the men, check the food staples and if we need to stock up, ask my tenants if they harvested extra this year and are willin' to part with whatever they dinnae need. See Giles for coin to pay them for their generosity.

"Have the smithy work overtime on weaponry. We need as much as possible. I am sendin' word to a few of our nearby clans to the south, informin' them of what's to come and to join us."

CHAPTER 22

L IAM SAT FOR A moment more, making a mental check list of what he needed done before taking his leave from Rhys. He headed to the kitchens, instructing the Mistress to record what would they'd be needing extra of, and to provide him with a list in an hour. He moved onto the smithy then onto Giles for coinage.

He spotted one of the soldiers lounging in the courtyard and motioned for him to follow. "Gather up a few of the men, and those carts there, have them brought out and emptied. Gather as many grain sacks ye can find."

Liam motioned the man to go about the task given, and continued on to seek out the accountant Giles. Giles was in the back room going over ledgers and taking notes. Liam stood before him, waiting for the man to look up and acknowledge his presence. When he didn't, he cleared his throat a couple of times.

"I ken yer there Liam, so be about it then. I have work to do." Giles said without looking up from his writing.

"Rhys has sent me to collect two bags of gold to pay out to the tenants." Giles raised an eyebrow at this and Liam ground his teeth.

"Ye can waste time by sendin' yer apprentice here to confirm this, or ye can be about it and get them now." Liam ground out.

Giles sat another minute, then had his apprentice retrieve the two bags, and then proceeded to count them, finding them of equal value. He flipped open a ledger and tossed it to Liam, instructing him to initial the withdrawal. Liam did so then stormed out, impatient to get going.

He found Jessie outside holding the reins to his mount. She had a strange look upon her face; almost as if she was scared for him, or something.

"Thank you Jessie. I'll be back in a couple of days to drive ye crazy. Dinnae worry lad." He winked at her. That startled her and she gave him a strained smile. So, apparently he was into boys; bummer.

Watching him ride out, I couldn't help but feel worried. A nasty feeling ran up my spine and I tried to shake it off but it only nagged me more. I busied myself with my daily chores, and once done, I was sent to the kitchens to see if they needed tending to. Since there was nothing to do there, I went back and spent some time with the black lamb. Once done, I checked again on the horses before heading out. I stopped by one in particular who had been brought in a few days ago.

"Be careful with that one lad, he's a bitter." Sean swaggered over to me and leaned against the stall door. I looked over the horse myself, but he only nuzzled my arm for more affection.

"My father had a gift with horses. It didn't matter how obstinate they were, he would break them. I wonder if it passed down to me." I said to Sean.

If in understanding, the horse whinnied at Sean and I couldn't help but laugh. "All right lad, if ye think ye got the 'gift' then let us see what ye've got."

I blanched at the man's comment. "I don't know how to train a horse!"

"I'll teach ye. First ye need to bridle him, like this." He struggled with the horse, the horse refusing to open his mouth to have the metal bar shoved into it. Eventually Sean won the fight, sweat dripping down his face onto his shirt.

The horse nipped him in the ear so Sean shoved him back. I rolled my eyes at the two, thinking how the male species in the animal kingdom were all the same; stubborn and pigheaded.

"What's his name?" I asked.

"This pain in my arse, is Lucifer." He handed me the lead and opened the stall door, instructing me to lead him out. I gave a tug and Lucifer actually followed.

"Well I'll be damned. I guess ye do have a gift. Take him out to the training arena. Ye ken where that is?" he asked and I nodded, leading Lucifer out into the courtyard and up a hill where the horses trained.

He pawed the ground when he smelled fresh air and felt the wind run through his silver mane. Nostrils flaring he shook his head, his body vibrating with contained energy.

Sean followed us into the arena, taking the lead from me. I stood back and took in Lucifer's magnificence. Lean muscles and strong legs moved fluidly. He was bred for speed.

Sean trotted Lucifer around, keeping him close, releasing a foot at a time of the reins after each lap Lucifer completed without struggling. Silver main and tail seemed to float in the air and his coat, almost blinding in the rare peek of sunlight.

This stallion was meant to be min and I his. As thought reading my thoughts, he sauntered over to me with Sean digging in his heals in the dirt to stop him, but was unsuccessful.

"Who's a good boy, you are aren't you, yes you are." I rubbed the bridge of his nose then leaned and touched my head to his. Yes, this was to be my stallion.

"Stubborn horse! Good luck trainin' the beast!" At hearing Sean's sour tone, Lucifer nipped Sean's coat as ye walked by, causing Sean to shove at Lucifer's nose before leaving the arena.

"You wicked beastie aren't you. Well, he deserved it didn't he. Come on, let's get to know each other. Show me what you got boy." A sneaky gleam smoldered in his eyes before he took off running.

Rhys stood on the wooden balcony, monitoring the goings-on in the courtyard. Liam had left hours ago and the place seemed vacant, what with Jasper and his group of men gone, and now with even more of his men out with Liam.

He caught Sean heading to the kitchens, grumbling to himself. He wondered if his grumblings had anything to do with Jessie. He scrubbed at his face in exasperation then followed a bit behind him.

He found him in the main room of the kitchen, nursing a tankard of ale and talking to Mrs. Drummond, the head mistress of the staff and running of the Keep. He stood back out of sight and eavesdropped.

"Bless it all to hell and back Annie, that beast had it in his mind to ignore my demands, then bites me. The lad is going to is goin' to regret all of that, that demon's nonsense."

At the mention of the 'lad', Rhys perked up and was appalled to here this news. He marched over then to over to Sean, demanding to know what had happened.

Sean tsk'd then went into explaining, "...the boy sayin' his da had the 'gift' with horses and maybe he would too. So I had him take Lucifer out to the arena and..." Sean relayed everything to Rhys, who couldn't help but grin. So, the horse bit him and not Jessie, that made much more sense.

Rhys left him to his complaining and went to check on Jessie's progress with Lucifer. She was leading him at a mild gallop around the arena. She pulled on the lead, bringing the horse to a stop then tugged again, having the horse trot up to her.

Nostrils flaring and sides heaving from his exertion, Jessie stuck out her hand for him to smell her. He shied away instinctively then slowly walked up to her. She procured an apple out of her coat pocket and Lucifer nipped it cleanly off of her palm.

"So, I see ye've met our Lucifer. What's yer bite count?" He watched Jessie brush the horse's mane with her hand.

"Well, I had to bite him about three times so far but we have come to an understanding, haven't we my friend." When I didn't get a verbal reaction, I turned and looked at Rhys' shocked face and I had to laugh.

"I am just jesting, Rhys. I would never harm an animal, no matter how feisty it may be." I reassured him. "He hasn't bitten me yet, but, the pigs though, I'm sure there is a special hell for them." I glared in their direction.

He laughed at that one so I guessed I was off his shit-list after my first comment. "Sean has told me yer doin' well here, that yer a hard worker, harder than the rest."

I blushed at the compliment and I turned away, appearing to be busy. "Yes, well it seems the others feel that frequent breaks are needed to get through the day, but…" I shrugged and began my walk back to the stables to clean Lucifer up.

"Jasper will be back in a couple of days. I'm sure ye'll be a sight for sore eyes I can imagine."

"I suppose. Has he been successful out and about?" I missed his grumpy face and surly voice.

"Aye, but it isnae good news as I feared. I'll say that ye and Jasper may stay on here longer, but I need Liam to stay here. I dinnae ken for how long either. If yer in a hurry, then ye'll have to go without him."

I didn't like hearing this news myself. Jasper and I would need to sit down and discuss what our next moves were to be. I had been lost in my thoughts when Rhys' voice snapped me out of them.

"If ye decide on stayin' a bit longer, I ken Sean would be grateful for it; as would I." When a snuffle echoed down the stable aisle, Rhys and I turned to see Lucifer hanging his head over his stall door.

"I take it Lucifer would enjoy yer stay too." Rhys winked at me and I rolled my eyes. "I'll let ye get back to it then, lad." Rhys about faced and left me to it.

CHAPTER 23

THE MEN, ALONG WITH Jasper, arrived looking disheveled and weather beaten. A couple of the younger ones were passing jokes between themselves, but the rest were somber.

I met him in the courtyard expectantly, but all he did was toss the reins of his mount to me, followed by an absent-minded "Thank You" before walking off. It was as if he hadn't even noticed me; so lost in his thoughts.

I didn't follow, but took charge of his mount and another rider's as well. I'd let him decompress before I would search him out. The horses needed tending to anyway and then all the bells and whistles that went along with that job, so I didn't linger over my thoughts about Jasper.

Once done with my job, I checked over the rest of the gear from all the returned mounts, making sure they were cleaned properly and organized for easy access. They were subpar at best, and I would have to come back and do it myself, correctly. For now, I was starving and it was near supper time.

Most had come in and had started eating before I had come myself. The room was filled with mostly murmured whispers, with the occasional bark of laughter here and there. Rhys had not attended dinner, but Jasper was here and seated with Liam in deep discussion. I let them be and sat where I could find a seat.

Thankfully, because everyone was in a less than cheerful mood, I didn't have to deal with the razzing I was usually subjected to by the others at the table.

Once I had had my fill, I turned to find that Jasper and Liam had already left and so I went about in search of them. I asked around and was told in which direction each had gone but, as to the where; they had no idea.

I felt guilty about my sneaking around, opening doors, and hiding in dark alcoves whenever another person was near.

Voices could be heard, muffled behind Rhys' private study doors. There were at least four men in there, by the different pitches in tones. The door was closed so I couldn't make out exactly what they were saying. I slowly opened it a crack and listened in.

"...the villages are horrid. The people cannae pay more rent. Their homes are fallin' into disrepair and cannae afford to fix them. Some are in rags, other on the verge of starvation."

Jasper paced while Rhys and one of the other men were seated and drinking. Silence filled the room and had I not seen them there myself, I would have thought they had left.

"All right, so what do ye suggest we do?" The one man I couldn't see asked.

Rhys sighed then got up to refill his cup. He went to his desk, rummaged through his papers trying to find pen and ink. "Most likely he will follow through with the rent increase. The people will have no choice but to pay it. It's too late to go anywhere until winter is over."

Jasper and the other men nodded in agreement. "As for now, we will have to wait on doin' anythin' rash. Send Ian to Rowen as Liam's replacement. We need eyes and ears in there."

"So, what have ye heard," a close whisper said into my ear.

So distracted was I, that I immediately began to answer the question posed to me, then squeaked when I realized that there was indeed someone behind me.

"What are *you* doing here? Don't you have to practice or…something, instead of sneaking around eavesdropping?" I snapped harshly in a whisper.

"What, me? I was just walkin' by and saw ye here. Yer the one eavesdroppin'. Ye should be ashamed of yerself." Liam smirked at me. I wished I could have slugged him, but we weren't supposed to be here, and I didn't need him announcing that we were by yelping in pain.

The sound of shuffling feet came through the cracked door. Liam and I both jumped back and scurried along the wall, trying to find a hiding place since there wasn't time to run. I slid behind a full length tapestry and held my breath. I didn't know where Liam had gone to.

Jasper and the other men left the room, closing the door behind them. They took a minute to continue their discussion in the hallway, and my lungs began to burn from holding my breath. I slowly let it go through my nose, and then in a whoosh once the men had moved on.

They passed by me impossibly close but thankfully they were so engrossed in their conversation, that they didn't see the vertical lump in the tapestry. Or, if they had, it wasn't something uncommon to be concerned over.

Once the hall was quiet, I stayed put just to make sure they hadn't decided to come back. Liam took it upon himself to startle me yet again, and this time my fist connected with his face.

"Mac Ghalla!" *Son of a bitch*, he cursed loudly. "Why did ye have to do that for?" His angry voice sounded next to me. It was dark behind the tapestry so I couldn't see what my fist had connected with.

"Well, stop sneaking up on me and that won't happen!" I said back, annoyance plain in my voice.

"I'm going to find Jasper. Go find your own business and leave me be. Good night." I said smartly to him before leaving.

I hurriedly went in the direction Jasper had gone, hoping to catch up to him, however, what with the time I had spent slugging Liam, the other men had gotten much farther ahead and I'd lost them.

I sought out Sean to let him know that I would be cleaning up the men's gear from earlier, and if he saw Jasper, to tell him to come to the stables.

It infuriated me how the stable hands left things after "cleaning" everything. Once all was done to my specifications, I went into the main kitchen, grabbed whatever I could find then went back to the stables.

The animals talked amongst themselves, and, I found of late, that I preferred their company over the people. They were blissfully unaware of what was to become of them in the near future and I wished I had the same ability.

I settled down next to my little friend who again, was lying in the back corner by himself. I handed him my apple core and he happily ate it, foamy saliva dangling from his mouth as he chewed.

Here I could talk about anything and not worry about it getting back to anyone; there were no human ears to listen in on me. The animals didn't cast judgment whereas people would. I absently rubbed the lamb's fuzzy head. It nuzzled my knee then relaxed its head on it.

Lucifer grumbled down the aisle which reminded me that I needed to take care of him too. I bid my lamb good night, and headed on down to check on him.

It was strange hearing a horse complain. He was so opinionated too. I handed over a carrot which he had sniffed out immediately and pushed at my pocket, demanding it. Once consoled, and the stables quiet for the night, I headed up to bed myself.

Jasper found me in the training arena with Lucifer, practicing his jaunt, trot, gallop, and canter. "Good God, Jessie, he's twice yer size! What did ye do to get stuck with him?"

I stood in the middle, lead in hand, lengthening it by a foot each time he made a complete lap. "He picked me honestly. I guess I have Jon's talent with horses too." I said without glancing at him.

Jasper entered, not realizing just how rogue a horse Lucifer was, and backed out again when Lucifer reared, eyes going wild, and began to charge at him. I pulled hard on the reins, my feet dragging on the dirt as he pulled me. He stopped shy of five feet from Jasper and I brought his head down to my chest, the bridge of his nose pressed against my breast bone. I cooed to him quietly, and stroked the side of his face.

"Jessie, get the hell out of there! He's too wild, he's goin' to kill ye!" Jasper bellowed at me but I had Lucifer now under control so there was nothing to worry about.

Lucifer glared at him, nostrils flaring in warning. Once calm, Lucifer looked at me, imploringly for a treat for his good behavior. I laughed at him and complied.

"If I were you, I'd high-tail it out of here, at least until I bring him back to his stall."

Jasper stood there glaring still at Lucifer, who all but ignored him now, happily chewing on another apple. I shrugged and began to walk him to the gate. As suspected, Lucifer snorted in warning, which had Jasper quickly moving away a good distance.

"I'll be in the main study. Find me there when yer done with the Devil." Jasper made a face at Lucifer before walking off.

I couldn't help but snicker after him, and I could have sworn I saw amusement in Lucifer's eyes. I got him cleaned up then sought out the old man.

I found him sitting in the master library instead, reading something in Gaelic, but he put it down when he saw me stride in. As I sat, he got up and put the book on the shelf, skimming the spines of others.

"Thomas is causin' problems for the tenants on his lands." He selected another one and returned to his seat.

"And how does this affect our plans?" I raised a brow at him but he didn't see, what with his nose in the current book.

"Rhys said he needs Liam to fight in the Rising which means, that we would have to leave without him, or we stay. And if we stay, then I will be joinin' as well."

"You can't just *join*, Jasper! You're older than dirt and will probably keel over and die after running someone through." I argued with him.

"Oye, lass, I still have a good fight in me. I willnae die on this field." He countered back.

"Yeah, probably get hung instead." I said under my breath but from the glare he shot at me, I hadn't been quiet enough.

"I think you're asking for a death wish, Jasper. What would happen, God forbid, you end up maimed or dead? What if both you and Liam get hurt, or die, then how do I go about finding Jon?"

"Ye dinnae go on, lass. Ye go back to where Jon and I traveled to your time, and go home to yer gran." He said mournfully.

"Why must you join it? You don't live here, you haven't pledged fealty to Rhys." I wasn't going to give up without a fight of my own.

"No, I dinnae pledge fealty to him, but I did to Jon, and as far as I'm concerned, he is the rightful Duke of Devonshire."

I rolled my eyes at that and blew out an exasperated breath before replying, "Oh please, there's no one to prove yourself to. Jon isn't here and the remaining people who would remember him, wouldn't expect you to save them. As far as they're concerned, you're with Rhys."

"There's the matter of what he did to ye if ye've forgotten. He cannae get away with that alone! I should have killed him on the spot." Jasper's anger radiated and filled the room.

There wasn't anything I could say to that. I wanted to kill him myself; remembering that night had my back going stiff. Jasper told me the last time he treated it, that it was barely noticeable, however, the tug on my skin here and there said otherwise.

"I appreciate the noble gesture Jasper, but it's not worth your life. You're not exactly a spring chicken."

"I'm goin' whether ye like it or not. It's not yer decision to make. It'd be my last fight to be sure. How I miss bein' out there." When he didn't say anymore, I looked up to find that he was gone.

CHAPTER 24

I WAS DETERMINED TO convince Jasper not to go. I was just as stubborn as he and I had my work cut out for me. I had to find Liam and ask for his help.

The Keep was quiet now and I snuck out and headed to the armory. The sword I had used against Liam was an easy one, but I needed to get my body stronger if I was to protect myself. If anything, after what occurred at Rowen, I needed to keep my eyes open and my guard up.

I was amazed with the selection of weaponry. I strolled by the claymores that were as big as I was tall, and quickly wrote those off my list.

Clubs and maces were on wooden wracks. Lances, hammers, arming swords, and broad swords were on several other wracks. Hanging on the walls were long bows, overlapping each other for space efficiency, quivers just below them.

Further back, the room opened wider. The wracks were in long rows, holding different types and sizes of daggers. To the side, my favorite weapon, were the rapiers, gleaming in the torch light just above them. I handled a few of them, loving the familiar feel of the hilt in my hand. Hearing the seductive whistle they made when I swung them back and forth.

I put them back after trying each one, reminding myself that I was there for something with a bit more heft. I went for an arming sword that was a couple feet shorter than myself. It was heavier than it looked but I managed.

I headed out to the secluded field that was on the south side of the Keep, where there was enough tree coverage to hide me from sight. A few times I turned around every now and then to check to make sure no one was following me. I kept feeling a prickle on the back of my neck, but no one was there.

I followed my training of fencing, all be it slower since the sword was way heavier than a rapier. Within ten minutes I was sweating heavily and I took a break to remove my coat. Snow was falling around me but I paid no notice, only concentrated on killing my current foe; a tree trunk.

"Open yer legs," came a male voice and I squeaked, losing my balance and landed in the snow.

"I beg your pardon!" I admonished the man. Then I rolled my eyes at my proposed assailant.

Liam stood over me, arms crossed over his chest, and his own legs in a wide stance. "I said open yer legs, wider when swingin' a sword. Otherwise ye'll lose yer balance just as ye did now."

He extended a hand but I shoved it away, and got up. I ignored his instruction, my stubbornness kicking in. I had to do this myself. I soon wore myself out, but hid it as a show of taking a break to drink water.

"How did you know I was here?" I asked, corking my canteen.

"I saw ye go into the armory and either ye were plannin' on raidin' the Keep or just browsin'. I wanted to make sure we were all safe." He said this with a smirk on his face.

I stuck my nose up and tried to continue to ignore him again, which was hard to do, with him standing there in the dim moonlight. What I could see of him in the light, was the heated gleam in his eyes and his jet black hair moving in the wind. I shivered but not from the cold.

"Here, I brought these out for ye to try." He handed me one of the two anelace, and one of the two small dirks as well. He removed his cloak, and laid it over my own.

He was suddenly behind me, his chest brushing my shoulder blades. He grasped my right hand which held the anelace. "Dinnae wave yer hand only. Yer strength comes from yer arm and shoulder; use the whole of it."

His breath caressed my neck, causing goose bumps to rise over me. I didn't feel the cold anymore, his body being in close proximity to mine, generated plenty of heat.

He took my left hand next, directed the blade to lay along my forearm. I tried to bring it back to point outward but he tightened his grip painfully, telling me to keep it tucked in.

"Dinnae show that ye have this, otherwise yer opponent will strategize the best way to fell ye," he warned me.

My breath came out harsh but not from the exertion of the training, but from his closeness to me. Sensing this, he stepped away and I felt a little disappointed over it. I'd have to think that over later.

"Follow my lead, lad." He stood next to me, slowly instructed me on how to move the sword correctly. He lifted his left hand, the one holding the dirk, and made a slashing motion with it. The whole time he did this, I never once saw the it.

I followed as he instructed, practicing these moves for what seemed like hours, but only about half of one. Sweat dripped from our faces and our shirts were plastered to our bodies.

"Up for a friendly duel?" he asked once we took a break.

"I guess." I rolled my shoulders which were now killing me, but I wasn't going to wimp out of the challenge.

"Let me see what ye got, *lass*." A wicked grin spread across his face and I gasped.

"How dare you sir! I'm not a '*lass*'! Now, raise your sword so I can actually have an excuse to run you through!" I hissed angrily.

"Okay, mo chridhe." The smile somehow got broader as he raised his own sword. I didn't know what the hell he'd just said but from the look on his face, it was yet another way of calling me lass.

I lunged for him and he stepped to the side easily. I turned around and tried again, only for him to move aside again, as if avoiding a pile of shit.

"Dinnae let yer anger get the best of of ye, lass. Ye'll make mistakes which could cost ye yer life, or the life of someone else."

"Ugh, why are you so damn annoying? Isn't there some skirt you should be under, or is buggering your kind of thing?" I countered. At his startled then furious look, I took my opportunity and swung, nearly taking off his left leg.

"Och, lass, these were my favorite pair of breeches! I guess ye'll just have to sew them for me later." He winked.

I shushed him, not wanting anyone to find us out here. Our little dance continued until he caught me close, the dirk pressed against my abdomen. Both our breaths were angry puff in the cold air but I didn't feel the cold anymore; and neither did he.

I backed away, only to be reminded that the dirk was still there, and if I so much as moved an inch, my guts most assuredly would be on the ground.

I shoved him away instead, causing him to stagger back, almost falling into the snow bank around us, but he caught his footing quickly. He flung his weapons aside, anger plainly on his face. I took a step back, in fear that I had finally gone too far.

The quiet was deafening and I tossed my weapons next to his in a truce. My body had begun to shiver from the cold now and my muscles tightened up miserably. Without talking I collected my coat and cloak, preparing to bundle up and go back inside. Instead, I found myself face to face with a very pissed off Highlander.

His eyes were jet black due to the night, but I could feel them burn into mine and I really did want to leave then. My breath caught in my throat, intending to scream for help however, reading my mind, he sealed his lips over mine in a fevered kiss.

When I broke the kiss I asked him firmly to let me go, his answer was a single word, growled out between clenched teeth, "No." His lips crushed mine again and I tried to struggle but soon gave up, telling myself that my body was too tired after the exercise I'd just gone through.

The best defense I could do was a slap across his face. It didn't seem to cause him enough pain to back off. I finally got loose when we came up for air, putting distance between us by going in the direction of where my weapons laid.

"How dare you, sir! Who the hell do you think you are? Go find another boy to bugger. I'm not interested." I hissed at him.

"I am not into boys and ye are no 'boy', Jessie, or should I call ye Jessi-ca?" He quirked an eyebrow at me; waiting for an answer. When he saw my reaction, he was quite pleased with himself.

He began to stalk towards me like a lion on the prowl. His eyes glittered fire and lust when the moonlight touched him for a moment, and my traitorous body clenched in anticipation. I side- stepped away from him, swooping down for my belongings while keeping my eyes on him.

"My name is 'Jessie', *sir*, and you'd do best to remember that for the future." I warned.

"But 'Jessica' is such a pretty name, it suits ye so well too." A rakish grin quirked at the right side of his mouth; making him even more impossibly handsome. What the hell was wrong with me?

"That's it! I warned you but you must have lost your hearing somewhere and now your head will follow."

I slammed into him, knocking him to the ground, landing on top of him with my knees on either side of his ribs, my dirk at his throat. I glared down at him, daring him to move. I pressed the dagger harder than I had intended and a trickle of blood oozed from the mini cut.

"God yer beautiful." He whispered either from the air being knocked out of him or from the sting from the cut I had just done.

At my stunned look, he took the opportunity to flip me over onto my back, loosened the dirk from my hand then trapped my wrists in both of his hands. His body covered mine and I was sure that what was currently digging into my lower abdomen was not the hilt of a dirk.

I squirmed until he let all his body weight lay fully on me and my breath left me because of it. "Are ye goin' to settle down wench? Or should a nice spankin' do the trick?" He teased against my neck. His lips felt so good on it, like warm velvet that whispered across a sensitive spot. I shuddered, cursed then tried again to get free. No such luck.

I looked up at him finally, calm and collected. He grinned down at me then crushed his lips against mine, but not in anger but in full desire to taste. I fought it for a minute but there was no use. My body went lax and I kissed him back. I soon found my hands freed and now running through his black mane, loving the feel of it.

The kiss seemed to go on forever, or at least it felt like it and I didn't want it to ever stop. It had been so long since I'd been kissed like this, even with Nick it had become scarce. This full passion exuding from Liam fueled my own and I craved for more.

At some point we had rolled again and I was now lying on top of him, hungrily kissing him, nipping and biting then plundering. But, reality kicked me sharply as Liam's hands began running up under my shirt at the hips, heading for my back. I was off of him as if I'd been shot, and I wiped my mouth across my sleeve, trying to catch my breath.

I stood up too soon and my vision blurred from becoming dizzy so I bent over again until the feeling went away. Liam rose himself; and brushed snow off of his backside and shoulders, out of breath himself. I needed to get away from here, from him. He was dangerous to be around apparently.

I flung my cloak over my shoulders, then looked around for the sword I'd brought down with me to train with. I kicked the snow, trying to locate it but couldn't find it.

"Jessica, it's alright, calm," Liam slowly walked over to me, treading carefully as though I was a scared animal.

"No! I will not calm down, it's not alright, Liam. And don't call me 'Jessica'. That's not my name, not anymore." I sucked in a breath at my stupidity. Now the cat was for sure out of the bag.

"Jessi," he held up his hands in surrender before continuing on, "Jessie, I dinnae mean to scare ye."

"I'm not scared Liam, I'm pissed off! How dare you take such liberties of me." I kicked at the snow some more cursing, "Oh fuck it all to hell and back! You find the sword." And with that, I strode off back to the Keep, angry with Liam but mostly at myself.

He watched her go, a scared rabbit lost in the snow. He circled around, collecting the dirks and the two swords he'd brought. He kicked at the snow as she had, looking for the sword she had brought with her, but couldn't find it either.

"Damn it, where are ye little bugger," he hissed out between his teeth, then cursed in Gaelic when the tip of his foot connected with the buried hilt of the sword. He suspected the woman would be causing him more pain and trouble in the near future.

How dare he, how dare he!! How did he know? Who would have told him? *Jasper*. He was the only one who knew that I was a woman. I'd been very careful when disrobing and binding my breasts, so it had to be him.

I stormed past my room and straight to his, throwing his door open where it banged against the wall. "What the hell?" Jasper jumped out of bed, pretty agile for an old man, a short dagger at the ready.

CHAPTER 25

"Why did you tell Liam about me? How long has he known?" I yelled at him, chest heaving and fists tightly clenched.

"What? I dinnae tell him! Why would I risk what we're here to do? I dinnae ken how he kens but it was not I who told him. Did ye strip down to yer knickers in front of him? Ye two have been spendin' a lot of time together recently." He glared back at me.

It just dawned on him that he was standing before Jessie, naked as the day he came into this world and quickly wrapped the bed sheet around his waist. He prayed she hadn't seen anything.

"I did no such thing you bastard and how dare you accuse me of such. I'll beat the truth out of him tomorrow and so help me God, if you did Jasper, you'll be next."

"Dinnae be threatenin' me, *lad*." He exaggerated the last word. "Ye'll be comin' back to apologize if and when ye do find out how he kens. Oh and dinnae be stormin' my room again. I might have had company with me!"

"Ha! In your dreams old man." I crossed my arms and rolled my eyes.

"Wait, why are ye not abed yet? Where have ye been and who have ye been doin' it with?" Jasper crossed his own arms, turning the tables on me.

I shuffled my feet, the blood finally flowing through my body again now that I was indoors. Jasper took it as stalling. "I'll ask ye again, Jessie, where have ye been tonight? I willnae ask again."

"I was restless so I went on a walk to check on Lucifer, in case he needed another blanket or something." I said defensively.

"And I suppose *he* just happened to be there?" He raised an eyebrow at me.

"No, Liam wasn't there. He caught up with me when I was walking in the field, on the south side of the Keep."

"Ye shouldnae be out there alone at night, lass! What were ye thinkin'? Ye werenae thinkin' were ye." He cut me off before I could answer him.

"I wasn't alone. Liam was there and I felt perfectly safe." I said more to convince myself than to assure him.

"What if he was a rapist?" he looked at first horrified, then angry at the thought. I would have laughed but he would have killed me where I stood if I had.

"Does it look like I've been raped? Wake up Jasper. I'll find out tomorrow how he knows. There isn't any point doing it tonight since there's nothing to be done about it at the moment. Go back to bed."

I closed his door a bit quieter than I had when I stormed in. Liam had some explaining to do in the morning. I entered my own chamber, thoughts of what took place tonight outside, racing through my mind. What were we going to do if he told someone; anyone?

We'd have to leave, right away. Maybe this was our way out from joining the Rising that was bound to come. That had been the plan before meeting Liam anyway. I'd talk with Liam in the morning then with Jasper and go from there. Hopefully we'd be on the road by afternoon.

I didn't see Jasper anywhere after breakfast, nor Liam for that matter, which didn't bode well. I had hoped that Jasper had heeded my words, and that I would be the one talking to Liam about the matter of knowing I was a woman.

Thankfully, there were no excited words of a potential duel so I carried on with my usual work. Lucifer was more excitable than usual so I took him to the arena to stretch his legs for a bit. I brought along a training saddle for him to try out, hopefully he'd get used to wearing one.

He didn't seem all that enthusiastic to wear it and shied away from me several times before I took him to hand, tying his reins around one of the fence posts, almost touching his nose to it. There'd be no horsing around today. Once I'd gotten it on over a thick blanket, I made sure the cinches were taught before letting him loose.

Immediately he went to bucking wildly but I refused to give in to his tantrum, instead just let him buck around until he wore himself out, which took some time. Time was all I had at the moment so I leaned against the fence and watched. I pulled out a carrot and chomped on it, making sure I made enough noise for him to hear me.

It took a couple of bites but then his ears pricked up and he stood stock still, and looked at me. I looked back at him as if I didn't know what he was looking at then feinted shock at seeing the carrot in my hand. I held it out in offering and when he didn't come, I shrugged and continued to eat it. His nostrils flared and spit dangled from his mouth.

I wasn't going to go to him with it. He had to learn that he wasn't in charge, that he would have to submit to me in order to get rewarded. I finished the carrot then pulled another one out, began to munch on it. He shook his head and flicked his ears but decided to come and get it himself, slowly, step by step.

He got to me in a few strides and just stared at me. At first I could see his annoyance then watched as it turned to pleading. I handed it over and he grabbed it hungrily, nudging me for another when he practically swallowed the damn thing whole. I took his reins and proceeded to walk him, but he dug his hooves in the dirt, refusing to move.

I pulled out an apple, took a bite of it then walked off, not turning to see if he would follow. I got a few feet away before I heard his indignant snort, and hooves clomping on the dirt.

We got one lap in before I gave in and let him have the rest of it. Eventually, I didn't have to entice him with food.

"Lookin' good, lad. Soon he'll be ready to ride." Sean beamed of mostly toothless smile at me. I smiled back, inwardly cringing at the sight of the remaining teeth that were rotting away.

"He has potential but he's not ready to ride, far from it. We just battled it out about wearing a saddle. As you can see, I won." Lucifer snorted then stuck his nose in the air. I patted his neck in praise. "He definitely has come a long way over the past few months." God, it had been months that we'd been here. Where did the time go.

I spotted Jasper in the distance, striding to the mess hall so I took Lucifer back to his stall, cleaned him up then fed him, and left the stables to Sean before I went in search of both Jasper and food.

I plopped down next to him and found myself ravenous and got a platter and filled it with meat, cheese, bread and grapes. He grabbed a tankard and filled it with ale before handing it to me, telling me to slow down or I'd choke. He continued on with his meal as if I weren't there at all. That kind of pissed me off. What the hell did I do?

"I think we should head out considering Liam has figured out what I am." I casually whispered to him.

"Keep yer voice down. Did ye talk to the man yet or should I do it?"

"I haven't seen him all day, in fact, I thought you might have had the talk with him. You haven't seen him then?" I asked worried.

"I havenae see the lad all day myself." He replied.

I ate a little more, thinking this new development over. Where the hell was the man anyway? I looked around but he wasn't in the room.

"We were on our own before we met Liam, not expecting a tag along with us, so there shouldn't be any problem for us. Rhys needs Liam in case there is a Rising. It might be harder but we don't know for sure we can trust him to guide us in the right direction anyway."

"We're not leavin'. I'm still join' the cause. Thomas has it comin' to him, whatever that may be." He continued on eating without looking at me.

I growled at him, my frustration at its limit with this man, and my fists clenched. When he didn't say anything else, I went to seek out Liam. So far this day had been crappy all around.

I had found Liam lounging in the stables, petting my little lamb. I came in to check on the little guy and Lucifer when I couldn't locate him after searching the whole Keep, but here he was.

"What are *you* doing here? Shouldn't you be with Rhys, planning or whatever you men do to prepare for war?"

I crossed my arms, nerves on end from remembering our last encounter the night before. My cheeks grew warm and I turned away, paying too much attention to a chicken. How ironic I thought as I rolled my eyes. I moved on to Lucifer, not caring whether Liam followed or not.

"I heard ye've been lookin' for me." I turned in his direction as if just noticing him for the first time; started to speak loudly so my voice would carry down the main aisle then yelped.

"What the hell, Liam! Back Off!" I shoved at him but I might as well have been pushing a brick wall, a very handsome one. To cover my thoughts, I slugged him instead, causing his nose to bleed.

He laughed while holding his nose with his handkerchief to staunch the small trickle of blood. "Is that all ye got, lad? Surely ye were bein' gentle. Ye dinnae even break it."

I glowered at him. "Consider it a warning. Next time I won't be so gentle." I hoped he wouldn't try and provoke me because honestly, that was the strongest punch I had ever done. "Since you're here, I need to get some information."

He executed an exaggerated bow before replying, "all right, ask away then." As he waited, he rubbed Knightly Fellow, one of the other fine specimens of stallions here on Rhys' property.

"How did you find out about me? Jasper is the only one besides me. So, let's hear it." I finished grooming Lucifer and settled his feed bag around his head while waiting for Liam's answer.

"I'll tell ye but not here. Ye dinnae ken who might be holdin' up the walls with their ears around here. I'll see ye tonight for practice."

"Fine, but only training and talking, got it? There'll be nothing else." I stood with my arms crossed over my bound chest and tried to look serious.

He hesitated and I saw a quick sparkle light his eyes, but just as quickly, it faded. "I dinnae ken what else we'd be doin' there, *lad*." A rakish grin spread across his face and my heart fluttered. I tried to tamp the feeling down but it only got stronger. Stupid girly hormones.

"Go away. Go do something productive and leave me be. I have my friend here to see to." I had finished with Lucifer but he was going to have to be my escape goat for now so I got the grooming brush out.

"There are several '*productive*' things I want to do, but for now, I have to meet with Rhys. Good day, Jessie." He gave a short nod then left me to my thoughts.

"Lucifer, he's going to be some kind of trouble for me, just like you. You're lucky I'm already in love with you pal." Lucifer whinnied as if in understanding, sending oat dust puffing out of his feed bag.

Liam kept his word, that we would only train and talk, no extended kind of physical workout. However, he had yet to tell me how he knew of my being a woman. The more I asked the more he evaded the question, only announcing, "All in due time, all in due time, lass." I had to admit, it was a bit erotic, carrying around the knowledge that he, and *only* he, knew of what I was. How he felt for me but could not act upon it because of the secret.

Jasper was all but absent, rapidly eating meals then hiding away somewhere, emerging again only to eat again. I gave up trying to get a hold of him. It had seemed that I was no longer a blip on his radar. He was my only connection to my time and I couldn't feel anymore alone as I did now.

Sean was my only daily companion, the two of us working side by side, breaking the new horses that had come to the keep. They had to be ready when we had to leave for the Rising. Thankfully, the mares, bays, and stallions were more cooperative than Lucifer so it seemed to go by faster. Lucifer was none too happy about his attention being taken away, and nipped at me when I would walk by or groomed him.

Our nights together got longer, training for what seemed like hours, sweat dripping from our faces and clothing clinging to our bodies. But instead of parting ways, we sat and talked about anything that came to mind.

I looked honestly looked forward to our nightly rendezvous, enjoying the secrecy of it, the thrill of potentially being caught. Not that we were doing anything wrong; just two men training, in the dark.

We sat tonight, training over, and the snow fell gently, dusting our eyelashes and hair. This spot felt magical when it was just like this. Anything was possible in the quietness of the night. I couldn't help but feel it falling over me.

"I'll tell ye now, how I came to ken ye were a lass." He unearthed a twig from somewhere and poked at the banked snow in front of him. I stayed quiet, looking out over the white pristine field. I began to fidget with the queue that always came out during my training; wrapping it around my finger then releasing it.

"Do ye remember our first night camping together; the three of us?" I shrugged before answering, "Not really, no. I was just glad to be away from Rowen Keep and Thomas. I know I was very tired and still in a lot of discomfort. Why?"

"Aye, ye were, lass, ye were. Only a few people ken what had happened. Had I'd ken it myself when it had, rather than just before we had left, I would have killed him for it. There is a matter of Rhys also bein' assigned as babysitter to Thomas while Lord Jon is away." He continued to doodle in the snow, trying to find the next words.

I didn't rush him, enjoying the mood of intimacy our physical closeness brought. I could feel his heat still radiating from his workout and I scooted closer to him, hoping he wouldn't notice.

"I dinnae ken ye were a *lass* until that night in the woods. I had gone to retrieve water for the horses and for us and, well, other business to attend to." He said sheepishly. "Anyway, Jasper I guess took it to be a good time to change your bandages and clean ye up while I was gone.

"On my way back though, I came up short when I saw the two of ye. It was then that I had found out."

I looked at him confused, trying to bring back the memory of that night but couldn't. I couldn't recall anything unusual. He looked at me for a moment before continuing on.

"Jasper was tendin' to ye and he needed somethin', so you directed him to it with one of yer arms; in doin' that, your shirt had fallen away and well…" He looked at me then shifted his eyes down towards my bound breasts. I followed his gaze then, and realization came at me like a hard slap to the face.

Instinctively, I crossed my arms over my chest as if to hide my already covered breasts. Immediately, he took one of my hands in both of his, gently cupping it. He gave it a squeeze but didn't let go of it, but rested our joined hands on my knee.

"I then ken what had happened at Rowen, and that it had been to ye. Fresh anger filled me and I would have turned back to kill the bastard, had it not been for my promise of helpin' the two of ye."

I shivered then, which he took as my being cold, and, grabbing my cloak, he wrapped it around me for added warmth. But, I had not shivered because of the cold, no, it was from the fresh wave of terror from that horrible night with Thomas. Without thought, Liam took my hand in his, braiding our fingers together, giving me strength from him.

It felt right; having his hand in mine like this. It had been some time since I had held hands with anyone, even Nick. I shoved that thought away quickly, not wanting to ruin the peacefulness I felt currently. All too soon, he broke contact to gather up the weapons we had trained with, then helped me up.

We walked in companionable silence for a bit, digesting our conversation from a few minutes ago, and where to go from here. I couldn't help the worry that started to creep up my spine.

"How many others know about my being a woman, Liam? It's not safe for me to be here if others know." I stopped him mid stride with a hand on his bicep. He didn't answer me fast enough and I felt my patients wearing thin from being tired, both emotionally and physically.

"Rhys is the only one who I ken that kens yer a woman."
He stared down at me warily, waiting for something not so
good to happen to him.

"Why did you tell him? Why would he care to know
this about me?" I asked pleadingly up at him. He touched
my cheek with his fingertips and I instinctively turned
into them.

"He's been watchin' Thomas for some time now over the
years, paying closer attention of late due to hearing about
such matters similar to yer own, some have been much
worse. I felt he needed to ken, to assure he ken ye were not
a spy for Thomas. Jasper, he's well past his prime and could
be taken down easy enough, but ye could slip away without
anyone noticin'. I was protectin' ye, lass."

I didn't know how to react to that information so we
continued on back to the keep, changing the subject back to
Rhys' business with Thomas. "The Crown thought it best
to leave Thomas for the meantime, as the temporary Lord
of Rowen Castle until his brother Jon returned. He would
be in charge of the keep, the tenants and surrounding lands.

"The Crown kens of Thomas' misgivings, and
charged Rhys with the watchin' of him, being reasonably
compensated for his efforts. It wasnae choice really, but the
money was enough to keep Rhys from arguin' about it. He
dinnae need it mind, but it never hurts to have more."

"So, why hasn't anything been done about Thomas and
his ruthless actions against others?"

"*If* Thomas is caught and found guilty of his crimes,
and most likely not since the Crown dinnae care about us
and our 'tiffs' as they call them, then his title will be given
to his heir while he would most likely be exiled to one of

the smaller properties. If he somehow should parish during the Rising, then the lands and title will go to his heir also, which Rhys will handle until the heir reaches of age to take them over."

We were approaching the keep and unclasped hands, just in case one of the night guards were to see us returning. I couldn't help but feel sad that it had to end so soon. I shook it off and walked faster to the armory.

"Why are you telling me all of this? You don't even know me; let alone Jasper for that matter." I asked as he unlocked the armory door. He entered and placed back the weapons we used, and then exited just as quickly, locking the door behind him.

"Where did you get those from?" I said as we headed into the main building.

"What, these? Every senior officer has a set. Why do ye ask?" He had tucked them back into a hidden pocket within his coat.

"The first night I went out, I just walked in, thinking nothing of it that it should have been locked. It makes sense now however." We both grew concerned over this information, giving each other worrying looks.

Once inside, the halls were quiet but for the occasional servant scurrying about, seeing to things before retiring themselves. "Where's Rhys." Liam demanded of one of the servants. She immediately pointed down the hall to Rhys' private chambers then hurried away.

When he proceeded to go in that direction, I hurried next to him, trying to keep him from going to Rhys with the matter at hand. There was nothing we could do right now about it.

"Wait, we can't just tell him!" I whispered harshly to him, panicked. I grabbed at his arm with both hands but he only dragged me along because I wouldn't let go.

"Why not? There's a possible traitor amongst us and he needs to ken this now."

"If you tell him, he'll want to know how we know and we'll have to tell him what we've been up to." I warned him, trying to change his mind.

That did get his attention and he stopped short of Rhys' chamber door. I blew out a sigh in relief. "All right, I'll come up with somethin'. In the meantime, we'll keep our nightly appointments as usual. Tell me if ye see anythin' unusual."

I gave him a grateful smile then headed to our designated rooms for the night. His being the first, we parted ways, saying good night then I rushed off before he closed the door in my face. I started feeling as though I was a school girl with a crush on the hottest guy in school. I rolled my eyes in disgust at myself. I really had to get a grip.

I had intended on crashing onto my bed, clothes and all, so tired that I was, but for some reason, balls of nerves rushed through my body causing excess energy to pulse through me.

I knew why if I'd been honest with myself, which made me even more anxious. I had to get out of here and go somewhere; anywhere.

I stormed out and back down the hall, stopping in front of Liam's bedchamber door. I stood there fists clenching and unclenching. My heart was racing madly.

Something the size of a small cat scurried near my foot which had me jumping, bringing myself back to what I had planned to do.

I pounded on the door and waited for him, tapping my foot impatiently. I knocked again and the door suddenly opened, presenting a half naked highlander who didn't seem all too pleased to be bothered once in his room.

His face immediately changed from annoyance to surprise when he saw that it was me standing there in the doorway. Since he had yet to ask me to come in, I took the initiative and walked right in. "What are ye doin' here?"

I turned to face him, chin held high and hip cocked with a hand resting on it. "Close the door Liam. We have business to attend to." I answered with a sultry smile.

Nerves forgotten, desire filled me at seeing him vulnerable, shirtless and in bare feet, the throng keeping the front of his breeches hanging slightly untied. That was the only thing that was loose where his breeches were concerned.

Liam quirked an eyebrow at me. "What kind of business?" His grin slowly spread and fire entered his eyes.

"Liam, close the door."

CHAPTER 26

"Cannae wait until mornin' eh? It must be important. Let's hear it then." He did as I told him, locking the door behind him, and turned back to me. I rushed him then, causing both of us to stumble, knocking him into the door as we went. He recovered quickly and matched the heated kiss I had started.

My hands found their way into his hair, curling my fingers into it and tugging, trying to get him ever closer. His hands grabbed my butt and squeezed, then curled behind my thighs; lifting me up and wrapped my legs around his waist. His lips burned a trail down my neck and across my collar bones, licking the hollow area between them.

He felt so damn good. I remembered the day I'd seen him shirtless and how it had taken my breath away. We somehow got to the bed and he came down on me, never breaking our kiss. His weight felt right above me and I could tell he was trying hard not to crush me fully.

His skin was wonderful. Hot, smooth; with a fine sheen of sweat coating him. The fire that burned across the room lit his skin, turning it into the color of amber.

I couldn't wait to see the rest of him. He seemed to have the same thought on his mind since he'd stood up and began to remove my boots and socks, before untying the strings at the waist of my own pants. I had double knotted them and after having some trouble untying them, growled before removing a small knife and cut the strings.

With a wicked grin, he ever so slowly glided my breeches down my legs, his fingertips caressing my bared skin as he went. I wanted to rip them off myself but I let him have his fun. All I could do was stare at him myself.

Once they were off, he ran his hands slowly up my ankle, stopping just behind my knee and caressed me there before continuing. All I could do was moan as my body vibrated with need. He gripped my hips and tugging me closer to the edge of the bed. My shirt had hiked up to just below my breasts, leaving me completely bare from the waist down. For some reason, I felt shy all of a sudden, but I wouldn't let that stop me.

He dropped to his knees, running his large hands over my thighs and hips, kissing my knees before opening them fully. I blushed which brought out his wicked grin before he settled between them and tasted me.

His tongue was pure magic and I couldn't remember ever being teased in such a way that I'd want to stay here forever. His hand came next, caressing where his tongue had just been and I sucked my breath in as the first wave of pleasure rolled through me. His fingers were warm against my heated flesh and I wanted him to do more.

His tongue returned to tasting and with one quick flick, my orgasm hit, fluid roll after fluid roll, rippled through me. When I finally came down from it, I looked at him with dazed eyes and a half smile of my own. He removed his own pants then and I could feel my eyes go heavy with desire, my mouth water at the sight of him. I couldn't wait to get my hands on him.

I got up on my knees on the edge of the bed, touching his chest and shoulders, his stomach, tangling my fingers the black curls that settled just below the trail down from his belly button. That was always my favorite part of a man.

I kissed him slowly and deeply, wrapping my hand behind his neck to keep him there, while the other hand grasped him, fingers curling around him then slowly moving with his slight thrusts. He groaned against my neck, holding onto my bottom, his fingers flexing on and off as they held on.

He went to remove my shirt but I pushed his hands away, placing them where I wanted them to be, avoiding any chance of seeing my back at any time. He complied for a little longer, grasping my hips as I grasped his erection. I couldn't wait much longer myself.

He pulled away though and I reached for him, nearly falling off the bed in the process.

He gave a little chuckle and said, "Aye, lass I want ye just as bad but a few moments more and ye'll have all of me."

He was magnificent to look at. Black curls dusted his chest with a line trailing down a tight abdomen and down to his groin. Strong muscular legs stood slightly apart, while his shoulders and arms flexed just by moving them. I had to remind myself that I wasn't in a romance novel but damn he sure look as if he were on the cover of one.

"Lass, I willnae take ye unless I can have all of ye. I ken what your back looks like and it doesnae bother me. Here, look at all of me."

He ran fingers over old scars that marred his skin and had turned white over time. He turned around and I gasped at what was there. Jagged scars ran every direction they could on his back; from shoulder to hip. I reached out and touched one but quickly removed my fingers when he gasped.

"Och, lass, it doesnae hurt anymore, you tickled me is all. Dinnae be tellin' the other men about it though." He winked at me before coming back to me.

"Let me feel yer body Jessie, all of it."

I sat on my knees, worry written on my face I was sure, but I thought about what he'd just shared with me and I knew he wouldn't tease me about it. He knew what it was like to be scarred as I was.

I nodded then and he untied the laces at my neck, loosening them to open the shirt's V neck collar. He took it by the hem and pulled it gently over my head and tossed it aside.

He looked at me, asking permission to continue his appraisal and I hesitantly nodded, trying hard not to cover myself. His eyes trailed down my neck as his fingers were doing and rested on my breasts, feather light caresses following the shape of them.

His thumb grazed my nipple and it hardened even harder, causing a pleasurable ache between my legs. He tugged on it before replacing his fingers with his warm mouth. I nearly fell over and would have if it hadn't been for his hand grasping the back of my neck and one arm holding me tightly against him.

He tortured the other breast and all I could do was arch and press him closer, wanting him to take more in. He flipped me onto the bed, following on top of me and our lips met again feverishly. Hands went all over each other, not able to get enough. I could feel him pushing against me, asking to take his fill. I wiggled my hips, opening for him to nestle between my thighs but he hesitated, brushing soft kisses across my cheeks and neck.

"Jessie, I need to be inside ye," he took a shuttering breath as I thrust my hips upwards to press against him, "but I dinnae want to hurt ye, lass. I can do it quickly, get it over with if ye wish it, or take it slow."

Sweat dampened his forehead and his upper arm muscles quivered with need, and all I could do was tear up and smile at his sweetness when he was obviously suffering.

"Liam, this will not be my first time, I am not a virgin. You may have your fill with no worries." I assured him.

With a stunned look then a wicked grin replacing it, he crushed his lips against mine in thanks. Just as he had the night before, he trapped my wrists above my head with one hand, but the other guided himself into me before grasping my hip tightly.

He smiled down at me then thrust deeply into me, filling me fully to the point of a mixture of pleasure and pain. We moved together as if in a race, meeting thrust to thrust.

He suckled hard on one breast then nipped and that sent me over the edge completely. I held my breath as it washed over me, then another one, stronger than the first before coming down on aftershocks. He continued to thrust, bringing himself to climax, then slowly lowered himself to lay on top of me, both of our lungs starving for air.

He gave one more thrust, as a reminder of what we had just gone through together then kissed me again, gently this time as a lover would. When he exited me I whimpered and he immediately went pale.

"Are ye alright, lass? Did I hurt ye after all? Let me check ye to make sure yer alright."

I gave a weak laugh before replying, "I'm alright, really. I didn't want you to leave quite yet is all. I like you there, inside me."

"Well in that case, give me a couple of minutes and I will be happy to serve ye again; fully." His wicked grin appeared before replacing it with his mouth on mine. It was going to be a very long night.

I rose before dawn, dressing quickly in the dark, tripping over something in the process. I cursed what I thought was quiet enough but Liam must have heard it and rolled over and reached for me.

I leaned back and kissed him, lingering there for a few moments before breaking it. "I should go before the Keep wakes. It wouldn't look good for either of us if a boy came out of your room, disheveled looking." I rose from the bed but leaned over one more time, placing another kiss on his lips before heading to the door.

I shall see ye soon, lass." I nodded a dreamy smile on my face as I closed the door behind me. I couldn't wait to see him again either.

I crept back to my chamber, enjoying the achy soreness between my legs, and my sensitive nipples being caressed by my shirt, reminding me of the night. I couldn't believe I was actually getting turned on again, so I rapidly changed my thoughts to what laid ahead for Jasper and me.

The sun touched the hills and sparked a red line through my window slit, igniting my room with warm light. I stood in it with my eyes closed, letting it cover me wholly. I felt energized and wanted to tackle the world at that moment but settled on changing my day old clothes and cleaning myself up before dressing again.

The first sounds of movement came from the other side of my door, the servants flitting back and forth, getting ready for the day and the inhabitants here at the Keep. The scent of food assaulted my nose as it came in through my window, causing my stomach to growl loudly.

I joined the early risers, sitting down at a table that was empty for the moment, enjoying my quiet time. The large hearth had a roaring fire going and the room was warm and cozy for a change. I went through two servings of the food and washed it all down with goat milk, which was warm and thick, something I had yet to get used to, but didn't care at the moment.

"Good mornin' to ye laddie. How did ye sleep last night?" Liam plopped down next to me and I blushed madly at his question.

"That well eh? Me, since ye asked, slept verae well. Like a bairn at his mother's tit." He sent me a lazy grin which only had my cheeks flaming more now.

"I slept very well McGuinnis. Glad you slept well too." He was shocked to hear me use his last name, but we had to keep up appearances of my being a boy.

"Uh, yes well, workin' with that beast again I would presume? Why ye waist yer time 0n that one is beyond me. He hates everyone." Liam said in between bites.

"He seems to like me fine all right, maybe there's something wrong with all of you?" I smiled around a chunk of warm bread, tearing at it like a beast myself.

Liam laughed at that and patted me on the back, making me cough over the piece that was making its way down my throat. I chugged my wine that had replaced my milk, and then glared at him once I'd stopped coughing. He only smiled at me.

We ate in silence then went our separate ways, he pinching my ass before walking away. I jumped then looked around to see if anyone saw it then relaxed when no one seemed the wiser. I'd get him back somehow. For now, I went about my usual daily tasks.

CHAPTER 27

WE SPENT THE NIGHTS together, either training or just keeping each other's company in bed, making love often, but sometimes just cuddled under the covers and just being. We talked about everything and sometimes nothing, soft kisses and sometimes not so soft.

I hadn't told him about Nick and Sophie, wanting to keep it at bay for a little while longer. Sooner or later the question of how I was not a virgin would come up and then I'd have to tell him. For now, we were in our little bubble with no concerns, broken hearts, or worries of war. Every morning I would dress and return to my room, missing the feel of him against me.

We waited for word in regards to the Rising but still nothing, yet. Agitation flooded the Keep to the point that some were turning against others, looking for any reason to fight. Fights turned into stabbings which kept the infirmary busy.

Rhys came out onto the wooden balcony overlooking the courtyard and bellowed, "Enough! I willnae tolerate this behavior! Our fight is not with each other, but with Thomas and his men. I cannae have ye all bleedin' to death before then. Now, pull yerselves together for Christ sake!"

Rhys glared at all who had congressed in the courtyard. The men looked like little boys being scolded by their father and, in many ways, he was.

If he was to come out of the rising victorious, then he needed all his men hale and hearty. Liam had his head in the clouds of late and I hoped it wasn't due to our, I don't know what to call it; but most likely because of our time together.

Word came the next day that Tomas had rallied up men from the north, gearing up for the Rising. The halls of the Keep were all abuzz with the news and adrenaline and nerves replaced the agitation, suffocating me.

I hated to admit it but anticipation flowed through my own veins. Lord knew I had been training for it with Liam, with Jasper being none the wiser. Lucifer had gotten used to my derriere on his back and now we raced the hills, and practiced jumps which he seemed more enthusiastic about than me. He was magnificent though.

He ran like the hounds of hell were snapping at his hind quarters, racing to an invisible finish line only he could see. This magnificent beast was my spirit animal if there ever was one.

The people, especially the men of Rhys Castle; had found appreciation for my being the one to break him. But I hadn't broken him in. I had earned his respect and he; mine. We were a formidable team.

We returned to the Keep to find wagons being loaded with food stuffs and kitchenware, barrels of ale or wine, and others loaded with weaponry.

"What's going on?" I stopped one of the soldiers walking by and he informed me they were heading north now.

Five other clans had gone on ahead of us once receiving word from Rhys a week ago. I searched out Jasper, finding him with Rhys and Duncan; Rhys' Captain.

"Most of our resources are headin' out now to catch up with Clans Campbell, Drummond, and Graham. Ruthven and Montgomery are not far behind us." Jasper updated Rhys.

"Good. Saddle up once all the men are mounted themselves." Rhys ordered both of them.

Jasper caught my eye and strode over, grabbed my arm and dragged me away from the others. I squirmed, trying to break free but he had a surprisingly strong grip.

"Jasper, stop it! You're hurting me." I pulled at my arm and eventually he let go causing me to almost fall over. There would be bruises later.

"Where have ye been, lass? I practically tore the Keep to shreds lookin' for ye." He said low enough only for me to hear.

"If you had looked in the stables,"

"I did go in there! It's the first place I looked. I found Sean around here and he told me ye'd taken that beast out for a jaunt." He looked around to see if anyone had turned to hear him yelling at me, but with all the noise going on currently, we were ignored.

"We're headin' out now. Pack up yer things and come back straight away. I'll have Sean ready yer mount." I started to tell him I was taking Lucifer, but he'd already stalked away barking orders.

I hunted down Rhys and found him in the main hall, handing out his own orders. Well, there was no time like the present I guessed. I needed to see a man about a horse and I wouldn't take "no" for an answer.

"Laird Rhys, I have a matter to discuss with you if you can spare a minute." I said rather bravely I thought. I was very determined to have Lucifer no matter what.

"What is it lad? I'm verae busy at the moment." He moved on to the main study, gathering up maps and books of some sort.

"I've come to purchase Lucifer from you." I dropped a pouch of coins onto the desk and waited for his response.

He looked up at that to find it was me standing there and not a boy. "Lass, that horse isnae ready to be ridden, by anyone and I willnae risk yer life with him."

"He is ready. I've spent every day training him. He will not let anyone else near him and I've ridden him plenty. Ask Sean, he'll vouch for me." I said more confidently.

"That horse isnae ready I said. Now be gone with ye. I have much to do and yer keepin' me from it."

I balled my fists before snatching up the money and headed to see Sean. Thankfully I didn't have to search far for him, him being in the stables.

"Sean, how much would you say Lucifer is worth?" I asked nonchalantly.

"He's a pretty penny to be sure lad, comes from good stock. Why? Lookin' to buy him for yerself?" He winked at me but when I didn't join in with his joke, he stopped what he was doing and looked at me seriously.

"Seriously? Lad, I ken ye've done well with him, and yer verae fond of him too but, he's not nearly ready to be anyone's mount."

"How much," I said flatly.

Sean looked at me, trying to gauge whether to tell me or not. I could see he didn't have a very good poker face, contemplating how much he should quote me, hoping the amount he told me would be way out of my price range.

"A hundred and fifty pounds." He said firmly. "Ye got that much on ye lad?" He smirked then returned to his business.

I left at a run and found Giles was sitting, ledgers opened and facing away from him. I could see he'd been busy this morning signing out funds.

"I'm here to purchase a horse." I tossed one hundred pounds; leaving the amount open for negotiations. He didn't blink at that, but fingered the coins in front of him. His eyes took on a greedy gleam.

"Which horse are ye thinkin' about?" He tossed a coin back onto the small pile then laced his fingers together.

"Lucifer." I stated.

"Remind me which one that is?"

"Really, all right the white demon." I crossed my arms to try and hide my nerves.

He smiled then, borderline evil before speaking, "Oh aye I ken the one. Ye have a good eye for horse flesh. Rhys hasnae told me he was for sale. I'll need to speak with Rhys, of course, to make sure all is in order."

"If you haven't noticed, he's a bit busy getting ready for a war. Do you really think he'll take kindly to you interrupting him?" I stepped aside with a sweep of an arm towards the door then crossed my arms again.

When he didn't comment or get up, I stated, "There is enough money there for at least two horses so I don't see why we're still discussing this."

"If yer quite sure it's that beast ye want, then sign here and our business will be concluded." I was surprised that he hadn't tried to raise the amount on me. He handed me the quill and ink and I signed the ledger before he could change his mind. He handed me the receipt and I left, straight to my room to pack up, pleased that I now owned the Devil. It was time to show everyone what he was made of.

Most of the men were mounted now, and a few of the women, most likely wives and daughters, were seated side saddle on their own mounts, grouped together and chatting. I missed my own girlfriends; especially Kate. I was surprised and felt a bit guilty that after all this time here, this had been the first time she had come to mind.

I mounted Lucifer in a fluid movement, something I'd practiced with him, so he wouldn't get spooked. I needed to be able to mount and dismount quickly in case something should call for it.

Jasper canted over on his own mount, double checking to see that my gear and bags were secure. Once he was satisfied, he nodded and gave me a proud smile. I nodded back but didn't return the smile.

"Why are ye on this beast when I had yer mount made ready for ye?" He inquired firmly.

"I have her as a pack horse. I needed extra supplies." I stated, chin up.

"Like what, yer girly stuff?"

I sent him a sideways glare before answering, "If you must know, coffee for both of us, an extra tarp for Lucifer since he can't be near the others without starting trouble; among other stuff."

"Aye well, as long as Rhys is fine with ye takin' his prized stallion, then I have no complaints." He trotted off to join Rhys at the head of the line.

We headed out, traveling slowly behind the soldiers, bringing up the rear. Sean was left behind to take care of the remaining livestock while the rest of us stable hands were sent to take care of the horses, and livestock to used for food.

Jasper and I didn't speak much about what was to come with the Rising. Probably thought he'd scare me to death and wanted to save me from that. He'd forgotten about the wars we American's had gone through and the devastation left after them.

What I hadn't told him was that if I was at any point in danger, I wouldn't be running from it, but toward it. When Liam and I were out training or in each other's arms, he gave me strength and courage that I never knew I had.

I felt stronger, emotionally and physically. I had something to fight for if for no other reason than to preserve what was our family history.

We had three weeks ahead of us due to the thick snow covered ground. But where I was once terrified of every little thing, I felt no fear now.

My ass no longer hurt when in the saddle, from all the training with Lucifer. The cold still sucked but I'd toughened up to it. It was but an annoyance rather than a promise of a peaceful death.

Liam stayed mostly with Rhys' group, both when riding and when camping. Occasionally we'd pass each other, a secret glimmer of desire being exchanged when secretly brushing hands.

It was difficult for us to sneak off and train, and being together alone, was nil. It gave me time to think on where our relationship was headed, if anywhere at all, then reality would set in. I would have to remind myself that Jasper and I would be going back to our time once we found Jon, and Liam couldn't go with us.

The thought of losing Liam hurt my heart and I was afraid that I was falling in love with him. I tried to harden my heart but every day it got harder and harder.

Jasper rode with me a few times, usually quiet, his mind on other things. I stopped asking about the progress of what was to come, trying to carry on a conversation to break the silence. But instead he'd just ride off, evading my questions.

Rhys was a little more forthcoming with information, whether he knew it or not, what with my sneaking around close enough to hear it in pieces.

Jasper caught me twice and gave me a warning look to back off. I stared back at him in defiance, but reluctantly backed off. A few of the stable hands rode with me, which was a distraction at least, even if their conversations were mainly crude. A few times I had to blush at what was coming from them.

For this trip, I was thankful that I had my own tent, and didn't have to share with Jasper. He and Liam had camped closer to Rhys, readily available if needed. However, the nights grew mournful when silence was around me, leaving me to my thoughts.

The only assurance of knowing I wasn't completely alone was Lucifer blowing his nose and the clomping of his feet in his own tent.

When we had tree coverage, I'd wonder off a bit to train in the darkness, Lucifer blocking any sight of me to the others with his big body. I had decided long before this trip, that I would be fighting for no other reason than to kill Thomas myself.

To this day, Jasper had no knowledge of my nightly training with Liam, nor now. He thought me holed up with the women and children since he considered me meek. I'd show him when the time came.

Lucifer whinnied that he was hungry, again, so on my way back, I managed to pilfer some lettuce and a couple of carrots for him. At least I had him for company. Two loners supporting each other.

CHAPTER 28

We arrived at the border a week later than expected, no thanks to a wheel on one of the wagons breaking. There were three clans already there and set up, leaving us to camp behind them, which meant being further away from the main headquarters; again. It was late in the day and my stomach growled when it caught a whiff of something cooking close by.

I thought the wagons would never get here and we'd all starve to death but they'd arrived with us before dusk and cooking fires brought to life quickly, sending splendiferous scents in all directions.

My stomach churned a bit at the thought of the plain bannocks and cured beef strips we had eaten while on the trail. It was too bad I hadn't packed enough of my coffee otherwise I could have had coffee and biscotti.

I found out where the main tent was without any problems. It was the largest of them all, with the clans' flags fluttering in the wind. Shadows played against it, silhouetting at least ten large figures. I couldn't tell who they were but I had an idea.

I settled in the shadows next to it, trying hard to listen to what was being discussed. I got bits and pieces, but not enough to put together anything. I looked down and wondered if I could lift the edge up just enough to...

"What are we doin' here?" Came a hushed but familiar voice. I still let out a squeak, startled from being found snooping. I elbowed him in the shoulder which was met with some Gaelic curse word, but it barely moved him.

"Shhh, I'm trying to hear what's going on in there." I said over my shoulder.

"I can probably help ye with that, Jessie." Liam murmured behind me.

I hadn't thought of that. I got up, brushed my butt off then held out a hand to him. He didn't hesitate, seemingly all too eager to take it.

"Come with me, lass." He whispered while looking around. All too quickly, our hands separated and I curled mine into a loose fist, trying to keep the heat from his a little longer.

We found a vacant campfire to occupy, far enough from listening ears. It felt strange spending time with him, after a couple of weeks of rarely seeing each other at all.

"So, what do ye want to ken?" he asked.

I stared at him then answered, "Everything."

I listened patiently, waiting to hear it all out in the open. Once Liam was finished, we sat quietly, the fire forgotten so lost in my own thoughts. He cleared his throat which brought me back to the present and I apologized for my momentary verbal absence.

"How many men does Rhys have?"

"We have six clans with us, roughly twenty-five hundred; possibly more. Thomas was only able to convince three clans up north to march for him, but there are many."

At least we had numbers on our side. As to how those numbers performed, was another matter. The thought of war was getting all too real for me and my nerves were on edge at the idea of it coming.

"Malcolm joined us today; and Graham, Drummond, and Campbell are at the border already. Rhys is sending Duncan and Nearwell in to gather information from Thomas' men. Hopefully they'll come back with somethin' useful."

One of the wives working another cooking fire, brought us each a bowl of something warm and fragrant, all-be-it unpleasant to look at. Bread was our only utensil for eating the stew, but we still wolfed it down.

"Where did ye set up camp? I noticed Jasper has set up near Rhys. I assume yer close too?" He asked over a large bite of stew.

I swallowed my mouthful, wishing I'd brought my canteen to wash it down. "Actually, I camped on the outskirts of our encampment. It's much quieter and I feel more comfortable letting the girls loose."

At his confused look, I elaborated by looking down at my flat chest and he barked out a laugh. I tried to not laugh myself but I couldn't help it, I snickered.

He looked around, trying to find my tent since I hadn't directly told him. He spotted Lucifer standing under a grove of trees and figured it wouldn't be too far from him. He'd be paying her a visit tonight once the camp grew quiet for the night.

"I'm camped near Jasper myself if ye were wonderin'." He provided even though I hadn't asked.

"I assumed you would be in case he'd have need of you." I answered back, not looking up from my food. "I'm going to see if I can beg another bowl of stew from one of the women. Want more yourself?" I quirked a brow up at him, waiting for a response.

"No thank ye, ye go on ahead. I best get back to Rhys anyway. Good night to ye if I dinnae see ye before ye retire." He winked then went about his business.

I shrugged and walked off in search of more food. I turned and watched him go, hoping he'd turn around too; he didn't. I shook off my disappointment and rolled my eyes at the silly school girl feelings. I told myself that he couldn't acknowledge our relationship without giving himself away.

I was able to charm a second helping from the woman, along with a couple of vegetables for Lucifer before I headed back to my little camp. I fed Lucifer first and checked his own makeshift tent, making sure he was protected from the elements.

I went through my usual routine for the night then settled down with my stew and bread and my furs wrapped around me. I pulled the photos of Sophie and Nick out of my satchel, the corners now dog-eared from being taken out so many times. I had decreased the amount of times I'd take them out, trying to keep them safe from any more wear and tear; they were all I had of them.

The camp had grown quiet, and the occasional snore here and there and some other sounds, could be heard and were all too familiar. Those sounds brought back the nights with Liam and I longed for him. Distance really did make the heart grow fonder as they say.

Loneliness had become an unwanted companion of mine since leaving Rhys Castle, and I certainly didn't want to keep company with the other stable hands. There was only so much lewdness in a day. I even missed Jasper's grouchy face.

A cough sounded too close for comfort outside my tent, and I removed the small dagger Liam had given me before we had left the castle. I kept it under my pillow just in case I needed to use it.

Footsteps sounded just outside the flaps of my tent and I clutched the dagger and my fur more tightly around me. "Who's there, answer me right now." I said rather bravely considering how scared I was.

"Jessie, it's me, Liam." He entered my tent and I breathed a sigh of relief and a bit panicked.

He looked at the dagger I had forgotten to put down and he smiled. "Good lass. Yer learnin' well but, ye should hide it better so yer assailant dinnae see it comin'."

I blushed then quickly sheathed it, placing it back under my pillow. I looked up at him, not sure of my next move or of his. I didn't have to wait long to find out. He fell to his knees and I instantly reached for him, our lips devouring each others. Our clothes were removed in a frenzy, wanting to feel skin against skin. His tongue was magic on my breasts, the first wave of pleasure flitting through me in anticipation.

His fingers worked their magic inside of me and the first climax was soft and slow. As I came down from it, he gave one strong thrust and filled me completely. I'd missed this, missed us being together.

We clawed and bit each other, tasting each other's skin and mouths. A feral growl erupted from him as I met each thrust he made, our bodies battling it out for a release that seemed just out of reach.

I shoved him onto his back and took control of the rhythm, setting a faster, deeper pace than before. His hands clasped my breasts then moved to my hips, guiding me, tugging on me, both of us trying to get closer. I arched my back, feeling him go deeper still and I felt the first roll of pleasure surge up and out.

I held my breath and the orgasm got stronger and stronger then turned into multiples. I thought I'd died and gone to heaven. He flipped me over and took control, his own climax hitting him soon after mine and he groaned as if he were in pain.

He collapsed on top of me, both of us out of breath, sweating despite the chilled air around us in the tent. He withdrew from inside me then wrapped me against him, covering both of us with my furs. He ran his fingers up and down my back as if he'd done it all his life. He lightly kissed my forehead and it brought tears to my eyes.

Once we'd caught our breaths and were relaxed enough to move, he leaned over me, gently kissed me before brushing away my tears. I could so get lost in his expressive eyes, which were intently watching me at the moment.

I gave him a watery smile and he smiled back briefly, but then grew serious again. He gently kissed me and I him, before he pulled slightly away.

"I dinna ken when, Jessie, but I can tell ye now; I love ye. So much that it takes my breath away every time I look at ye."

More tears came and I openly sobbed now, causing him to withdraw away even more. I quickly brought him back and kissed him. When the kiss, broke, I smiled up at him as I tucked a piece of his hair behind his ear.

"I love you too, Liam. That is why I'm crying. I love you so much it hurts. I never thought I could love like this again."

His face looked relieved and we kissed as if to seal the deal. Instead of frenzied sex, we made love, gently and comfortingly. Afterward, we cuddled again in silence, enjoying the feel of each other.

"Now that we have that established, I'll be camping nearer to ye. I dinna want ye here so far from me."

I leaned over and kissed him in thanks. I started to doze off, feeling safe for once since being in this time, but it was soon disturbed by Jasper's voice outside my tent.

We scrambled to find our clothes and dress quickly, but Liam's shirt had gone somewhere so I threw one of my furs over him and told him to stay quiet.

Jasper threw open the flap of my tent without asking for entry, and I scolded him. "What if I had been bare assed naked."

"Then I'd guess we'd even then aye? Besides, why would ye be naked in this frigid weather, are ye daft woman?" he came back at me.

He had a point and I blushed because I had been naked moments ago. "What is it Jasper, I was going to bed. And close the damn flap for Christ sake!"

He turned, surprised he hadn't. Once done, he turned back to continue on with whatever he had to say but stopped short, looking down at something with a weird look on his face. I looked in the direction he was and saw Liam's foot sticking out partially from the fur that covered him.

A dark look crossed over Jasper's face and I actually shrank a bit, waiting for him to yell at me. I opened my mouth to distract him, to remind him as to why he'd come, but he held up a hand to silence me. He grabbed hold of the bottom of the fur and pulled it away.

I squeaked because I was half naked, wearing as it turned out, Liam's shirt that we couldn't find earlier. Before he pulled it away completely, Liam told him, "I wouldn't go much further than that my friend. We wouldn't want to upset the lady's sensibilities now would we."

"I thought I told ye to stay away from him. I warned ye." Jasper turned to Liam and bellowed for him to get dressed and meet him outside. Before I could say anything, he had exited the tent without a word to me.

"I'll be right back luv," he assured me. I only nodded saying nothing. "Och, lass, dinnae fash about him. A ghraidh, I love ye and Jasper can be damned about that." Liam kissed me tenderly then left me.

CHAPTER 29

JASPER AND LIAM WALKED off a ways from Jessie's camp. Liam knew he had some explaining to do but how much to tell, he wasn't sure. He nearly tripped over Jasper so lost in his thoughts. Before he could apologize, he found himself splayed out in the snow, nose bleeding.

"God damn it, what is it with you people and punching me in the nose!" Liam snarled at Jasper while wiping his nose on his sleeve.

When he got up, he was only met with yet another fist to the face; this time in the right eye and once again sprawled in the snow. The first one he deserved but the next one had him charging Jasper, bringing both of them to the ground.

"Ye only get one in Jasper for what ye found tonight but that was it. Ye want a fight then ye shall have it. I'd like to get back to Jessie."

That was all it took for Jasper's rage to reach boiling point and he swung out, connecting his fist to Liam's stomach. Liam barely felt it, landing a blow of his own to

Jasper's face in return. Blood splattered both men now along with the snow around them, making it look like a massacre.

"I should kill ye for this, ye bastard! How dare ye take advantage of her." Jasper landed another blow to Liam's ribs before kneeing him in the groin.

Liam rolled to his knees, grabbing at his groin and tried to take deep breaths through the pain. He vomited up this dinner, then spat out blood from a cut on his lip. He managed to get to his feet all be it still slightly bent over and out of breath. Jasper stood breathing hard himself, bent over with hands on knees spitting blood into the snow like Liam had minutes ago.

"Damn it man, I love her! Leave off already!" Liam exclaimed, trying not to vomit again. His balls had been tender from being with Jessie earlier, and now they were on fire. He doubted he'd be able to have children at this point.

"Ye dinnae ken her so how can ye love her?" Jasper went for Liam's face but Liam stepped aside and Jasper stumbled past him, off balance.

While Jasper was on hands and knees, Liam took the opportunity to return the favor and kicked Jasper in the groin, then landed a blow to his ribs by kicking him again.

Jasper's anger fizzled out a bit now that he was on the ground and rocking back and forth over his last two injuries. He had time to reflect back onto himself and felt ashamed for being too busy to have Jessie close by to keep an eye on. It was his own fault that this had happened.

"I'm plannin' on marryin' the lass, as soon as possible, after this Risin' business."

Liam pulled out the ring he had chosen from one of Rhys' tenants who owned the jewelry shop in the village.

He hadn't planned on it but as soon as he'd laid eyes on the ring, he knew it was fate that had brought Jessie to him and he was going to keep her.

"What if she's with child now? Have ye thought about that? Are ye prepared to take care of them both? Yer one of Rhys' soldiers mind, not some farmer who has all the time in the world to be with her and the child.

"She'd be alone most of the time while yer out gallivantin' around, doing business for Rhys."

"Whatever happens, I *will* take care of her, and any bairns we may have. Ye have my word on it." Liam swore on it.

They stood, breathing hard, sweat mixing with blood on their faces. Their clothes were torn and bloody and both men still stood bent over from being kicked in the balls. Liam flashed Jasper a grin but Jasper only scowled back at him.

"Go clean yerself up and get changed. Yer weddin' her tonight. Tell her to get dressed and get her arse out here in twenty minutes." Jasper stated then walked off towards his own tent to clean up before searching out Rhys.

Liam blew out a few breaths and tried to stand straight. Unfortunately, Jasper had a strong fist and managed to do some damage to his ribs and other areas of his body. He limped back to his tent to clean up then headed back to Jessie. She would not be pleased with the news.

"Oh my God, what the hell happened to you?!" I looked him up and down, searching his face and then the rest of him, the concerned parent I used to be coming out.

He shifted away when my fingers brushed his sides and I reached to pull up his shirt, but he shoved my hands away and got up quickly. He told me that he and Jasper got into it but that he was fine.

"Jasper said we are to meet him in a few minutes outside here." He passed me my cloak and gloves signaling me to put them on. He turned and exited before I could ask him why.

My mind was racing as to what was going on and why we were to meet Jasper outside at this late hour. Surely this could wait until morning. I pulled on my cloak as instructed, grumbling to myself in annoyance at Jasper's behavior.

I met Liam outside, bundled up, shifting from foot to foot to keep my blood moving in an attempt to stay warm. The camps were all dark now, so Liam took me into his arms for warmth and to calm my nerves. I didn't know what was to come.

Jasper stalked to his tent to freshen up and changed his shirt, washing down his face until the cloth came away somewhat clean of blood. He bet he looked a sight but there was nothing to do about it. He only hoped Liam would look just as bad or worse.

Once cleaned up, he sought council with Rhys in his private chambers, which also acted as the meeting room during the day. He found him pouring over the maps that were given to him earlier by the five men he had sent to do reconnaissance of the area.

So engrossed in his current inspection and planning, he had not heard Jasper come in. Jasper stood for a minute then cleared his throat to get Rhys' attention. Rhys went for his knife that was on the table in front of him then relaxed when he saw that it was only Jasper.

"Sir, I am in need of yer priest to bless a union. I need ye to be there also as witness to the union."

Rhys raised an eyebrow at him in confusion. A union? For whom he wondered. "Who is to be married on such an occasion as this?"

Jasper cleared his throat and ground out between clenched teeth, "Liam and Jessie, Sir."

At that announcement, Rhys blanched. He could see Jasper was none too pleased about it. Just out of curiosity, he asked as to why. He had a good idea but had to hear it for himself.

Jasper only had to raise an eyebrow in annoyance then winced at the pull of the fresh cut running through it, and returned to scowling. Rhys did his best not to laugh, and covered it by coughing before turning to get something to drink to further squelch it.

"I presume your current physical state is due to the reason for said union. How fairs Liam then? Does he even ken he's to be wed tonight; and does Jessie ken?"

"Aye, he kens but if he hasnae told her, then she dinnae ken what's comin' to her, serves her right the little trollop." Jasper grumbled.

"Come now, Jasper ye ken she's no trollop. Yer just sore over the fact ye have to let her go. Does she love him then?"

"I am verae sure she does, but he pledged his own love for her to me in our scuffle; that he planned on marryin' her once we'd gone back to the Keep."

Rhys collected his coat and gloves, and both men headed out in search of the priest. He'd been brought to bless the men before going into battle. They'd have to record the marriage as legally binding once they returned to the Keep, but for now this would have to do.

Once found, the three men joined Liam and Jessie at the appointed spot, just a few feet away from her tent and under a cover of trees. When the priest saw the two forms holding each other intimately, he gasped in outrage before being assured that it was indeed, a man and a woman standing before him, and not two males.

"Calm down man, the smaller one is a lass, disguised as a man for safety." Rhys said.

I looked over at Jasper then to Liam, not liking the feeling of what was to come. Rhys smiled at me kindly and took one of my hands and tucked it around his upper arm, leaving his large one tightly over it. I apparently wasn't going to be going anywhere.

I cannae marry them just by yer word that 'he' is really a lass. I need some proof of yer word, Sir." The priest told Rhys.

I shot a look up at him and he only smiled back, patted my hand as if I were a child, and turned to speak to Liam and the priest. Marry? Who was going to be married? There was only one woman here and that was…Oh!

"What fresh hell is this?!" I demanded.

"Blasphemy!!! How dare you speak such filth!" The priest looked as if he was going to faint on the spot. If I hadn't been so pissed off, I would have laughed and tried to find other ways to make his day. However, this was going to stop right here.

"And just who am I to marry, Jasper? Rhys, Liam, or the priest?! I'm not marrying anyone period. Any you have no say in the matter. I am a grown woman and make my own choices." I said hotly then crossed my arms and sulked.

"Dinnae be daft woman, yer to marry Liam of course," Rhys informed me, but by my look, he realized my question had been a rhetorical one.

I pulled Jasper aside, far enough away so the others wouldn't hear what I had to say about the matter. "Jasper, I can't marry Liam, or anyone else for that matter. We came here to find my grandfather and bring him home." I whispered harshly to him, hands on my hips.

"Ye have to, lass. It was a matter of time that ye two would have been caught. What if yer with child? Did that ever cross yer mind?" At my astonished look, we both realized I hadn't.

"Aye, well, ye have to whether we end up goin' or no. If we cannae go back, then ye'll need protection. I dinnae plan on livin' forever. Yer marryin' him and that's final."

When tears rolled silently down my cheeks, he softened a bit.

"Lass, for now ye need someone to look after ye, especially if I'm not here after the Rising. This isnae the time for the faint of heart, especially for women."

He walked back to the group, leaving me alone in the snow with my thoughts. I looked around but Lucifer was too far for me to run to. I wanted to be somewhere, anywhere but here, and at this moment.

Tears filled my eyes in despair but Jasper had a point. What if we couldn't get home, to Nana, to my father. What then? I didn't want to hurt Liam. I loved him too much. But what choice did I have? I turned back to them and looked at him. My heart broke at the thought of leaving him, but I couldn't picture being without him either.

For now, I would take him for as long as I could, and figure out the rest when the time came. I walked back to the group, taking Liam's hand in mine and nodded my agreement. He brought me into my tent to talk and was followed by the priest.

"What the hell is he doing in here?" I bellowed. The priest crossed himself yet again while looking at me sternly. I didn't have the time nor the want, to sooth his religious sensibilities. I needed to talk with Liam.

"He needs proof that yer a woman to marry us."

I looked at him confused then in horror at what he was suggesting. "You've got to be joking. And exactly what should I do to prove it? Flash him my tits or would he like to see a bit more, maybe drop my drawers while I'm at it."

I didn't wait for a reply from Liam, but turned to face the priest and pulled up my shirt, exposing my breasts to him. When I went for my breeches, the priest stormed out; his face red as an apple. Liam actually laughed at that but soon sobered up.

I scowled at him too then blew out a breath, exhausted from all the drama. He took me into his arms, saying nothing, but held on tightly. It was just what I needed at that moment.

"Liam, we can't do this. You don't know anything about me, nor I you. What if we end up hating each other?"

He took my hands in his and squeezed. "I may not ken who ye were before I met ye, but from the first day we met until this day, I could only love ye for who ye are now. Somehow, I've had this feelin' that we were meant to be together. Call it fate if ye will."

He planted a gentle kiss on my forehead then led me out to join the others again. The ceremony was simple and quick, Liam vowing to love and protect me until his last dying breath. As for me, I was in a daze and didn't hear much of what was said.

The ceremony was so very different than back in my time. Even as a civil one. Nothing elaborate, I didn't wear a gown and that saddened me. This would have been the occasion to wear Nana's gown which was back at the Keep. It was quiet and intimate with only a small torch to light our group.

The priest didn't give anyone an option as to objecting to the union, not that there would be any forthcoming anyway, but still, just to have someone on my side would have been nice.

Liam took my hand in his, eyes shining and a warm smile on his face as he slipped a braided band of gold onto my finger, officially joining us in marriage. It shimmered in the torch light and felt warm to the touch.

I looked at it and tears filled my eyes and spilled down my cheeks. I didn't know if it was because I was now a married to Liam or for the heartbreak I knew would come later when I would have to leave him.

"I got it few months ago, in hopes ye'd become my wife. I hope ye like it. It's nothin' fan," he began.

"Liam it's beautiful," I said in between hiccups and sniffling. "It fits perfectly." I turned it around and around on my finger, loving how it felt; as though it had been there all my life.

All too soon, the dreamy feeling was broken when Rhys spoke. "Now that that's settled, we'll leave ye both to it then. Congratulations man!" he said to Liam, giving him a hardy slap on the back. He took up my hand and kissed my newly ringed hand before leaving.

Jasper was next, skipping Liam all together and embraced me tightly. I stood stiff for a minute then hesitantly clung to him, wiping my nose on his sleeve since it was there.

"Lass, ye'll see, all will be fine. Oidhche mahath." He kissed my forehead then left us.

The priest practically made a run for it when Rhys said it was time to go, so now it was Liam and I only, standing in the snow, not sure what to do next. I pulled my glove back on, feeling the cold now and tightened my grip on my cloak.

"I need to walk, Liam. I need to clear my head and...I just need some quiet for a bit."

His look turned sullen but nodded. "All right but stay close. Dinnae forget where ye are, Jessie." He made a bow then walked in the direction the others had gone.

CHAPTER 30

I COULDN'T BELIEVE I was married again. I didn't even know if I liked the idea of it. I hadn't planned to marry again but here I was, nailing it. Jasper's words a month before we left; about people who are grieving seek out comfort in any way possible. To forget their pain for even a moment was human nature. That it was fine.

How dare him, the hypocrite! Here I was, doing just that with Liam and now Liam was saddled to me, the bastard. I'd be reminding him of his words then telling them all to go to hell.

That chance didn't come, nor would it come. Word had come that the negotiations didn't go well and so now war was upon us. I looked around me, seeing only stony looks on all faces that came into view, even with the women. The young boys who were to participate in this looked ready to shit their pants if they moved a muscle.

This would be it. Whatever it took, we'd bring Thomas down and fix the wrongs he'd brought upon everyone. If we were successful today, Rhys would take charge of all of

Devonshire's estates and lands until Thomas' heir was old enough to take over. That would be years from now.

Liam and Jasper informed me that I was not to go near any of the fighting, that I was to stay behind with the other stable hands to help them. We were to take the tired mounts and send fresh ones back out with the riders. I assured them I would, muttering under my breath to make sure they thought I would obey.

At their dubious looks I smartly said, "What, do you not trust me?" They didn't have time to argue with me about it. Rhys had called them to saddle up and head out.

"Please be careful, both of you," I whispered as I watched them ride off.

Once the camp grew quiet, I quickly donned my armor, secreted away small daggers underneath my leather thigh guards then belted on my sword. I mounted Lucifer then kicked him into a sprint.

I stopped a safe distance from the group that had left earlier, tracking their horses' footprints in the snow. Thankfully, the sky was clear so I had no trouble finding them.

When I got close enough, my heart dropped. Men upon men, blade against blade, hacked at each other. Horses laid bleeding and kicking, trying to get up only to stumble then fall to the ground again. Tired from their efforts, they eventually gave up in defeat. Some were legless from being cut down, some lay still.

I continued on by foot, Lucifer's reins in one hand and my dirk in hand. Men writhed on the ground, missing limbs themselves or suffering from a fatal wound to the body. I couldn't bring myself to help them along to quicken their deaths, so I did my best to ignore their pleas. It was bad enough that I had to silence their mounts.

I mounted Lucifer once I was assured there were no others to silence. Thankfully, I had not been noticed while doing the gruesome task, the men so focused on what they were doing to notice a "boy" roaming around.

I spotted Jasper who was no longer mounted himself, his blade swinging at the enemy. I watched him go at it, and for a moment I could picture the fierce highlander as he might have been long ago.

This wasn't an old man, but a force to be reckoned with. Blood, mud and sweat covered him, and the graying strands of his hair swung back and forth as he twisted one way then another. This was a warrior in front of me.

He cut and slashed any man that dared to come at him, roaring with each blow that finally brought his foe to the ground. He really did miss this. If fighting was his thing, why hadn't he joined the military back in our time? He would have been a good soldier. On second thought, probably not. He would have been a rogue soldier.

I knew then that he wouldn't be going home with me nor with Jon. This was his home, his time was the here and now. My eyes misted and my heart tightened at the thought of not having him come with me.

My vision cleared in time to see one man sneak up near him as Jasper sparred with another, and I kicked Lucifer into a dead run. Before he could come to a halt I lunged off of him and slashed at the man. Lucifer ran off somewhere, hopefully away from any danger.

The man was huge but I was stealthy thanks to my own size and slim frame. I tripped over something and landed on my back. He smiled down at me before raising his claymore to finish me. I smiled back before kicking him in the balls, causing him to drop to his knees and howl in pain.

He grabbed his groin then vomited. I crouched, pulled out two of my long daggers and just as Liam had taught me, laid the blades crisscrossed against his throat. I didn't wait for the man to recover from my ball busting. I swung my arms outwards, slitting his throat and almost decapitating him. Blood spray struck me in the face but I hadn't noticed it.

Another man swung out, trying to grab me but I was too fast. With each lunge he took, I swiped at him, sometimes cutting him or his armor. I couldn't help but enjoy this little game of cat and mouse, but my enjoyment was cut short thanks to my cockiness. A beefy arm came around my neck and my arms pinned against my sides with his other one.

My vision began to blur from lack of oxygen and my lungs burned painfully. I could feel my heartbeat slow with every beat and a sense of calm filled me, knowing this was to be my end. Somehow I was all right with that.

I suddenly found myself sprawled in the mud, face down and air trying to enter my now freed body. It hurt something awful but I sent up a thank you for giving me a second chance at life, at least for the moment.

The man, who had been my captor a moment ago, now lay sprawled and twitching, and very much headless. Now all of this was too real and I had to put my guard up from now on. A hand patted me twice then hauled me up to my feet.

"Och, lad its but a head," the voice trailed off when he recognized who he was helping up.

Jasper stood there, a stunned look on his face from seeing me. He backed up a step then glared at me. I could see he was considering running me through himself for my disobedience. But his look changed from white hot anger, to shock and then pain before collapsing to his knees, the point of a sword sticking through his chest.

We both looked down at it as it pointed skyward before being removed from him. It made its presence known again only this time through Jasper's stomach.

"No!!!" I screamed and grabbed him as he laid down fully on the ground.

Blood ran from his mouth each time he breathed, bloody foam trailing down the sides of his mouth. Someone near us ran the man through as I sat next to Jasper. All my thoughts had left me but for one, to keep Jasper alive.

"You, you're going to be ok, you're going to be all right. Do you hear me, Jasper? Just hold on." I looked around me for help but everyone was too busy to come to our aid.

He chuckled then coughed, spraying my face with blood but I didn't care. My hands shook but not from the cold, but from seeing how much blood he was losing with each breath he took.

"Lass, it's alright now. Dinnae cry for me. I told ye this was to be my last fight, and see, I dinnae disappoint."

"This is not funny Jasper, how can you make light of this?" I said angrily to him, as deep wracking sobs emanated from me.

He squeezed my hand in fear of what was surely to come and I squeezed back, trying to give him my strength to hold on. My tears streamed freely and he brushed them aside shakily.

"Ye should have stayed where I told ye to, lass. Now look at ye, covered in blood and god only kens what else that's happened to ye." He coughed again and more blood ran from his mouth.

"Shut up old man. When have I ever listened to you." I gave him a watery laugh.

"Ye mind yer husband, Jessie. If not for me," he laid his hand down over my belly before continuing, "for the wee bairn yer carryin'."

I looked at him, startled, then back at his hand that still laid over my stomach. "I'm not pregnant you dolt! I think I would know seeing how I have been before. You've gone daft in the head from loss of blood is all."

He gave me a bloody smile and nodded in assurance. "Aye ye are, lass, I ken the look now. I wasnae sure until last night."

I wasn't going to ask exactly how he knew this information, but I gave myself a moment to think it over. Could I possibly be? That made things even more difficult for me now.

The fighting continued around us but no one paid us any mind. Just a kid crying over his dying or dead grandfather. He arched in pain and he looked to the sky, wanting it to be over; wanting peace.

He looked so tired now, and his face had gone pale. My knees slid around as I tried to get closer. When I couldn't I looked down and found that I was kneeling in blood and mud.

"Jasper don't leave me. Please don't leave me. I can't do this without you." I laid my head over his heart and sobbed. He patted my head weakly, then let it lay by his side again. I kept repeating that he couldn't leave me.

"I ken yer scared, Jessie but yer not alone. Liam has instructions as to where yer to go. I havenae told him why though."

I shook my head no. "I'm not leaving you here, damn you! I have Lucifer and we can get help."

He squeezed my hand so hard that I yelped in pain. "Jessie, ye'll do as I say for once!" he growled. I nodded, seeing that just yelling at me was an effort.

"Get on yer beast and wait for Liam to come back." He swallowed and tears ran down the sides of his face.

"Jessie, my lass; I've loved ye from the moment ye were born, as my own granddaughter. I am so proud of ye, girl. Never forget that."

I sobbed harder now, my body wracking from them. "I love you too, old man."

He gave one last gasp then quieted as his last breath left him. He was gone from me.

CHAPTER 31

I CLOSED HIS HALF opened sightless eyes then took a few breaths, hating the feeling that I could do so and he no longer could. Numbness was all I felt now. I picked up my daggers and with a loud growl, started swinging away, not caring if I made contact with a body or not.

I didn't much care if they were even on our side or the others; the rage ran so deep in me. This, this was all Thomas' fault.

I didn't know how many men I took down, nor did I care. Nothing seemed to matter now. My family was gone and I was alone.

It seemed like days had passed but only half of one. There were less screams now, or maybe it was because the blood was rushing in my ears, causing a loud hum in them.

Miles of bodies from both sides littered the once pristine, snow covered field, the field that was now a mixture of blood and mud. I sank to my knees and sat next to Jasper's body, not remembering how I had gotten there.

My daggers laid next to me, fallen from my numb grip on them. I didn't feel the snow that had begun to fall gently. Lucifer had found me and he nuzzled my hair and shoved at me to get up. I didn't move though. I just couldn't bring myself to move. Maybe this was my end too.

Liam and what remained of the clans, were searching for any men they could help, and wrote down the names of the ones they couldn't.

That's when he'd seen Jessie, Lucifer standing close to her asking for attention. His heart plummeted at the sight of her slouched form, kneeling with her head hanging down. She didn't move a muscle and the terrifying thought that came to him was that she had died like that.

He wasn't surprised to see her here. He suspected that's why they had trained all those nights, not just for protecting herself. It hadn't occurred to him that she would want to participate in the war, but it all became clear as to why now.

As he climbed over bodies, he kept his eyes on her. It felt like eternity until he reached her, but once he had, he knelt down, wanting to collect her into his arms. He stopped short, afraid to touch her and find her dead.

"Jessie?" He said her name gently but she didn't respond.

She took a breath and he nearly wept, thankful it wasn't her corpse in front of him. She stayed still, hands at her sides, and he noticed most of her was covered in drying blood. He prayed none of it was hers.

He took one of her hands loosely, trying to give comfort but also to let her know that she could move away freely if she needed to. Her hand was ice cold and limp in his and she made no move to take it away. He sat silently with her, waiting for her to look up and see him. She eventually did, and the grief there was heartbreaking.

"He's, he's gone, he's actually gone!" She said hysterically then broke into bone breaking sobs.

He gathered her into his arms, cradling her, holding on tightly as she sobbed. He whispered endearments into her hair as he stroked it, wishing there was something he could do or say to make the pain go away.

Rhys stood over them and was soon joined by more, silently grieving over their own that had perished that day. They surrounded the two of them, heads bowed, some with silent tears running down their cheeks.

"Did ye see how the lad fought against the others?" One of the men said under his breath to another.

"Aye, I did and what a fighter he is now. Not some stable hand any longer but a right proper highlander." The men murmured their agreement and continued their praises.

Rhys stood looking down at Jessie's small form in Liam's lap. The lass had really held her own today. He'd caught sight of her in between killing his own attackers.

"That is no stable hand, but Liam's wife. She is one of our own after today, treat her with the highest of respect."

The crowd grew immediately quiet at Rhys' words. A few manly gasps filtered through the small group. Liam picked Jessie up, intending to ride with her, but her sudden scream had him halt his movements.

Jessie clasped her side and blood oozed freely between her fingers. He had gone just as pale as Jessie currently was, but for him it was from panic. There was so much blood.

Rhys bent down on the other side of her, inspecting the wound. It thankfully was not so deep, just enough to split the skin apart. What concerned him was how much blood she was losing. He followed the slash and it ran further up, along the ribs, just next to her breast.

"Shite," Rhys cursed and signaled to one of the men carrying a torch. He instructed another man to fetch any alcohol he could find, the stronger the better. He ripped her shirt further up to her shoulder to get a better view of the gash.

"We're too far from camp to get her there alive. This needs to be tended to before we head back." Rhys said more to himself than anyone within earshot.

The man returned with a flask of whiskey, thank God, and then stood back and fidgeted. Rhys removed his short knife then snatched the torch from the other man.

"See if she'll take any of this, the more the better. This isnae goin' to be pleasant for her."

With shaky fingers, Liam managed to get the alcohol into her and hoped that it would be enough to take the edge off of what Rhys was about to do. When she tasted it she drank greedily and Liam had to pull it away before she drowned in it.

"Easy now Mo Chridhe. Just lay back now and we will fix ye up." Liam assured her but she made no move as to acknowledge she'd heard him.

Rhys instructed Liam to pour the whiskey over the gash to cleanse it, something he'd seen done by the women who dealt with this kind of thing. Jessie screamed as though the hounds of hell were chasing her. She tried to move but one man held her down by crossing her arms over her chest, and another man sat on her legs.

While Liam prepared Jessie, Rhys sat close by, knife in the torch fire, heating it until it turned bright orange-yellow. Once satisfied with it, he counted to three, placing the knife against the gash to seal it closed. She squirmed and cursed then passed out cold before he removed the hot blade.

The men all sighed with relief once she was out. The seared flesh looked ugly but at least the bleeding had stopped. There was still the possibility of death if it got infected. Fingers crossed that it wouldn't.

"Liam, have her ride with you and take Lucifer with you. He willnae go with anyone unless she's nearby. Mrs. Graham is at the camp, seek her out to see to Jessie. Return once she's settled. We have many bodies to bring back for burial and I need every man to help load them."

Liam nodded then picked Jessie up and carried her to his mount. He took up Lucifer's reins and tugged at them but the horse wouldn't budge. "Ye can either go with her or die out here; yer choice ye demon. I would gather yer lady would verae much miss ye if ye werenae there when she wakes."

Liam mounted up; Jessie seated but slouched in front of him. She moaned but still slept. He moved on not waiting for Lucifer to make up his mind to come or not. Surprisingly, the damn horse joined them albeit at a distance.

When Lucifer came near enough to check on Jessie, Liam took the opportunity to catch up his reins and tied them around the horn of his own saddle. Lucifer didn't seem to notice, so focused on his owner. He nudged her leg and she groaned loudly and he shied away.

"Leave off ye beast! She's hurt for Christ sake." Liam glared at Lucifer who ignore the look but didn't touch Jessie again. He did however ride closer to her as if to protect her.

Liam had never seen the likes of a horse caring for its owner but here he was, hovering like a nanny over Jessie.

Liam knew then that Lucifer would die for her if it meant keeping her safe, even from him.

Camp was a couple of hours away at the speed they were traveling, and Liam tried not to jostle Jessie too much. He checked her leg and even though he'd fastened his leather belt around it, it still bled freely albeit slowly. This gash had been found once the wound on her side had been taken care of.

Snow had started to fall heavily by the moment so the choice had been made for him. He spurred his mount and Lucifer into a hard gallop, thankful Lucifer hadn't given him any resistance. It took an hour but they got to camp just as the only tell tale signs of it were of the fuzzy glows of the cook fires.

He took her to one of the larger tents, instructing the men to vacate and find Mrs. Graham and send her to him. Once the tent was empty, he ripped her shirt open and removed it, followed by her breeches, socks and boots.

Her body was quite a sight, and not a good one. Black and blue bruises were appearing before his eyes and he averted them to the still bleeding wound on her hip. He found a cloth that looked reasonably clean and tied it around the gash as best he could then flung a fur over her to get her warm.

"Liam, what do ye have for me?" Mrs. Graham asked, already rolling up her sleeves to get down to business.

She'd come with the camp to be with her husband, but also to act as nurse for the wounded men. Her daughters were there as well to assist, along with a few other women whose husbands were there for the battle.

Liam pulled aside the fur to expose the bandage on Jessie's hip but didn't reveal the rest of her body. He wanted it to stay quiet that Jessie was in fact a woman, and not a stable hand, as everyone knew her to be.

She pulled the bandage aside and looked at the wound, hmming and hawing over it but didn't say anything else, just replaced the cloth and moved on.

"Poor lad, one so young shouldnae be fightin'. What was Rhys thinkin' lettin' the boy on the field." She tsk'd.

"He dinnae let him. The lad disobeyed orders and went in himself." Liam said rather sharply. He lightened his tone at Mrs. Graham's stern look.

She returned to looking over the parts of Jessie that were exposed, finding nicks and a few longer cuts along her collar bones, one on the right shoulder and down the right forearm. None too serious like the two major ones.

She cleaned those quickly, placing salve over them but left them un-bandaged, then moved on. She went back to Jessie's left hip, removing the cloth once more, and thankful that she had made it tight enough to stop the bleeding.

She flushed it with water then whiskey before stitching it up, placing salve then re-bandaged it with a clean cloth. Happy with her work she proceeded to remove the fur to find any more injuries but Liam halted her.

"I can do the rest from here. We took care of another one at the battle site. Let's let the lad sleep." Liam insisted.

"Nonsense, I've had six of my own boys and I ken what's under there. Ye called for me so let me get about it. The lad isnae the only one needin' tendin' too."

Before he could get to her in time, Mrs. Graham pulled the fur away from Jessie, leaving her naked. She gasped then shot a look at him. He had the good grace to blush.

"I can explain. This is my wife, Jessie. She's one of Rhys' stable,"

"I ken who Jessie is, but not that he was a *she*, Liam. Does Rhys ken of this? I'd have a right mind to go and tell him right now if she didnae need more tendin' to."

"He's the one who had us marry last night. If ye dinnae believe me then go ask him yerself." Liam scowled.

She scowled back at him then looked Jessie over, not finding anything that warranted fixing. She did find the burnt slash along her left side, from the side of her breast to the last rib.

"Rhys, he did the best he could considerin' where we were. She was bleedin' heavily and we needed to stop it. Is there anythin' ye can do for it to make it less...ugly?" Liam asked.

She looked over the seared flesh then went to work, what little that could be done with it now. A couple of stitches had to be placed since the knife hadn't sealed it completely, then more salve was applied before bandaging it. She crossed herself and said a prayer for Jessie then left without a word.

CHAPTER 32

IT FELT LIKE HOURS had passed where he sat, holding Jessie's hand. She hadn't moved, not even when Mrs. Graham stitched her up, both hip and side. Her hand lay limp and hot in his but he held on tight to it.

He scrubbed at his face then got up and asked one of the women to sit with her so he could attend to other business. The woman was to fetch him if there was any change, good or bad. He took his leave and saddled up, intending to go back to help retrieve the bodies, but found out that Rhys and the others had returned already. Thankfully there were very few bodies to bury.

The thought of death had his mind turning to Jasper. They could not bury anyone due to it being winter and the ground frozen hard. The only good thing at the moment where the weather was concerned, was that it was cold enough to keep the bodies from rotting quickly.

He joined Rhys and a few of the other men in the main tent to go over the events for the day. Rhys was pleased that their numbers were greater than Thomas', however, it was brought to Rhys' attention that Thomas hadn't even appeared today, sending his men into a battle without instruction.

That was probably why his men retreated so quickly, but most of them lay dead on the field. He hadn't even sent wagons to retrieve the bodies that fought for him, but left them to rot where they fell.

So many lives wasted today, and for what, money. Money was the root of all evil and today proved that. The men sat quietly, reflecting on the events that occurred and drank as much whiskey as they could to try and forget it all. Liam however, as much as he'd wanted to join them, excused himself to return to Jessie.

"How is she doin'?" Rhys later asked Liam when all had calmed down the next day, leaving him some time to check on Jessie himself.

"She hasnae woken yet. Yesterday's activities are terrorizin' her in her sleep."

One of the women, who'd been taking turns with the treatment of Jessie, was currently checking and cleaning the hip wound. It looked ugly, swollen, blood red and angry. Infection seemed to have set in during the night.

"She's a strong lass. After the way she fought yesterday, there is no way she's goin' down without another fight and not winnin' it too." Rhys patted Liam's shoulder but Liam didn't reply, just sat there and watched.

Liam hoped she would pull through but with the two wounds she suffered, most men larger and stronger than here; died from such wounds. He didn't want to lose her, but he'd started to harden his heart to the fact that he just might and there was nothing he could do about it.

Mrs. Graham made an appearance after the woman who had just seen to Jessie, and had informed her of the possible infection. "We have to open it and drain the puss. Flush it frequently until it runs clear."

She dug for her small dagger and cut through the stitches. After the first three, the puss ran down in a thick streak to collect on the table top.

Liam grimaced then felt his stomach turn but he refused to leave her side. He cooed to Jessie, stroked her hand and massaged her fingers all the while Mrs. Graham cleaned the wound. She cut away the death flesh which did have Liam heaving into a well placed bucket next to him.

"I'll pack it with linen and leave it open to make sure the flesh inside heals enough, then I can close it up."

She glanced at Liam when she didn't hear a response and found him passed out cold on the floor. She rolled her eyes and shook her head then went back to her ministrations. Once done she left the two of them alone, leaving Liam where he passed out. No sense in hurting her own back lifting a highlander.

Liam stretched his sore legs then his back after waking to find himself on the dirt floor by Jessie's sickbed. He wondered how he managed to be on the floor, and then it all came back to him and he nearly vomited again. Thankfully the sight that greeted him of Jessie wasn't so gruesome this time.

She slept fitfully and was hot to the touch. Fever had set in because of the infection in her leg but all he could do was place cool rags on her forehead for now.

He fed her snow since she wouldn't wake to drink, which seemed to work fine. He bathed her and spoke to her when they were alone, hoping all the while that she could hear him.

Plain exhaustion had taken him and he slumped in his chair, unable to sleep but too tired to do anything else but try. Once the next rotation of women had changed, he let himself out to seek out food and fresh air.

He found Rhys with a couple of others, eating and talking near one of the fires. He helped himself to a bowl of stew then joined them. It felt good to be out in the fresh cold air, even in the snow.

"She fought well our Jessie, even better than some of the men here. Any chance ye had somethin' to do with that?" Rhys asked Liam.

"Aye, for the past few months we've been trainin' out in the field at night. She told me she'd had fencin' lessons."

"The way she was movin' through those men who had the good graces to get in her way, that was nothin' like fencin'." Rhys eyed Liam for some kind of reaction but got none. The boy looked as though he'd fall asleep standing up.

"I dinnae see her until I found her so I cannae tell ye. I would have liked to have seen her at it though." Liam eventually answered.

Once done with his food, Liam stood then stretched, wincing as his tired and stiff muscles protested the movement. He hadn't liked leaving Jessie for so long so he bid the men a 'good day' and went back to Jessie.

Rhys stayed seated after Liam retired for the night. Thoughts plagued him on how it had been easy to take down Thomas' men. They were mere farmers who had been shoved into it, followed by the higher ranking men from the northern clans. Most didn't have fighting experience. Disgust filled him over the thought of so many lost.

He'd have bet on it that the farmers and their sons who'd fought in the battle, had been threatened with the loss of their lands if they hadn't. He wouldn't put it past him either to take the lands back now since the farmers had perished and since the women couldn't handle all of the care, he'd kick them out.

They'd found a few of Thomas' men who were injured and so brought them back to the camp for questioning at a later time. Preferably when they weren't screaming and bleeding all over the place.

His thoughts came back around to Jessica. She'd run down at least fifteen men if not more, including two of Thomas' officers. All her pain and rage spoke volumes in her strikes. She'd been as wild and fierce as a rogue stallion, like Lucifer.

Speaking of Lucifer, he'd spotted him in the field close by to her, waiting for her to come to him. They really were one and the same to each other.

Exhaustion finally settled in and he sought out his own tent, loosening his tartan so he could remove the thick leather breast plate that had kept him protected. He dropped everything that could come off easily before wrapping himself back into his tartan, then collapsed onto his pallet for the night.

There was something he'd have to discuss with Liam but it could wait. Sleep came to him almost immediately, his snores filling his tent and escaping through the tent flaps to join the others flowing over the campsite.

CHAPTER 33

Liam entered Jessie's tent to find there had been no change. She slept fitfully, tossing her head back and forth and her brow tightly knit together. Beads of sweat coated her skin and it shimmered in the candlelight. The occasional tear escaped the outer side of her eyes, running slowly a trail into her hair. The tears were for Jasper, he was almost sure of it.

One of the men had reported that she had been with Jasper when he'd fallen. She'd stayed with him until the end, then just started swinging away, blades shining, even in the gloom.

He pulled a chair up to the pallet she was on, thankful that someone had taken pity on his bottom and took the stool away. He grasped her hand in his, thumb stroking the top of her smooth skin.

He prayed and prayed for what seemed like a lifetime, praying she would live, praying that God would take her pain from her and bestow it onto him since he was stronger.

No answer came, she lay there still, and he laid his head onto their clasped hands.

He hadn't realized he'd fallen asleep until Mrs. Graham made a noise and he'd shot up straight as a board in the chair. He scrubbed at his eyes then stretched, watching her go about her business with Jessie.

"She has the fever, but it's a mild one now."

Mrs. Graham confirmed to him as she mopped at Jessie's brow and neck, then went about checking Jessie's hip and upper side. The wound on the hip was still a tad bit angry but since she'd been constantly changing out the packing, the infection seemed to have gotten better, if not altogether gone now. Another day and she'd sew it up for good this time.

The burn was healing nicely and she crossed herself in relief that at least something had worked well. She'd let Rhys know of the fine job he'd done, even if it did look awful.

Liam helped with the ministrations that Mrs. Graham instructed him to do, giving luke-warm tea to Jessie to help ease some of the pain. He returned to his seat, clasped her hand again and began praying.

"Nick, Sophie!... please don't leave me, please don't go!" Jessie whimpered in her fevered state. Liam tried to sooth her by caressing her hair and whispered endearments but nothing worked. All he could do was hold on tight to her hand, feeding strength into her to fight her demons.

Who were Nick and Sophie? Why did she need them to stay? There were many questions but for later. Once she was well enough and strong enough for them. When she called for Nick again, he posed as this Nick, assuring her that everything would be all right, and instantly she quieted and her face relaxed.

He wouldn't lie to himself that it hurt that it wasn't his name she called for. He pushed the surge of jealousy aside as best he could and concentrated on attending to her comfort, however small it was.

Mrs. Graham had shown him how to tend to Jessie's hip and side, something he wasn't fond of, especially the hip wound, but he did what he was told and soon she was confident in the healing of it and time to stitch the hip wound closed. Liam gave a sigh of relief and a mental pat on the back for his efforts.

The fever had left Jessie and she slept soundly for the first time since she'd been brought back to the camp. Once Liam was satisfied that she was out of harm's way and resting comfortably, he left her to find fresh clothing and to get some much needed sleep on a much needed pallet.

I awoke in complete darkness. The smell around me was pleasantly familiar so I lingered where I was for a few moments more. I went to rise but stopped immediately, pain shooting through my whole body. What the hell had happened?

I must have made a noise because the darkness was soon gone with the drawing of a curtain and a young woman stood before me. A candle flickered next to me on a bedside table and the roar of a warm fire sounded behind her.

My body felt like it was on fire the pain was so great. I couldn't quite make out the woman's face, my vision being a bit blurry, but she spoke gently to me and I settled back down against a soft backing. I must be on a bed, but whose and where?

"Easy miss, we dinnae want to split a stitch now." The young servant said gently.

"Where am I?" I stuttered to her, my voice unrecognizable to my ears. My throat burned from dryness and I coughed. She instantly had water against my lips and I drank greedily.

"Easy now, not too much or ye'll vomit it all up. Yer at Rhys Castle now."

She helped me sit up against more pillows, careful not to have me bend too far forward. A sharp tug at my hip had me gasping and I went to lift up my gown, but she pushed my hand away and covered me up quickly.

"Ye've been asleep for the past three days here and yer husband will be verae happy to see ye've woken. I'll summon Mrs. Graham to see to ye along with some food. Ye must be famished." She turned to leave but I stopped her with my question.

"My husband?" Nick was dead and in the future, not here with me. What the hell was going on?

"Aye miss, yer husband Liam. Ye dinnae remember yer husband?" At my sheepish look she gave me a wan smile then hurriedly made an exit, leaving me to my thoughts.

Liam was my husband? The memory slowly came into focus of the two of us, along with Rhys, a priest, and Jasper, a ceremony in the woods just outside of camp.

A few minutes had passed when another woman, a few decades older than the last one, came straight for me, a 'no nonsense' look on her face. I shrank back into the pillows the best I could but there was nowhere to go.

"So, yer finally awake then. Alright, let's be about it then. Turn onto yer side." She threw back the covers and my legs and feet were instantly met with cold air so I reached for the blankets. That was not such a smart move on my part.

She tsk'd tsk'd me then rolled me over when I didn't obey, hiking up my nightgown all the way up to my shoulders.

"What the hell do you think you are doing? Stop molesting me and leave off woman." I hissed at her but she ignored my complaints and went about removing the bandage around my hips.

I looked down as best as I could but with my arm in front of me, I couldn't see anything. It was probably for the best after hearing a gasp coming from a much younger servant.

The she-devil poked and prodded around which had me sending out curses, curses for the pain and curses to her for causing the pain. The young servant gasped again, louder it seemed this time, and the old woman only grinned.

"Well, it's good to ken at least somethin' on ye has mended fully. Yer hip looks good, a few more days and I'll remove the stitches. Now, let's see this one." She lifted my arm up until I hissed and cursed some more, not touching this wound thankfully.

"Ye'll be up and 'bout in no time, lass. Finella, bring over the salve and some clean linens then go and get the lass here some food and drink." She winked at me then went about washing her hands again.

After what seemed like a lifetime, she was finally finished cleaning me up and setting new bandages over the salve. Maybe I was losing my mind but both areas felt much better.

If reading my mind, Mrs. Graham commented, "There is willow bark infused in the salve. It helps with the pain. Ye drank it while ye were out cold."

Just as a fresh gown was pulled down to my ankles, Liam burst through the door, unsettling the servant who ended up dropping my tea.

"*Mhar na galla*, Liam! You didn't need to charge in here like a pissed off bull. I'm not going anywhere any time soon." I snapped at him.

He ignored my anger and continued to stride to my bedside, smoothly landing on the edge of it, making me wince, and took my hand in both of his. "How are ye feelin', *Mo Chridhe*? Do ye have much discomfort?"

Before I could get a word in edgewise, he began barking orders to both the young servant and Mrs. Graham, whom did not take kindly, nor obey his demands. The servant girl ran off to fetch wine for me along with some food.

"The lass is healin' fine and should be up and about in a few days. If she needs to use the privy, call for a servant to assist ye darlin'. Liam, stay off her, she needs rest, not coddlin'." She looked at me over his shoulder and gave me a small smile and a wink.

I hid a smile, clearing my throat in hopes of hiding it from everyone within view. Mrs. Graham continued to straighten up her things before adding more peat to the fire. She handed me a glass of water, ordered me to drink the whole thing then left the two of us alone.

He started fussing with the blankets around my waist and I instantly slapped his hands away, half amused but growing more impatient with his mothering. Getting the hint, he went to the other side of the bed and stretched out next to me, careful not to touch me anymore. I pushed his bangs out of his eyes, not certain what to do next myself.

"So, Mrs. Graham says I'm fit as a fiddle now. The long rest did me some good." I gave him what I hoped was a bright smile.

"Aye, well ye've been down for four days, two of them battlin' a fever. Honestly Jessie, how do you feel?" His look of concern warmed me and I assured him I was doing fine.

"I feel like I've been hit by a MAC truck," at his confused look I quickly rephrased, "like a herd of cows ran me over, and my left side I'm trying to ignore all together.

He still looked a bit concerned by my first comment, but I distracted him by asking how he fared from the battle. "Not to worry, lass, nothin' but a few scratches here and there. I'll say I will be verae jealous of yer own battle scars once they've healed."

"I highly doubt that. Before coming here, from the States, I had but one sizable scar and now, well, I have so many I can't count them all."

"Aye, well one is in this harsh land, ye can bet on gettin' a few." He traced the veins that were faintly visible on top of my hand, but that was it. The seriousness of what had happened showed on his face, the humor removed to be replaced with sorrow.

Bits and pieces came back to me in the waking hours, but my dreams haunted me every night, and I couldn't be sure what had been real and what hadn't.

The men around me were faceless and I couldn't be sure who was friend and who was foe, all were covered in blood and blindly swinging.

I saw myself in the melee, everyone and everything in slow motion around me. Even the snowflakes seemed to stand still in the air, easily brushed aside by an absent minded gesture.

In others, I stood my ground, meeting blade after blade with my own strokes, slashing away at any person that got close enough. Several of them were collapsing to the ground.

Liam snapped me out of my dark thoughts by brushing a strand of hair out of my face then wiped away the stream of tears that had fallen while I had recalled my nightmares.

"How's Jasper? Has he come to visit yet?" I asked in hopes of changing the subject.

He gave me a slow smile and took my hand again in his before answering me. "He's recoverin' himself otherwise I'm sure he'd be here bossin' me around and motherin' ye to death.

"Dinnae fash, lass. Get yer own rest so ye can be back on yer feet for trainin' again. I miss our midnight meetings of foreplay. For now I must leave ye for a bit." He kissed my hand and gave me a wink and I felt my cheeks go rosy at the thought then all too soon he was gone.

CHAPTER 34

I was up walking in a week albeit with a cane. I made my first appearance in the courtyard and I immediately breathed in deeply, enjoying the cool crisp winter air that assaulted my nostrils. I never thought I'd miss the smells of the outdoors, including manure but here I was, gulping in the air.

The courtyard grew eerily quiet but for the exception of a few young children running around playing tag. I looked around and found all eyes were on me. None of those faces were smiling, just stone-faced.

I proceeded to step back in the way I had come out but found a hard wall behind my back, instantly stopping me in my tracks. Within a heartbeat, a tall man in the far corner to my left, fell to one knee and bowed his head. More soon followed, with women curtsying.

"What the hell is going on? Is Rhys behind me or something?" I said under my breath. I turned to find out what I had backed into and sure enough, it was Rhys standing there now looking down at me.

He caught me instantly as I nearly fell over from being so close to him and looking up at him at the same time. He set me back gently then walked passed me into the courtyard himself.

Rhys turned and faced me then fell to one knee himself, right arm crossed over his chest then bowed his head as well. I mouthed 'what the fuck' in complete confusion. Once Rhys stood up again and joined me on the top step, I still couldn't speak.

"They were not bowin' to me, lass but to ye. We have much to be thankful for due to ye and the honor is all mine." Rhys gave me another bow before heading off to do other business.

I stood there, still as a dummy, trying to figure out what the hell I'd done to deserve this treatment when Liam found me standing there like an idiot.

"Something strange just happened outside. Everyone there just…bowed to me. Why would they be doing that?" I looked imploringly up at him.

"Well ye did fight for Rhys firstly. Second, a woman who fought in any battle and came out of it alive should be commended for her noble actions, even if she did disobey orders. And lastly, ye did take down over twenty men all by yerself like a savage. There are some who are quite scared of ye." He said the last part with a wink.

I felt the blood drain out of my face and panic set in. He took me into his arms and assured me the ones, who did fear me, were very glad that they were on my good side. I shivered and my hip ached badly so I headed back to my room to chase all of it away.

Once Liam tucked me into one of the fireside chairs and handed me a glass of wine, my body felt better but my conscience was even more worked up.

What had I done? But my mind wouldn't allow me entry into it. Maybe I didn't want to know and in the not knowing, kept myself safe from something far more horrible than I could imagine.

"Liam, what did happen, at the battle I mean?" He sat across from me, ankles crossed and hair loosened around his shoulders, a whiskey in hand. At my question, he looked at me a bit shocked at the question but cleared his throat.

"I wondered if ye would remember or not. I hadnae wanted to delay yer recovery over it, so I didnae want to talk with ye about it. I see now, that it was due to yer not rememberin' at all what took place. Are ye sure ye want to ken?"

I looked into the fire's flames, not answering right away. Did I want to remember? Not really, but a part of me felt absent from everyone else, like the butt of someone's bad joke or something.

"Yes, I want to remember, no scratch that, I need to know what happened that day; everything, Liam." I sat up straighter and stared at him, hands folded and waited.

It seemed my nightmares were very much real after all. Liam retold the day's events the best he could from what others had told him of my heroics in the field.

"There is somethin' else. I was not truthful to ye when ye asked about Jasper." Liam said hesitantly.

I squirmed in my seat, unease filling my throat with bile. "Go on," I insisted.

"He fell while fightin' beside ye. Ye were there until his end, and that's when it's said ye turned into a madwoman. He is here however, and I am willin' to take ye to see him. We cannae bury him, or the others until the first thaw."

"Why did you lie to me about him? What good did you think it would bring me to wait?" I demanded. Tears spilled from my eyes and he held out a handkerchief and I snatched it from him.

"Ye'd suffered horribly from yer injuries, Jessie and it took ye a whole week to finally wake for Christsake! I wasnae bout to have ye slip back into oblivion, and not ken to when ye'd wake again; if ever. People have died from such heartbreak!"

"It was not your choice to make, Liam! You don't know what I'm capable of. How dare you, take me to him now." I got up, and headed for the door, not turning to see if he followed.

If I had to, I would go to Rhys or anyone else who would help me in finding Jasper's body. Thankfully, I didn't have to wait for Liam to decide on whether or not to come.

"This way then."

I followed silently behind him, tears still streaming from my eyes and dripping onto my chest. He refrained from saying anything to me until we reached the room where the bodies were being kept. "I must tell ye, lass, he suffered much and is not a sight I would wish for yer eyes to see. Are ye sure about this? Would ye not rather keep the memory of him before the battle as yer last memory of him?"

"Open it; now." I demanded, and Liam signed then unlocked the door, pushed it open and signaled for me to enter. I followed him down the main walkway. I avoided looking at the bodies on either side of me laid out on tables.

We entered another room off to the right, one more private, where Jasper and a couple more high ranking officers were laid out. While I had been convalescing, someone had taken the time to clean the bodies, and dressed them in finer clothing than I had ever seen.

Jasper laid there, his complexion grayer than the clouds outside, lips blue and cheeks sunken in. Shadows had settled around his eyes, making them seem hollowed out. His jet black hair had been brushed and retied behind his head.

This was not the man I knew. There was no life. I could not mourn the body in front of me. Jasper had long since left us. My eyes didn't shed tears at the sight, but my heart tightened and grew hard, filling me with anger instead of grief.

I placed a coin over each of his eyes before laying a kiss upon his brow. "I will see to it that Thomas is given his rightful due penance for your death, and for our family. This I vow to you, old friend."

It was then I felt the first flutter of life in my womb and I instantly covered it with my hand, offering comfort and strength. I took it as a sign that Jasper had heard my oath, and had sent me a reminder of who I needed to protect now for the future of the family. I would do all I could to do just that.

"I need to meet with Rhys as soon as he is available. Send this to him and come back with his response." I instructed Finella, the young maid servant assigned to me, handing her the sealed parchment.

"I will be down in the stables." I informed her as we both left my room. She curtsied then rushed off in search of Rhys as I slowly made my way down the main staircase. I snuck into the kitchen, snatched an apple here and a carrot there, and some sweet meats and tarts. I would need all the bribing food I could get to get back onto Lucifer's good side again.

I hobbled into the stables and down the walkway between the stalls, stopping to look into the sheep pen. I'd come to say hello to my little fluffy black friend, only to find he was not there. A sinking feeling sat in my stomach and I quickly walked on until I reached Lucifer.

"Hello, old friend. I am sorry it has taken me this long to come and see you. As you can see, I've had some mending of my own to do."

Lucifer gave me a bland stare before looking in the other direction, blowing harshly out of his nose. I could only assume it was his way of showing his displeasure. I snickered and he caught wind of that which only made him even angrier.

He rolled his eyes at me and flattened his ears before neighing at me. Puffs of breath blew out of his nose with each breath and pawed the ground loudly. I stood there, taking my verbal punishment as seriously as I could, all the while trying my hardest not to straight out laugh at him.

Once I was done getting my tongue lashing from my horse, I informed him that I had brought him a present to say I was sorry. He didn't like hearing this and turned his head away from me, nose stuck in the air.

"Alright then, I guess I'll just have to eat this all myself. Good day to you Lucifer. Hopefully you'll be in better spirits to receive me tomorrow." I turned to leave, pulling out the apple tart I had brought with me. I bit into it and loudly exclaimed my pure enjoyment in the treat.

I nearly tumbled to the ground when a loud crack echoed through the whole stable, the sound of wood splintering behind me. Thankful for once for my nuisance of a cane, I was able to regain my footing immediately and turned to find Lucifer face to face with me.

Tart forgotten I stared into his dark brown eyes in absolute shock. Taking this opportunity as a good sign, Lucifer quickly nipped the tart from my hand and slurped it up, leaving slobber on the palm of my hand.

He sniffed my skirts and shoved at me when he caught the scent of another tart and the apples and carrots I had pilfered from the kitchens. I backed up a bit, shoving at his nose to stay put since he had taken a step forward.

"Leave off you beast! I'm getting them I'm getting them. Now, here's a beauty of a red apple for you my love." I held out my hand and he nipped it off my palm, crunching into it immediately.

"There's my good boy. I knew you couldn't stay mad at me forever. I am sorry I haven't been able to come until now to visit. I am very glad to see you survived the battle and came out of it unscathed. We lost Jasper though."

Sensing my sadness at the thought, Lucifer shoved at my shoulder, his way of asking to be held. I held onto his neck and he wrapped his head around my back to my waist. His familiar smell assaulted my nose and I couldn't help but smile. Someone had been taking very good care of my dear friend here.

"I see Sean has been taking good care of you while I've been gone. Let me have a look at you, sir. He's been using the special soap I made for you, hasn't he? Look at how shiny your coat and mane are. Such a handsome stallion you are."

Lucifer seemed to enjoy the preening I was giving him and all but puffed out his chest and held his head high, striking an impressive but also an imposing pose. I kissed his nose and scrubbed his cheeks before burying my face against his strong neck.

"Oye! What fresh hell is this?!!!" came a familiar Scottish voice around Lucifer's large backside.

I couldn't help but laugh at the use of my own favorite phrase, said in an angry Scottish brogue. I scooted past Lucifer to see Sean standing at what had once been Lucifer's stall. I stopped quickly once I had seen the damage my horse had caused.

"Damn the large Devil! This is the third time he's done this since comin' back. Why do I bother with the likes of ye, ye bloody bastard!" Lucifer looked blandly at him, still crunching on another apple while Sean's face turned the exact shade of said apple.

"I am so very sorry Sean, really I am. I didn't know he could do this, and you said 'third' time? I will be happy to pay you for the troubles this beast has caused you." I looked over at Lucifer who whinnied at me and I scowled at him.

"I'll pay to have a separate stable made for him so he will not be any more trouble for you. I'll see to it."

"Aye, make sure that ye do missy. I cannae have this behavior in my stables. The others will think it proper and start tearin' down their house. Idiots the lot of them."

At seeing me for the first time since entering the stables, he looked abashed at seeing me there, as if he'd seen a ghost. "So, ye finally came to see to this demon have ye, *lass*." He raised his brows at me and I blushed.

"Sorry?" I said sheepishly but he rolled his eyes then looked me up and down.

"How in God's name do ye plan on takin' care of him wearin' this thin'? And ye can forget about ridin' him side saddle. He willnae stand for that nonsense for sure."

"I wouldn't be wearing a dress for Christsake, Sean. I'll have to find some more appropriate attire for my job here."

Lucifer came back over, looked into his stall or what was left of it then shoved at me again for more food.

I shoved him back this time then glared at him. "And just where do you plan on sleeping tonight sir, now that you don't have a place anymore?" I scolded him. He looked away.

"I'll put him in with the carts for the night. Ye'll be sleepin' alone now. How do ye like that! That'll teach ye!"

"All right, I'll be heading in. I have to get off this hip. I take it you'll be able to take him in hand for now? And if you see Finella come to look for me, would you tell her I'm in the mess hall for supper?"

Sean nodded while he glowered at Lucifer who, in turn, glowered back at him. I could only roll my eyes, pat both of them on their cheek then hobbled out.

Finella found me in the courtyard on my way to the mess hall for dinner. Rhys had some time to see me in the morning before breakfast on the next day. I guess I'd have to wait until then. I sent her back with my confirmation of the meeting time. For now all I could do was eat.

Liam had seated himself with the men, and due to my female status being known now, well I was no longer allowed to sit with them. I turned and headed in the general direction most of the higher class of the fairer sex sat for dinner, but thought better of it after the searing looks most of them gave me.

I would assume it was pure jealousy that Liam had selected me as his wife, and being a new-comer to Rhys Castle to boot. I inwardly smiled back at them, feeling smug.

Since there were no other spots available for a lady to sit, I headed for the kitchens instead, looking forward to having some time to myself after learning everything about what had taken place a week ago.

My heart squeezed tightly in my chest as I thought of Jasper, lying there cold and alone. I hoped to God I would find Jon and tell him what a wonderful and loyal friend he had been to both of us and that he fought for our family's name and rightful place.

As I entered the kitchens though, Mrs. Graham saw me and quickly escorted me out and back down the hall to the great room.

CHAPTER 35

"A LADY DOESNAE SIT with the help. I am sure there is enough seats for all out there."

I growled in frustration and just went up to my room where I could truly be alone. I rung for Finella and asked her to retrieve a platter of supper for me along with wine. Also, for a bath since my hip was hurting terribly. She curtsied, something I hated but would have to get used to now.

I really hated being a woman at this moment in time. Once my purpose here was done, I'd ride day and night to get to the doorway back to my time. Hopefully it would be sooner rather than later.

The tub was brought and put next to the fire. Six servants, mostly men, carried and poured their buckets of hot water into it. Just seeing the steam rise from it made my body relax a bit. I couldn't remember the last time I'd had a bath, or a shower for that matter. Definitely not in this time that was for sure.

I disrobed with the help of Finella, pulling on my nightgown while waiting for the water to cool just a bit. She left to see where my food was and for a few minutes, I had blissful quiet.

I shed the gown and stood in front of the long mirror, looking at my naked body. So many scars but quite a bit of muscle on it too. My biceps were taught and detailed and my shoulders a bit broader. Thighs tight and sinewy and a nice tight ass.

My breasts had begun to fill and firm up due to the pregnancy, and at the reminder of it, I cradled the tiny bump that now bore proof of it. I gently caressed the skin over it, then over the five inch scar just below it. That had been a good scar.

The thought of Sophie's birth filled me with such love and excitement for this one to come. I never thought I'd have another child again, or a husband for that matter. But here I was, with both.

Then I realized what being here and pregnant meant. No pain relief and most likely death for the mother, child and or both. I vowed that I would not have my baby in this time and in this hellish place, come hell or high water.

A shiver ran over me and even though it was not from the cold in the room, I stepped into the bath and was instantly relieved of everything. For an instant, I felt as though I was back in my home, soaking in my large claw-foot bathtub with only candle light. The scent of chamomile and roses filled my nose and imagined myself in a bubble bath.

A soft knock on my door had me opening my eyes and bidding the person to enter. I was shocked to see Mrs.

Graham walk in with my tray of food and drink instead of Finella.

"The lass told me that ye've had some pain in the hip so I thought I would tend to it, and I'd bring ye yer dinner too. Ye shouldnae be bothered by those frilly sissy-pants down there, lass. They bark but dinnae bite; much." She winked at me.

"I wasn't bothered by them, just didn't want to sit there and have to endure the verbal suffrages of being a lady without a purpose until she weds, blah blah blah," I said then rolled my eyes.

"Aye, they do complain a lot about that for sure. They are hoppin' mad now that Liam is spoken for too. He was the best lookin' one left of the bachelors around here." She said and we both laughed.

She went about setting up her salve and clean linens on the bed and straightened out my nightgown and pulled the covers back. Once done, she handed me a goblet of red wine, one that was pleasantly fragrant for once.

"Very good wine tonight Mrs. Graham, my compliments to the wine maker." I drank and moaned in pleasure.

I heard a scrapping sound behind me and I turned to find Mrs. Graham had brought a stool up to the tub and motioned for me to turn back around.

"Ye relax dear, and I'll wash yer hair for ye. I am sure yer side protests much too." She said before I could decline her offer. Since she was right, I did as I was told and lounged back and closed my eyes.

It felt good to be pampered for a change. "You're very kind, Mrs. Graham. I've missed this for a long time."

"Yer vera' welcome, lass. It's somethin' I've missed myself. It's rare in this time to be able to enjoy the finer things in life, don't ye agree?" She asked.

"Yes I'd agree to that. I miss sleeping in on the weekends, pancake Sundays with my husband and daughter. It is very hard here." I was so relaxed I hadn't thought to watch my tongue. "Aye, I can relate. How I miss Pepsi and a good pint of Guiness. Fish and Chips, and burgers with all the fixin's. Good times they were." Mrs. Graham said reminiscently.

I sat up slowly and turned to look at her. From my knowledge of this dark time, there were none of those things, especially Pepsi. She smiled at me and I returned it with a hesitant one of my own. So, I had a friend after all.

"So you're from…" I trailed off, hope filling me that this was in fact real and not a dream; that I hadn't fallen asleep in the tub and was dreaming.

"1972, Scotland. There are only a few who ken from where I'm from, or rather *when* I'm from. It's not somethin' ye go about announcin'. Does Liam ken yer situation?"

"No, I haven't told him. I'm not so sure I should either. I don't plan on staying once I find my *seanair*. I promised my *seanmhair* that I would bring him home to her, if you know what I mean.

"How do you know about me? Did I talk in my sleep while I was recovering? Please don't tell anyone. I don't want to find myself strung up and burned to death, nor my baby." Panic filled me and I tried to get up but she stilled my attempt with a touch of her hand on my shoulder.

"Hush now, lass. Dinnae fash yerself. While tendin' to ye, I looked over yer scars as I looked for more fresh ones and saw the scar along yer belly. I ken that scar was from havin' a C-section, somethin' that isnae done here, especially in this time.

"Then there's yer accent. It's verae much American but not of this time's America. What year do ye come from, lass?" She asked, still scrubbing my hair.

"2017," I stated, waiting for her to call blasphemy for it.

"Really? What is it like then? I am sure much has changed since I had last been there. Please dear God tell me they still have Pepsi, pizza, and chocolate and good alcohol. None of this horse piss they serve here."

I laughed at that, something I hadn't done in some time. "Yes, those are still around, although I prefer Coke. It has changed quite a bit since your time. We had a black president who served two terms in the Whitehouse. Homosexuals may marry now, although it's still an issue among many states.

There are vegans, vegetarians, gluten free eaters," I rolled my eyes and snorted at that and continued, "many different types of music, some good and some you'd ask yourself 'what the hell is this?'"

Mrs. Graham chuckled at that. Of course, the kind of music she had back in her time was probably considered in that list of 'what the hell is this'. She rinsed my hair then handed me a towel, lending a hand for me while getting out of the tub.

"We've had a few wars too, both in America and in other countries. It's quite sad really." Silence fell in the room at this last statement. What could be said about war? It sucked no matter what year we were in.

"I've noticed Liam has not been to yer room since ye've been home. A man shouldnae be away from his wife for so long. They start sniffin' around other skirts for attention."

At my shocked look, she quickly assured me that Liam was not such a man, just that there are many who would turn to others for their needs.

"I'm not sure as to why he's stayed away. Maybe he wants to give me time to heal, both emotionally and physically." I said absently.

"Aye, that would be our Liam, but sometimes he needs a good smack in the head to wake his ass up and take charge. Maybe ye should do that one of these days soon?" She said with a brow raised.

What neither woman had known was that Liam would enter her bedchamber and sleep next to her, taking her into his arms as her nightmares played over and over again, only to rise before dawn as to not startle her when she awoke.

"The boy does love ye, lass, dinnae be mistakin' that in the least. When he loves, it's for forever. His parents are verae much the same way; most likely how he came to be the same. His brother and two sisters are just alike too."

I looked into the fire, a bit disappointed that he hadn't mentioned his family. I only knew of his parents down south.

"So, where does his family live? He hasn't told anything other than his parents are down south, possibly where my *seanair* might be. That's why we were all traveling together in the first place. Come to think of it, I haven't told him anything about mine either. This is very much an arranged marriage I guess."

For some reason, that thought didn't trouble me. What did trouble me was the fact I'd eventually have to speak to him about everything about me, including my trip here.

"I can tell you that I am not so sure I should talk to him about where, or rather *when*, I come from. He knew Jasper at least and thought we were family, and in a way, he was all my life. What do you think Mrs. Graham?"

"Please, enough with this 'Mrs. Graham' nonsense. Considerin' our similar situations now, please call me Helen. Only the youngin' should call me by my sir name.

"As to talkin' with Liam about…everythin' ye've been through, he seems to be an open minded lad. I've never seen him act untoward to a person who dinnae have it comin', especially a lass of any age. Ye won't ken until ye do."

She brushed out the tangles of my hair, hair that had been chopped before coming here to this time, and now hung past my shoulder blades. I counted back the months and found that I had been here already for six months. It seemed to have gone by so quickly.

"Hmph," was all I could reply at the moment, so lost in my thoughts.

She plaited my hair for the night then slipped on my socks since I could yet bend over and reach my feet. I stayed silent as she took me to the bed and went about her ministrations for my pain relief. I hated the smell of the salve and every night prayed that that night would be the last night I'd ever have to smell it. It did make the pain go away though.

"Ye have black eyes, lass. Ye need to sleep more. Yer body is still tryin' to get better and it can't unless ye sleep. I will give ye somethin' tonight to make the dreams stay away."

I nodded in agreement and shifted down into the covers of my bed and lounged against the pillows. She began to untie the bed curtains but I begged her not to, that I wanted the light of the fire for comfort.

"All right, lass, as ye wish. I'll be right back with the tea for to help ye sleep." She left in a flurry of skirts and I sank back in relief for the privacy of my own company for a moment. I hoped the tea would work.

CHAPTER 36

I AWOKE TO SUNLIGHT streaming in through the window slits across the room. It seemed the tea had in fact worked. I couldn't remember sleeping so good in a long time. I lounged in bed for a few minutes more until my bladder demanded I get my ass up.

Once that business was taken care of, and maybe it was my imagination, but even my body felt good considering what it had gone through recently. I still couldn't quite raise my left arm all the way up yet due to the lack of use, and the pull of the burnt patch of skin there.

My hip gave little protest too when I sat down on the bed again. Today seemed to be a good day. I even convinced myself to dress all by myself too which was a bit of a feat even for an uninjured woman but I was determined to do it.

My hair was another problem all together. I took out the braids and brushed it out only to find that I wouldn't be able to contain it due to my injured side and lack of motion of my arm. I found a pair of hair combs and was able to sweep back the riotous curls just enough to keep them behind my ears.

I had to say, not a bad job if I did say so myself. Even my cheeks were pinker from the exertion of getting ready. I actually looked healthy and not so gaunt for a change. There were still shadows under my eyes but they were much fainter.

I found Finella on my way down for breakfast, letting her know I didn't need her assistance this morning. I asked if she could please bring my breakfast however, to the library since that was where I was to meet with Rhys.

She scurried off and I headed for the library, often quiet unfortunately, but to my enjoyment for sure. Reading was a luxury for the very few in this time, especially for women. Sewing and needlepoint just wasn't my kind of thing, nor idle chit chat.

The fire was roaring and candles were lit along the walls even with the sun streaming in through the window slits. There was still a chill in the air so I found somewhat comfortable chairs and brought them to the fireplace, along with a throw for my legs.

I wore a woven shall, mostly to keep the scars on my back hidden from prying eyes, but also for the cold and security of it. I walked along the bookshelves, searching for a good read. It was difficult considering most of it was either in Latin or Gaelic, and even though I was getting better with my Gaelic, I was no master.

"Hello there, now how did you get here?" I said aloud to myself. There, hidden between two large tomes, was a hardcover book with a wide spine and sky blue paper book cover.

I pulled it out and to my delight, it happened to be a novel I knew quite well from my time. However, how it got here was entirely another story all together; one I would have to ask Rhys about.

I settled down with a glass of wine and soon Finella came in with my breakfast, directing her to place it on the small table next to me for easy reach. Once alone, I pulled out the book from under the throw and began to read. I sorely needed an escape and this was perfect.

So engrossed with the book I hadn't heard anyone come in and I nearly jumped out of my seat when Rhys said, "Ah, I see ye found my favorite book among these dusty old relics."

I squeaked and he laughed before apologizing for the startle. Once I caught my breath I quickly took a sip of the wine then settled back.

"You've read the book?" I set it aside and moved to get up to replace it, but he motioned me back down.

"Aye, I have. It belonged to my *seanair*. My athair gave it to me on my thirteenth birthday. My *seanair* and I could spend hours discussin' the pieces in it. My *athair* never understood it himself. He dinnae have a heart of a poet I guess.

"Come to think on it, he wasn't much of a recreational reader himself; just correspondence and the like really. He chose other things to occupy his free time, which dinnae involve my ma or me."

The left side of his mouth quirked up in remembrance then moved on to get a cup of wine himself before settling down in the opposite chair from me.

"My seanair however was a dreamer, a philanthropist, and an optimist, which in turn he instilled into me. He'd written a few novels too, most were so beyond the imagination I often wondered where he got it from. Those have been put in my private collect since they are verae dear to me. Toward the end of his life, many thought he'd up and lost his mind, spoutin' about some kind of nonsense or another."

"But you kept this here. Anyone could pull it out and see that it's not like any other in here. It stands out like a sore thumb!"

"If ye havenae noticed lass, it isnae teamin' with people. Readin' is not a common thin' as it appears it is in America for you. But for a few, this room is usually empty. I keep it clean and a fire going for any visitor that may come in."

I nodded, absently sipping my wine as I picked up the book again. I flipped through the pages, enjoying the musty scent of it, noticing the edges had discolored to a light tan from age.

He began to quote one of the passages in the book:

> *"Some say the world will end*
> *In fire, some say in ice,"*

I finished for him without thinking:

> *"From what I've tasted of desire,*
> *I hold with those who favor fire…,"*

"Ye ken the poem then. It's one of my favorites, and somewhat suited for the day in age, wouldnae ye agree? What is interestin' to me is, why the publisher put the wrong date in the beginnin' of the book, verae strange in deed."

I turned to the very first page, and not only was the date there, but obviously the book had been through a printing press and not handwritten as is customary for this time. I was shocked that he hadn't mentioned how it appeared, just the date.

"Yes quite interesting indeed." I stated, not sure where this was going.

He sat across from me, elbows resting on his knees, chin on top of his folded hands and watched me. I started to squirm, wondering why he was looking at me so directly.

"It is verae interestin' too that this should be a poem you'd ken since this bein' the only copy in all of Scotland." When I didn't answer, he gave a small smile. It seemed I'd been caught.

"My *seanair* had told me fanciful tales when I was but a lad. They were quite colorful to say the least; I could almost imagine bein' in them. I sometimes feel it when I read his books from time to time," he said slowly.

"So what do ye have to say about it? I'm sure ye might have similar tales of yer own. I also ken yer not from here, nor are ye from the Americas of this time, and there is yer strange accent. I have met few Americans and I assure ye they dinnae speak like yerself."

I made no move to divulge any information of where and especially the *when*, to him. People who spouted out such nonsense were usually strung up on a stake and burnt to a crisp.

As if reading my mind, he took both of my hands in his and promised me no harm would come to me; that what we spoke of in this room would stay only in this room.

I took a few breaths, a couple of sips of wine for good measure, then told him of my own tale.

CHAPTER 37

Rhys sat there quietly and looked at my photos of Nick and Sophie, his face expressionless. I didn't know if that was a good thing or not and I twisted the throw between my hands, trying not to high tail it out of there.

"Well?!" I said a bit too sharp. I kept looking at the door, waiting for a stampede of soldiers to come storming through the door to drag me out to the courtyard.

"Does Liam ken any of this?" he asked, not looking up. He handed me the photos back a bit hesitantly then let go as if he'd been burned by them. I tucked them away in one of the hidden pockets of my skirt.

"No, I don't think he'd understand. I'm afraid he would take me to the stake himself and start the fire. People, as you well know, don't like talk of such things around here. I'd be considered either mad in the head or most likely a witch."

"Aye, but ye need to tell him. He's a verae open-minded person. Dinnae be so quick to judge him, lass."

He got up, took my goblet and went to fill it for me along with his own. "Do ye ken where these doorways are?"

I didn't feel the need to tell him of the map Nana had drawn up for me, showing me where not to go while on my hikes. The less he knew the better.

"Jasper told me about the one he and Jon accidentally went through, but neglected to tell me what to look for once I got there."

That part was true but if in fact it did work, then most likely it would have the same affect on me as it did on the other side. I wouldn't have too much trouble finding it.

"And not just anyone can go through them, only chosen people I guess."

"How do ye ken if ye are one or not?" he asked.

"Well, I'm not sure really. I think it's different for everyone. If Jon were here we could ask him what it was like for him. For me, it was a constant headache when I was at a great distance from it, then once I'd gotten close enough, then well...." When I trailed off, he looked at me and my cheeks went flaming red.

His look at first was of confusion but then he caught on he barked out a laugh. "Amazin' truly!"

"For Jasper it was a constant buzzing sound in his head. The closer he got the greater the noise level got, to the point he would shout even though I could hear him just fine. I think it has to do with the person having been selected to fulfill a purpose in another time. Jon's I'm assuming was to produce an heir to carry on the name and title and all that went with it. This being back in my time, give or take a few decades until I came along."

"There were no more Campbells of Devonshire in the time he traveled to which was 1949. I thought Jasper had just been a happy or rather a grumpy accident when he came through, but I think his purpose was to stay and raise my father, then to help me find Jon."

I halted and drank deeply of my wine then took a few more bites of my now cold breakfast. Rhys continued to sit there looking in the fire but obviously far away in his thoughts.

"Fate, if this is what it is, knew Jon would return and so left Jasper behind. From what I understand though, the whole time Jasper was in the future, the doorway still called to him instead of shutting off until he was needed again.

"The doorway never called my grandmother, and any information that Jasper and I had found in all the family ledgers, she could not see either. They're connected somehow. She thought it a cruel joke to tease her with the information when she could not see for herself."

At the thought of that day, it broke my heart again to see her so upset and how I had been the one to do it to her. So determined to forget my own pain of losing my loved ones, I obsessed over my grandfather's disappearance.

"And what purpose might it be for ye to travel all this way to our time? Surely it isnae to bring Jon home, even if he does live which no one kens that information. He'd be an old man now, most likely in his eighties and not fit to travel like that. Ye said it was hard for both you and Jasper. Plus, there probably isnae anythin' that important that he'd be needed again, excusin' yer *seanmhair*."

The same thought had crossed my own mind and my heart fell. Jon was not the reason I was here, and as much as I'd do anything to bring him back to Nana, that was looking less and less possible with each passing day. I had already been in this time going on almost eight months and hadn't made any headway as to retrieving my grandfather.

"I believe my purpose here is to take down Thomas. He cannot continue on as Jon's replacement, no matter how temporary it may be."

"And just how do ye plan on doin' this? Just walk in, curtsy then slit his throat?" He countered jokingly. When he saw my wicked smile he actually gasped, horrified.

"Ye've got to be jokin' lass, or yer truly mad in the head. Ye cannae just walk in there by or leave and expect him to welcome ye into his home. He'd recognize ye for Christsake! Does Liam ken of yer plan young lassie?" Rhys roared at me but by now, I had gotten used to it and didn't flinch from it.

"No, I haven't discussed this with him. I only came to this after seeing Jasper yesterday. Jon is my seanair, and since his son is not here to rein in his steed, then I would be the next heir to the dukedom and all that goes with it.

"I will not sit back and watch him destroy everything my *seanair* and his *athair* before him, had made of this land and everything on it. I will not stand for it!" I slammed my fist on the table next to me, upsetting the cutlery on my food tray.

I stood and began to pace, rage roaring through my body at the thought of Thomas. Ideas ran around in my head but just as quickly as they had come, the sooner I swept them aside, trying to find the right one.

"How long before the next thaw? My plan will work but it will take time and patience; two things I don't particularly have right now."

"Mid month I'd say but the roads would be slippery from the thaw. The snow has stopped and the rivers and streams are flowin' heavily already. Why do ye ask?" He hesitantly asked.

"We send a message that I, his cousin, and my husband wish to seek shelter for a few days while on route to Braemar, for family matters."

"But again, he'll recognize ye. Men like that who take pleasure in torturin' people, dinnae forget their victims." He insisted.

This was true, but it had been some months since I was last there. And, the way I planned on introducing myself, he wouldn't look twice at me.

"This would be true, if I were to come back as a boy, but I will be coming as Liam's wife who is in a delicate way." I placed my hands over the small mound that now slightly showed.

"My hair is longer and I'd be dressed appropriately for my station." I said trying to make this all sound affirmative.

Rhys sat there stroking his three days' growth of beard, thinking over all I had told him. It was a lot to take in, even for him. I was drained just from telling him all of it. I did have to say it had been very therapeutic to purge all of what I'd been keeping to myself.

"We need Liam to hear all of this, see what he thinks of it all." Rhys said more to himself than to me.

I began to shake my head no, but immediately stopped at the dark look Rhys gave me. "I ken Liam verae well lass, and he willnae go screamin' mad over any of it. The miniatures ye have," he gestured to my pocket that held the photographs, "the photographs as ye call them, they would back up yer story too."

"But what if he does go 'screaming mad', and brings down the keep with it, what then?" I felt my heart beat rapidly now and a chill run up my spine.

"Jessie, he loves ye to the moon and back. He'd accept anythin' ye'd tell him, even if ye told him ye had two heads!" He took my hands into his again, tightly this time in assurance and to lend me strength.

"Look, the short time ye've been here, has not been forgivin' and I can see why ye'd want verae few to ken who ye are. But for now, ye can put yer trust in me and in Liam. We will pledge our fealty to protect ye for as long as it's needed."

He slid to one knee from his chair and placed his right arm across his chest, over his heart before bowing to me. I placed my hand on his head as a sign of acceptance and he sat back into the chair.

"I'd like for you to be there when I tell him." I asked quietly but firmly.

He gave me a soft chuckle before answering, "of course I will. I wouldnae leave ye to fend for yerself if Liam decided to take ye to the stake. Although ye've proven that ye can handle yer own." He said with a wink.

My stomach rolled on the thought and I guess I had turned green from the thought, because he immediately apologized for his lack in judgment where words were concerned.

"And Mrs. Graham too; please. For moral support." I added quickly.

"Anyone else I should add to this list?" He asked sarcastically. I glared at him and he smirked.

"Now that's been settled, let's plan for tomorrow afternoon then." He squeezed my hand then placed it back into my lap before getting up.

"My dear, ye've got the look of exhaustion under yer eyes. I shall escort ye to yer room for a nice rest." He stood next to me and held out his arm for me to take. I stumbled a bit while trying to right myself with my cane and he caught me quickly.

"Just a moment, I will put this back and then join you." I began to walk to the shelf but he stopped me in my tracks.

"Jessie love, ye need not put it back. Please, take it with ye for yer enjoyment. I have not had many a day for a few years now to open it and most likely willnae until this Thomas business is dealt with.

"It would please both my seanair and myself if ye were to take it and enjoy it as much as we have."

My eyes misted over at his thoughtfulness, and so I took his arm and my cane while he carried the book for me. "How is it now that you do not have a wife and rug rats running around here?"

"I was once, many years ago. She was my heart. Like yer Nick, she'd been taken from me. She died while in childbirth, somethin' that happens quite often in these times. The wee bairn, our son, soon followed her in death. I havenae wanted to remarry since."

"I'm sorry, Rhys. Just as you have felt, I too feel the same pain; that is until I met Liam."

"Aye, there is that, and a wee bairn growin' in yer belly now." He beamed at me.

As if hearing it being spoken of, the baby wiggled and sent my uterus fluttering. "I think this baby already likes you." I gave a small laugh as I rubbed my tiny baby bump.

"Well as it should be! He'll be sayin' my name as soon as he's out!" Rhys' eyes sparkled at the thought and I couldn't help but feel the same humor.

"So you think it's a boy. What makes you think that?"

"I've always had a knack for this kind of thing my dear. Think of it as a gift really." He stated with his chest puffed out in mock pride. I burst out laughing and he shot me a stern look before laughing himself.

All too soon we stood in front of my door and we both sighed after our laughing fit. He handed me the book before opening my door. He signaled Finella to come and assist me then bid me a good rest until dinner.

Before he left me he informed me that he would seek out both Liam and Mrs. Graham and let them know of our meeting tomorrow. I nodded my thanks then entered my room.

"May I assist ye my Lady out of yer clothes?" Finella asked.

"Yes Finella, you may. Thank you."

CHAPTER 38

I TOOK SUPPER IN the library again, a glass of wine in hand and my borrowed book. I took my time, savoring each word and poem. The thought of not being able to read books like this ever again pulled at my heart.

Liam found me there after finding out that I was no longer taking any meals in the mess hall. He didn't know why but he didn't ask either, just sat across from me and talked about the happenings around the Keep.

"How's everythin' healin'?" he motioned to my left side.

"It's doing well actually, thanks to Mrs. Graham's skillful hands. I barely have any pain anymore. I can't wait to stop using this blasted cane though. How ridiculous I must look." I nudged the dreadful thing and it fell over to the floor.

He picked it up without my asking, smirking all the while. "Patience my love, patience. We'll be back to trainin' in no time." A rakish grin growing on his face, "I do miss our trainin' time." He winked at me and I actually blushed.

Truth be told, I had missed both types of training too, but I was not so sure how to go about starting it back up again with my hip being what it is now.

As if reading my thoughts, he took my hand and stroked the top of it, letting me know that he missed our time together too. We had had very little time since we had returned and it felt like we were strangers. I didn't look forward to tomorrow's meeting but it couldn't be helped if we needed his help. At least we could tell each other about what our lives were before we had met, to some extent.

"We haven't spoken of what are pasts were like, nor about our families. Do you have any interest in talking about them?" I asked hesitantly.

"Quite honestly, I hadn't thought to do so. But aye, we can certainly do that." He answered, cheeks flushing at his thoughtlessness; typical male.

"Shall I start then?" I asked.

"By all means, I'd like to ken all about ye, Jessie."

"Well let's see. I was born in the States and up until recently, have lived there all my life. My father and stepmother live there on the western side. Jasper and Nana stayed in Edinburgh all of her life. I do miss her so, I miss them all so much.

"Anyway, I went to school there, yes they are more accepting of girls and women participating in academia. Not much but we can still do it. My father was a philosopher of Geography which I never understood myself. I still can't tell north from south."

I took a sip of wine and a bite of bread as he sat there looking intently at me. "What else, I usually love to travel until I came here and all I want to do now is go home again." I didn't like the next part of my history but I had to tell him.

"I am-was, a widow when we had met. My daughter also had left me at the same time he had. They were killed in a carriage accident almost a year ago. His name was Nick and our daughter was Sophie. She was only three years old at the time."

He handed me his linen and I wiped my face and blew my nose. I sat quietly for a few moments, staring into the fire, trying to stiffen my spine again.

"I wondered who this Nick and Sophie were. Ye spoke of them often when ye were fevered and once here, in yer sleep. More like cried out for them. Now I can put two and two together. I am verae sorry for yer loss. Losing a husband is one thing, but to lose a bairn is entirely another."

"She was the light in my life. I couldn't remember my life before here and I couldn't imagine how I'd go on living without her once she was gone. I had thought many a time of joining them.

"Anyway, I came to Scotland in search of my seanair after my Nana had told me about him. She said I could stay there and I gladly accepted leaving my life for a while behind me.

"Being in Scotland, among its harsh mountains and beautiful green and purple fields, it's constant cool air and blistery winds, it has changed me for the better. It somehow has made me a stronger person and less naive of the world. I also have both you and Jasper to thank for that.

"I do hope our baby will grow strong like you to survive this world. I cannot bear to lose another." I covered my belly protectively and sent up a little prayer.

"Hmm, wait, what did ye just say?" he sat up in the chair, nearly tipping it over onto himself as he fell to his knees in front of me.

I touched his cheek as I placed his large strong hand over the small mound that was our child. It was too small for him to feel it but it knew who his father was by its little fluttering movement against the warmth that his hand created.

"Yes, our son, my love. At least Rhys seems to think it's a boy. There's a fifty-fifty chance of him being right." I smiled and joyful tears ran down both our faces now.

"How long have ye ken? Why did ye not tell me right away?"

"I found out from Jasper, just before he took his last breath. Jasper insisted I was with child, that he knew these things after being alive for so long as he had been. I doubted it but it's just started to move and tickles my belly when it does.

"It's been about three months, so right after our first time together. It does happen!" I insisted at his skeptical look.

"Well now, we must hold off our trainin' a few months longer, that is, the outside trainin' I mean. I must keep ye bed ridden from now on ye ken, to keep the bairn safe and all."

"You will do no such thing, Liam. I am with child but I am no invalid. In fact, it is best if women stay active when pregnant.

Keeps us healthy so there's no chance of becoming fat and lazy. Do you want a fat and lazy wife?" I inquired with one brow raised.

"No but what if ye get hurt or the baby gets hurt, what then? Ye cannae promise me that it might not happen. And ye'll not go riddin' Lucifer. I forbid ye!" he demanded. He got up and paced before the hearth and I tried very much not to laugh, but I couldn't help it. He was so much like Nick about this baby thing.

"You won't ride a bike, no rollerblading. Nothing but healthy food from now on. Are you on prenatal vitamins? What did the doctor say? When do we know what 'it' is…"

I could hear Nick's voice again in my head, and all the questions he had fired way at me. How he took such good care of me, being so involved with the pregnancy. When we found out we were having a girl, he couldn't be more excited.

My attention snapped back to Liam as he was still ranting instructions to me. I rolled my eyes which he caught immediately and I straightened in my chair, all seriousness.

The door swung open and Rhys walked in while Liam was continuing his rant. He looked at me then turned to exit when I said, "Hello Rhys, care to join us? Where you looking for Liam, well, here he is."

"Ugh, aye I was lookin' for him as a matter of fact. I came to tell him of our meetin' tomorrow afternoon. I already informed Mrs. Graham about it and she is willin' to be there. She has some idea as to what it's in regards to."

"What meetin'?" Liam stopped his rant in time to hear the conversation between Rhys and I.

"I came here to let ye ken that Jessie, myself, Mrs. Graham and yerself will be meetin' in my private study tomorrow afternoon. Yer wife and I have much to discuss with ye."

Before Liam could interrogate Rhys further, the traitor escaped, slamming the door behind him. I glared at it then turned back to Liam and waited for him to inquire about this issue now.

"Liam, leave off will you? You're hurting my head and giving me indigestion. Go after Rhys and rant at him for a while." I rubbed my temple, pretending I had one, but just wanted him to leave me be for now.

He thankfully shut up but still stood there in front of the hearth, glaring into the flames. I drank my wine until it was gone and wolfed down supper before losing my appetite all together.

"Go and rest and I'll be up in a little while. I'll have Mrs. Graham bring up some tea for the headache."

He leaned down and for a minute I actually feared he would hit me, sensing his anger vibrating through his body. But instead, he placed a kiss on my cheek and squeezed my shoulder before leaving me be.

I sat for another hour before retiring to my room, asking Finella to bring more wine and food since I was starving. This kid was going to do me in with all this food. It must be a boy. I'd never been this hungry when pregnant with Sophie. I settled by the fire and daydreamed, too tired to focus on a book but not quite tired enough for sleep.

When midnight came, Liam had not come to bed and so I went to bed myself, too tired now to stay up for him. He knew where his bed was and so with that, I blew my candle out and went to sleep instantly.

CHAPTER 39

I was already seated in Rhys' study when Mrs. Graham entered with refreshments and snacks. She went about setting all of it up then sat next to me, and I couldn't help but feel better about what was to come. We were a united front in this matter, and no matter what happened here today, we would stay that way.

Rhys entered with Liam and they both stopped short at seeing the two of us together chit chatting. They shook it off and took their seats before us, pouring both of us a cup of wine before helping themselves to whiskey.

"All right then, let's have this done and over with. The whole thing makes me testy." Rhys grumbled.

When I hadn't started talking, Mrs. Graham took my hand in her's and gave it a squeeze of encouragement. We linked fingers and I took a breath and began.

Liam sat quietly, staring at me intently. I didn't like the look at all. Rhys was more supportive along with Mrs. Graham as I spoke about where or rather, *when* I had come from. Both Rhys and Mrs. Graham already knew and Rhys seemed to take it as an absolution after hearing it twice.

Liam however, had a very good poker face and was revealing nothing. I wish I knew what was going through his mind. It was a lot to take in, I knew that, but the silence was killing me. Every minute that passed, had me concluding that he was not believing it.

I sat quietly once all was said and waited. My hand ached from squeezing Mrs. Graham's hand the whole time and I was sure hers was hurting her too, but she made no gesture of complaint.

"Why now. Why have ye waited this long to tell me all of this?" Liam said quietly. His neck had turned flushed and I knew now that he was very angry, maybe even hurt.

"It's not something you go around announcing to people. We don't know each other well, how was I to tell whether or not you'd turn me in to the magistrates to have me killed for my insane tale. Do you know what they do to people who are deemed to be witches? Do you?!"

"Of course I ken!" He bellowed back at me. "But ye should have told me before now. Maybe we wouldnae find ourselves in this position now if ye had."

"Do you mean married with a child on the way?" I countered back acidly.

"Aye! I mean no, not that. Ye ken what I'm sayin' and dinnae act like ye dinnae." He turned to Rhys imploringly, wanting his friend, his family to back him up in this. Rhys just sat there passively watching all of this madness.

My heart skipped and cracked at what he'd said. Tears filled my eyes and I looked to Mrs. Graham to confirm what I had just heard. Anger filled me, not for myself, but for my child and for Jasper.

"How dare you sir! None of this would have changed if I or Jasper had said anything of the sort sooner. Thomas would still have done what he has done, and we'd still find ourselves in this room. Maybe not married or pregnant, but here we are.

"I didn't ask you to marry me if you remember. In fact, I was against it from the start! And I didn't see you kicking and screaming to the 'altar' either Liam, in fact you were all for it, so don't put the blame on me." I yelled at him. Liam glowered at me and I back at him, both of us refusing to back down.

"Now look, fightin' isnae goin' to accomplish anythin'. What's done is done and cannae be undone so movin' on, we need to discuss Jessie's proposed strategy to get into Rowen Castle to finish what was started."

Rhys got up and paced as he spoke, not looking at any of us. I turned and looked away at Liam and he did the same. What the hell were we, children?

"She explained to me yesterday that her plan is to send a scroll, explaining that she is a cousin of his Lordship, and that she and her husband ask to stay for a few days before movin' on to Braemar to visit her parents.

"I am concerned that he will recognize her, if not immediately, then soon after her arrival. As for Liam bein' her husband and Thomas already kens him, it might be a little suspicious, so I pose an idea. I think it best that I pose as her husband instead, Liam would accompany us as my cousin." Rhys stated.

"Absolutely not I forbid it. She willnae do this; none of us will." Liam said matter of fact.

"It's the only way we can infiltrate the Keep and deal with him. I will send word myself, informin' him that not only are we travelin' to see her family, but also to discuss the current events, and what needs to be done to settle them."

"I still say nae to this! I willna stand for it, Rhys. She is in no way prepared to do this, and it would be puttin' her and our child in danger of bein' caught. He doesnae care about such matters and he willna be against continuin' where he left off." Liam demanded.

"It's not up to you lad. As much as I dinnae want to do this, the lass does have a good idea. I willnae leave her alone and I would put ye in charge of her when I have dealin's with him. I ken ye'll keep her safe." Rhys said sternly, putting an end to the conversation.

"That settled, I will send word immediately. The sooner the better so we can get this done." Rhys excused himself from the group, leaving them to do as they wished.

Liam however left me and Mrs. Graham in the study without a by your leave.

"Well I think that went well, dinnae ye think so?" Mrs. Graham said in amusement.

"The sooner the better we get this over with. I am not looking forward to this either."

Rhys received word that we were to be permitted to visit Rowen Castle to discuss the matters at hand. We were only give three days stay there which was fine by all of us. Liam had not joined in the meetings, still refusing to agree to this idea.

That left Rhys and I to go over the plans for this feat. Mrs. Graham would accompany us as my lady in waiting due to my delicate way, along with Finella as her assistant. We would leave in the next couple of days and it would take us about two week's time.

"I have villages that we may stay in during the nights for yer comfort, Jessie. I have sent word to the inns of our arrival so they are expectin' us. We willnae be travelin' heavy so be most selective as to what to bring with ye." Rhys instructed.

I had already done so, hating the fact that I could not fit into breeches any longer so I would have to travel in finer apparel. I really hated these dresses. However, they were quite warm and that would be very important while traveling.

"Ye willnae be ridin' Lucifer, but we will take him with us just in case we need to make a sudden retreat. I dinnae like the idea of ye ridin' period in yer state but…"

"I have been pregnant before and believe it or not, I am made of sturdier stuff, Rhys. The baby and I will be fine. There were much more intense vehicles back in my time."

"No" he said flatly and walked away. I rolled my eyes and glared at the door he closed behind him.

I sighed deeply and chose to relax in my oversized chair and read Robert Frost again. This trip was going to be exhausting in all aspects, and I couldn't wait for it to be done with and back onto my search for my grandfather. The fire soon had me dozing and for once, my dreams were kind to me.

COMING SOON

ETERNAL LOVE